MW00694563

SECRET MAFIA BILLIONAIRE

IT'S COMPLICATED - BOOK SIX

MAGGIE COLE

PULSE PRESS INC

This book is fiction. Any reference to historical events, real people, or real places are used fictitiously. All names, characters, plots, and events are products of the author's imagination. Any resemblances to actual events or places or persons, living or dead, is entirely coincidental.

Copyright © 2020 by Maggie Cole

All rights reserved.

No part of this book may be reproduced in any form or by any electronic or mechanical means, including information storage and retrieval systems, without written permission from the author, except for the use of brief quotations in a book review.

PROLOGUE

Dmitri Ivanov

THERE ARE THREE THINGS I DON'T HAVE TIME FOR.

Cowardly men.

Drama surrounding women.

Anyone trying to stop me from building my empire.

If any of those things get in my way, I deal swiftly with the issue and carry on with my life, even more focused to see my plans come to fruition.

So when I see her with him, I should stay away. It's a trifecta of everything I don't tolerate. But the moment she arrives, my attention is blurred. And I can't afford any distractions.

"This is getting old. What's the bottom line?" my older brother, Maksim, asks. For months, we've expressed interest and had multiple meetings to buy the land we need for our development.

Lorenzo Rossi, the Chicago Italian mob boss's youngest son, owns it. While he claims to be a legit business owner, my three brothers and I aren't stupid enough to believe it or let our guards down. But we also aren't going to back away from what we need. He bought the land from the city for next to nothing. Anything he gets is a huge profit. Before the ground can be touched, millions will need to be spent on cleanup. He knows it. We know it. But he's greedy. He also thinks he can string us along forever.

There's a loud surge of voices. It's only four o'clock, too early for the dinner rush, which is why we set our meeting for an hour ago. We should have finished by now, but Lorenzo doesn't understand the value of time.

Silver-spoon prick.

I'm bored and frustrated with his game. My brothers are, too, but I lack patience the most. Maksim, Boris, and Sergey all can wait things out longer than I can. But even they are fed up with this cat and mouse game Lorenzo's put us through. And I'm sick of looking at him and his three thugs' faces.

I sit back in my chair and cross my arms, glancing at the commotion, trying to stop myself from flying across the table and ripping Lorenzo to shreds.

A woman dressed in a bridal gown, the man I assume she just married, and people dressed up, arrive in groups. They all head toward the elevator, except one woman.

She has long, blonde hair that hangs in curls down her back. Her blue eyes remind me of Lake Michigan on a sunny day. A black, satin cocktail dress hugs her curves, accentuating her voluptuous breasts and round ass. Red stilettos match her pouty lips and clutch.

Hello, bombshell. Come to daddy.

She's not fat, but she's not a stick, either. I could grab her anywhere and not feel bones, which is what I like in a woman.

She walks toward our table, and I check her out. At first, she doesn't see me, but then she catches me staring, and our eyes lock. She blushes and looks away.

I look at her hand. *No ring. Good.*

When she passes, a light floral scent lingers in the air, and I almost groan.

I turn in my chair, watching her ass jiggle and sway just right before she disappears through the heavy wooden bathroom door.

"Dmitri?" Boris asks, pulling me back into the conversation.

I raise my eyebrows in question, and his face hardens. I'm sure I'll hear about this as soon as we leave.

Sergey clears his throat. "Our deadline is thirty days. If we can't make this happen in the next few weeks, we're walking. You can find another buyer."

Lorenzo calls his bluff. "You've got a lot of money tied up into land you won't be able to do anything with if you don't get my piece."

He's got us by the balls, and I hate it. "There are a lot of things we can do with what we have. Don't get cocky," I warn him.

The conversation goes back and forth. I'm getting irritated and excuse myself. "I need another drink. Anyone else?" The restaurant doesn't officially open until five for dinner, so the waitstaff hasn't arrived yet. Since we know the owner, he let us come in early but made it clear we needed to get our drinks at the bar, which we were fine with.

Maksim nods to get another round for everyone, and I go, happy to get a breather. The bartender is handing a man a beer. He's wearing a suit, has brown hair and eyes, and a scowl on his face.

"Bernie, give me four vodkas and four whiskeys," I order.

The bartender nods and grabs glasses and the bottles.

The man takes a sip of his beer then stares at the game on the television.

"What's the score?" I ask. I don't care, but Boris places bets on all the big games.

"Don't know. I've had to deal with shit all day," the man replies. He's dressed up, and I assume he's here because of the wedding reception upstairs.

"You part of the wedding?"

He scoffs and continues staring at the screen. "If you want to call it that."

I'm not sure what it is about him, but I don't like him. It's not his scowl. I know plenty of men who have the same look. But my gut is telling me he's a douchebag.

Bernie sets everything on a tray. "Sally should be in soon to wait on you guys."

"We're good. Thanks."

I throw a hundred down, tell him to keep the change, and spin with the tray in my hand.

"Oh, sorry!" The sex kitten from earlier jumps.

I check her out again, and she blushes, redder than earlier. "Not a problem."

"Sit, Anna," the man orders, as if she's a dog.

She's with him?

Anna.

My distaste for him grows.

Her face falls. She opens then closes her mouth. She shuts her eyes and takes a deep breath. "We need to go upstairs, Mitch."

"We aren't going until the game is over." He chugs several mouthfuls of his beer.

She bites her lip and quietly replies with a shaky voice, "But everyone is already there."

He spins on the barstool and, in a nasty voice, demands, "Sit your fat ass down."

She looks at the ground and blinks hard, her cheeks staining pink with embarrassment.

I put the tray of drinks down. "Don't talk to a lady that way," I growl. I shouldn't say anything. It's not my business. I don't need to get involved in this. There's a meeting going on and it should be my only focus.

Maybe it's the mix of how the meeting is going, my distaste for him, and the look on her face that makes me butt in. I usually steer clear of any domestic drama.

Anna's eyes widen.

Mitch spins and rises. "Keep your nose out of my business." He's not as tall as me or quite as built. My guess is I could take him out in one punch.

Not in front of her.

You don't need trouble. Walk away.

I lean closer to him. "My suggestion is you take your beer and move along to your party."

He steps closer. "What are you going to do about it?"

I glance at Anna. Her lip is trembling. I look back at Mitch. "I'm going to take these drinks to my brothers." I nod so he can see them. I could take him out myself, but a little intimidation never hurt. "When I finish, if you haven't escorted your woman upstairs, we'll be having a different discussion." Acknowledging she's his makes my stomach clench.

Why is she with such a loser?

I give her one last look and deliver the drinks to the table. When I turn, they step into the elevator. He has his hand roughly on her elbow. The doors shut, and I catch her fear-filled eyes.

I should follow him and rip his head off.

"Dmitri, Lorenzo seems to think we're willing to give him double what the property is worth," Boris seethes.

I groan inside. *You're here to close this deal. Get your head in the game.* The rest of the meeting only lasts another five minutes, but I can barely focus. All I want to do is go upstairs and learn everything there is about her. And I can't get her scared expression out of my mind.

Anna

Several Days Later

"WE DID THE BEST WE COULD WITH THE BLOODSTAINS, BUT WE couldn't get it all out," the woman at the dry cleaners says while holding out Mitch's shirt.

My insides quiver. "Are you sure there isn't anything else you can do?"

The woman shakes her head. "I'm sorry, but we tried it all. That will be forty-two eighty-three."

I stare at the faded, reddish-brown stains.

It's his favorite shirt. He's going to be so angry.

Why did I pack it?

We should have stayed home. This wouldn't have happened if we didn't go. I knew something terrible was going to happen before we left. I could feel it.

My good friends, Jamison and Quinn, got married. Mitch and I flew to Chicago, but he didn't want to go. Like all my family events, I had to convince him.

I shouldn't have. The last time my brother, Chase, and Mitch were in the same room, they almost got into a fist fight. I worried about it and even told my best friend, Harper, to help keep my brother away from Mitch.

The entire weekend was a disaster, starting from the first night when Mitch left me in the bedroom, waiting for him in lingerie. After so many hours, I put on clothes to look for him and found him in the hotel bar. A waitress was on his lap, doing shots with him.

It's not the first time I've caught him doing inappropriate things with other women, but like always, he claimed it was innocent fun.

The next day, Mitch woke up with a chip on his shoulder. He wasn't happy we were in Chicago.

We only lasted about fifteen minutes into the reception before Quinn's brother, Steven, and Mitch got into a physical fight.

The police came, Mitch threatened to press charges, and we went back to the hotel. I sat in the room all night, not knowing where Mitch was, and the next morning, he came into the room and told me we were leaving in ten minutes.

I didn't argue. I didn't question the perfume I could smell on his skin. I packed our bags and tried my best not to upset him.

If we can just get back to New York, we can fix things.

I'm not sure why I lied to myself. I had been trying to "fix things" between us for the last few years.

I slide my debit card into the machine, sign the screen, and take the items from the woman. It begins to rain on my way back to our apartment. By the time I get home, my hair and clothes stick to my body.

My nerves escalate. I set the clothes on the armchair then go into the bedroom to change before Mitch sees me. He hates it when I'm a disheveled mess.

I change and am in the middle of drying my hair when my alarm rings.

Oh God. It's so late, and I don't have dinner made.

I put my hairdryer down and rush out to the kitchen and open the refrigerator. The chicken still isn't fully defrosted, and my gut sinks further.

Can I do anything right today?

My appointment with my new interior design clients ran late. I should have been home two hours ago, but I also was almost to the apartment when I remembered about the dry cleaning.

Mitch has a demanding work schedule and wants dinner on the table when he comes home. I only started my business a few years ago, and he makes more money than me. I made over six figures last year, but he calls it "a glorified hobby." He's a financial advisor, and his job is more important, so he expects me to take care of anything related to the house.

And I want to make him happy, so I do my best to make sure everything is clean and as he likes it.

The door slams, and I curse myself for not paying better attention today.

"Anna," he barks.

I run out to the living room and attempt to kiss him, but he turns his cheek.

"Hi. Did you have a good day?"

He scowls. "Why is your hair wet?"

"I-I got caught in the rain and was drying it but went to the kitchen to start dinner."

"To start dinner? It's seven o'clock." He scowls.

"I'm sorry. I picked up a new client today and—"

"A new client," he growls.

I nod and force a smile. "Yes. And—"

He pushes me back so I'm against the wall. "Did you sleep with him?"

"What?"

He fists my damp hair. "You fucking whore."

Tears blur my vision. "Mitch, no! I would never—"

He slaps my face so hard, I wonder if my cheekbone cracked. His watch slices my lip.

"Ow!" I scream. The metallic taste of blood hits my tongue.

His brown eyes turn almost black. He yanks my hair and spit flies out of his mouth. "You're a fat, little—"

"Piece of shit!" my brother, Chase, yells and pulls Mitch off me.

What is he doing here?

Chase lives in Chicago. He moved there over a year ago.

"Chase, no!" I yell as he pummels Mitch in the face.

The two men roll on the floor as I scream. The fight seems to last forever. There's so much blood, mostly Mitch's, and I think my brother will kill him.

The neighbor comes over to try and break it up and also calls the police. It takes all of them to break up the fight. The next few hours are chaotic. Mitch, Chase, and I are all questioned.

They take pictures of all of us.

A female officer takes me into the bedroom. "There's a safehouse I can take you to."

"That isn't necessary," I tell her through my tears. "It was just a misunderstanding. He didn't mean it."

She tilts her head. "Ma'am, this isn't the first time he's hit you. We have the report when the neighbors called the last time."

More shame fills me. I glance out the window. "That was over a year ago and my fault."

She picks up my hand. "Nothing is your fault."

I turn to her. "You don't know. You don't live with us. It was."

"No," she insists.

A male officer, who my brother knows, leads Chase into the bedroom.

Chase goes into my closet and grabs my suitcase. "You have five minutes to pack, Anna."

"What are you talking about?"

"You're coming to Chicago with me."

"No, I'm not. Mitch is hurt. If I leave..."

"This is over," my brother yells.

"Calm down," the officer states.

Chase takes a deep breath. His hand is swollen and face is bruised. "Give my sister and me a minute, please."

I rise and go to the window.

I can't leave him. He'll be so angry if I go.

He's going to kill me.

No, he didn't mean it. He's under a lot of stress.

Why did I have to screw up today?

"This is a misunderstanding. I didn't have dinner ready. I got caught in the rain. I just...just..." I start to sob, and Chase pulls me into his arms.

He sternly says, "Anna, we're going to Chicago. Pack, or don't, but we're leaving in four minutes. You are not staying with him. And even if you tried, the police are requiring you to stay apart right now."

I can't talk. My brother's arms feel so safe, and I hate that they are his and not Mitch's. That I've failed to maintain my relationship, and Chase has to be the one to comfort me.

If he hadn't shown up, Mitch might have killed me.

He wouldn't.

His eyes were scarier than last time.

It only happened once before. Mitch promised me he would never do it again. But I've never seen his eyes so dark and so much hatred in them before.

I take nothing but my purse. In a haze, I get on Chase's plane and fly to Chicago with him. He tries to talk to me, but I can't do anything except cry.

I have so much guilt over what happened. And I'm embarrassed my brother witnessed everything.

When we land, Vivian is waiting in the car.

Her face falls when she sees us.

I cry all over again, and she hugs me.

When we get to their penthouse, Xander is waiting.

"Why is Xander here?" I ask.

Vivian's eyes are full of sympathy, and more shame fills me. "You're hurt, Anna. So is Chase. He's going to examine you both."

"No, I'm—"

"It's here or the hospital," my brother barks.

I shut my eyes. *Can this get any more embarrassing?*

I've known Xander forever. He's a doctor, but I'd rather have a stranger look at my face.

"It was only a slap. I'm fine," I insist.

"Only a slap? Do you hear yourself?" Chase growls.

Vivian puts her hand on his arm. "Chase—"

"No. Enough of this."

"Not now," Vivian says.

He opens his mouth then shuts it. "Fine. Tomorrow we're talking."

Why did I come here?

Where else would I have gone?

It's Mitch's apartment. I would have had to go to the safehouse.

"Anna, let me clean your face," Xander quietly says.

There's no point fighting this.

I sit on the table and let him, trying not to wince.

"I'm sorry. I know this hurts."

I can't look at him, it's too humiliating. So I keep my eyes shut.

"All done," he finally says then turns to Chase. "Your hand is swollen badly. I'd feel better if we took some X-rays."

Chase groans. "Is that necessary?"

"Yeah. I think you're going to need a cast. But I'll get you in and out. Let's go."

Chase sighs and gets up. He grumbles, "Fine."

"I'm sorry," I quietly say, closing my eyes again. I want this nightmare to be over.

Chase tilts my chin up. "Anna."

I open my eyes.

"This is not your fault."

I wish I could stop crying, but I can't.

Vivian clears her throat. "You should go. It's already late."

Chase pats my shoulder and leaves with Xander.

I ask Vivian if I can go to sleep. I don't want to talk. She hands me pajama bottoms and a top, but she's several sizes smaller than me, so they are skin tight.

I stare in the mirror, crying some more. *If you weren't so fat, maybe this wouldn't have happened.*

I'm the same size I've always been, but in the last year, Mitch started pointing out how big my ass and the rest of my body parts are. I've been eating a careful diet of portioned macros so I don't gain any weight. I tried to lose some, but nothing seems to budge.

Why didn't I bring clothes? What am I going to wear tomorrow?

I take my clothes to the laundry room. Vivian is folding towels.

"Hey. You want me to wash those for you?"

"Please. I didn't bring anything." I look down at my body, which is stretching the fabric of her pajamas as far as they can go. "I'm bigger than you. My fat ass isn't going to fit into your clothes, I'm afraid."

"You aren't fat. You have a beautiful figure."

I turn away, and more tears fall.

She quietly says, "Why don't I get out my laptop, and you can order some clothes? There's a service that delivers. It'll be here by ten tomorrow, at the latest, if you order tonight."

"Okay. Thanks."

We sit on the couch, shopping online. I select an outfit and go to check out.

"That's all you're getting?" she asks.

"I have enough at my place."

The sympathetic expression she's been giving me all night reappears. She puts her hand on mine. "Anna, you can't go back there. Chase isn't going to let you leave anytime soon."

"I'm not his hostage."

"Anna—"

"You don't know what happened. It's not Mitch's fault."

She sternly says, "Yes, it is. No one should ever hit you."

"He's stressed. He has a lot going on at work, and this weekend didn't help."

"I'm sure he's pissed. But it doesn't make it right. He could kill you."

I turn away. "He wouldn't." My voice shakes when it comes out.

Vivian stays quiet.

I rise to get my purse to pay for my outfit. I come back and enter my debit card info, but the order won't go through. *Insufficient funds* flashes on the screen.

"Something must be wrong with their system," I say, feeling embarrassed again but knowing I have enough money in my account.

I take my credit card out of my wallet and try to use it. It gets declined as well.

"I don't understand what is going on. I have plenty of money and credit available," I tell Vivian.

"Just put it on mine. The info is already in the system."

"I need to call the bank."

"Anna, does Mitch have access to your accounts?"

My gut twists. "Yes. We have joint accounts. Since he manages money, I let him do what's best for us with it. We keep two thousand dollars in it at all times, and he invests the rest."

"Do you have other cards?"

"No. Mitch doesn't like debt. This one is only for emergencies."

The color in her face drains. "Do you have access to the investment accounts?"

"I assume I do."

"You've never seen them?"

"No. Mitch takes care of it."

She furrows her brows. "Do you have online access to your account?"

"Yes." I try to log in to my bank account first, but I can't get in or reset the password. My credit card is the same. The air in my lungs becomes thick.

I pick up my phone to call the bank. There's a text message from Mitch.

"I'm sorry about tonight. It won't happen again. Call me."

I start to text him, and Vivian pulls my phone out of my hand.

"Do not talk to him tonight."

"Vivian—"

"No. He cut off all your access to your funds. Your money, Anna. Not his, *yours*. My guess is the investment accounts don't even have your name on them."

"He wouldn't do that," I claim, but the voice in my head says that she's right.

"Anna, I know this is hard for you, but you need to be honest with yourself about what is happening right now. If you go back to him, he will hurt you again, possibly kill you. He's cutting off your access to money so he can control you, thinking it'll drive you back to him."

I don't want to hear or believe it. Deep down, I know everything she's saying is true. "Why does this have to hurt so bad," I finally admit.

She pulls me into her arms, and I sob. When my brother comes back from the hospital, I'm still crying. His right hand is in a cast.

Mitch attempts to call me, and Chase grabs my phone.

"What are you doing?" I cry out.

He turns my phone off. "Anna, go to sleep. Tomorrow, we are talking."

"Give me my phone!"

"No. You can have it back tomorrow, if I can trust you."

"If you can trust me?"

"Yes. You aren't talking to him."

"I'm not a child."

Chase looks at me. All I feel is like I've disappointed him. "No. You're my beautiful sister who deserves someone to worship you, not hurt you. And if I have to lock you in a room to keep you away from him, I will. So help me, God, Anna, if he steps foot near you ever again, I will be in jail for killing him with my bare hands."

His words only make me cry harder. I don't know why I'm fighting Chase. I know Mitch crossed the line again. I saw what he was capable of in his eyes, which is far worse than what he did to me. If Chase hadn't shown up, I might be dead right now.

If my friend told me this was going on in her relationship, I would tell her to run. But I've put my heart and soul into the last five years. I love Mitch. Not the person he was tonight, but the person he is most of the time.

Except for the previous year, but that's from the stress of his job. Plus, you were growing your career and had less time to focus on Mitch.

He warned me I was putting my business before us. Tonight is a perfect example.

I had to think I could do it all.

Why am I thinking like this?

I put my hands over my face and sob. "I'm so screwed up!"

Chase pulls me into his arms again. "None of this is on you, Anna."

Then why do I feel like it is? Why can't Mitch love me without hurting me?

The thought that I've been pushing down for over a year, since the last time he beat me, rushes back. *Maybe I'm just unlovable.*

Dmitri

Two Months Later

"LADA'S RETIRING? WITH NO NOTICE?" I SAY IN RUSSIAN.

The barista sets my coffee down, and I pick it up.

Maksim replies over the phone, "Yep."

"She isn't going to finish our project?"

"No. She eloped and is traveling for the next month. She said she would refund our fees."

"We're in the middle of construction on a twenty-million-dollar building. She was supposed to go over materials with us today," I bark.

"I know. I'm walking into the meeting with Lorenzo. Figure it out. I can only focus on this right now. If this prick doesn't sell us this land, we're in trouble." He hangs up.

I curse, louder than I should.

"Bad day?" a familiar woman's voice asks.

I spin. "Vivian. How are you?" I lean down and kiss her cheek. We've worked together on several real estate transactions, and I've done some things with her foundation. Her baby bump is poking out of her jacket.

She smiles. "I think I'm better than you sound."

I sigh. "I'm in the middle of a new build, and our interior designer met some guy, got married, and flew the coop. She was already behind schedule. If I don't get materials ordered soon, we're going to lose millions."

Her face brightens. "I know a really talented designer who can help you."

"Who?"

"It's my sister-in-law. She's from New York and staying with Chase and me. She has her own business there but is relocating, so she doesn't have any projects right now."

"This is a twenty-million-dollar building. It's a large project," I say.

An amused expression appears on her face. "She can handle it. She's amazing."

"Any chance she's Russian?" I tease but also know my brothers prefer to keep everything in the Russian community if possible. Vivian is Greek and won't take it personally because she understands cultural issues more than most.

She softly laughs. "Nope. Grade A American."

I groan. "Guess it's time to expand my Rolodex."

Her eyes turn serious. "She's extremely talented, takes her work seriously, and will meet your budget parameters and deadlines."

There's no time to mess with this. If we don't figure this out, we're in trouble.

"Any chance I can meet her today?"

Vivian points to a corner table. A blonde woman sits in a booth. She's facing the wall. Her hair is in a messy bun, and she has a laptop open. "I need to go home and get ready for a listing appointment, but I can quickly introduce you if you wish. We just got done with yoga."

I motion for her to go first. "Lead the way."

"Anna, this is Dmitri. He's in a jam and needs an interior designer. Dmitri, Anna," Vivian says. "Okay, I'm going to be late if I don't go. You two talk. See you tonight." Vivian pats her on the shoulder and pushes past me.

"What?" Anna turns her head, and my heart beats faster. *It's her.*

I wonder if she ditched her loser boyfriend.

Vivian said she's moving here.

"Anna. Good to see you again." I slide into the booth across from her.

Her face turns red, and she opens her mouth to speak, then shuts it.

I hold my hand out. "I'm Dmitri. I don't think we formally met last time."

She looks at my hand and gapes some more. She finally takes it and mutters, "I'm so confused right now."

I chuckle. "I'm friends with Vivian."

Jesus, this girl is smoking hot.

She's wearing a yoga tank top with a wrap around her arms. She continues to gape at me.

I try not to stare at the little bit of cleavage showing and release her hand. "Vivian said you're an interior designer?"

"Yes," she whispers. She clears her throat and says louder, "Yes."

"I need you, then."

"You...you need me?" The red in her face deepens.

Yep. In my bed, sweating and calling out my name.

"For my building."

"Oh?"

"I'm in quite the predicament."

"What would that be?"

I should stick to the task at hand, but I can't resist. "I didn't think I would see you again."

She takes a nervous breath. "I'm sorry...about...um... I..."

Don't apologize for that dick.

I put my hand over hers. "You're moving here?"

She nods. "I think."

"With him?"

She bites her lip and shakes her head.

"Is it over between you two?"

She looks out the window then clears her throat. "What's your predicament?"

Guess I got my answer. Disappointment fills me.

I need to get this problem solved.

I remove my hand from hers. "I'm in the middle of construction on a multi-million-dollar building. Our designer bailed. We're already behind schedule and need to be ordering materials, or we're going to lose millions."

"And you want me to help you?"

"If you're as good as Vivian claims."

I'm sure you're way better than I could ever comprehend.

She has a boyfriend.

He's a dickhead.

She's still taken.

"Ummm... I...ummm..."

"Tell you what. Why don't we go to the building and do a walk-through then we can go to my place and review the blueprint."

She looks down. "I'm in yoga clothes."

I shouldn't flirt with her, knowing she's taken, but I can't resist. "Guess if we need to get dirty, that won't be a problem then."

Her eyes widen, and she turns crimson.

I push her laptop shut and lean forward. "Do you want to shower first? You look perfect to me, but I can make that happen if you prefer."

Her mouth hangs open.

I lean back. "My driver is out front. Why don't I take you to Vivian's? You do whatever you need to, I'll wait for you, then we'll go. Bring your laptop, and you can write up the contract for me to sign later today."

"You've not seen my work. How do you know I'm the right designer for you?" she blurts out.

I've never hired anyone without looking at their work before. I might be in a desperate situation, but I should still do my due diligence.

"Vivian vouched for you. She said you were transitioning your business and would be able to focus on me. Is she correct?"

"Focus on you?"

Yep. All day and all night.

"This project. And she claimed I could trust you to stay within my budget, meet deadlines, and create something amazing. Was she correct or wrong?"

"Ummm...yes, I can do those things."

"Good. Do you speak any Russian?"

She shakes her head. "No. Do I need to?"

I should at least warn her. "My brothers and I prefer to hire Russians and keep what we can in the community. You might have to communicate with some of them. Many of our workers don't speak English very well."

A line creases between her eyes. "I'm sorry. I don't know any Russian words."

"Will it bother you?" I ask her.

"Not understanding what they say?"

"If I need to be your interpreter."

She hesitates. "No. But are your brothers going to be upset I'm not Russian?"

And we're going to be paying you a fortune, and it's leaving the community? Yep.

I lie. "No. You're saving our asses." I shouldn't touch her, but I trace her fingers. "Maybe I should teach you some words?"

Her hand freezes. "Such as?"

I shrug. "The basics."

"Okay. If you want to, that would be helpful."

"Good. It's settled, then." I rise and hold my hand out to help her out of the booth. "Ready?"

"Where are we going?"

"To shower."

Her eyes widen. She swallows hard.

Yes. Me, you, and your sexy body all lathered up and rubbing against mine.

She's still with the douchebag.

But she's moving here, and he isn't.

"I'll drive you to Vivian's."

"She's only a few buildings down. I can walk."

I pick up her laptop so she can't change her mind. "I'll put this in the car and wait for you then. I've got several calls I need to make."

"Okay. I'll hurry so I don't waste your time."

Nothing with you is wasting my time.

"No rush, kotik. I've got at least an hour of calls to make." I don't, but I don't want her feeling stressed.

She tilts her head. "Kotik?"

Pussycat.

"I'll tell you later, over dinner tonight."

"Dinner?"

She has a boyfriend.

A loser who isn't moving here. Any guy who'd let her move across the country and not follow deserves to lose her.

You're asking for drama.

"Yeah. We've got a lot to do. You eat, don't you?"

She doesn't answer, takes a deep breath, and avoids my gaze. "I'm going to walk to Vivian's now."

I nod to her laptop. "Let me put this in the car."

"I can go myself." It comes out stern.

Back off. You're freaking her out.

"All right, kotik. I'll wait in the car." I motion for her to go first and grab the door before she can open it.

I don't get into the car. I stand outside the vehicle, ogling her perfect, juicy ass until it disappears inside the building.

My phone rings. "Maksim, did you close it?"

He sighs. "We're close."

"We're running out of time."

"I'm handling it."

"Fair enough. I just secured a designer."

"Who did you get?"

"A woman from New York. She's moving her firm here." I don't know how big Anna's business is or anything about it, really. My brothers will kill me if they find out I didn't do any due diligence.

"Who is it? Marisha? Yelena?" Those are two big Russian's in the New York community.

"You don't know her. Her name is Anna."

"Anna what?"

"It's Vivian Monroe's sister-in-law."

The line goes quiet for a moment. "Her husband is American."

"Yep. So are we."

"Not funny. That's a lot of money to withhold from our community."

"We're in a jam. We're going to lose millions if we don't solve this problem. She comes highly recommended and does amazing work," I insist, saying a little prayer that everything Vivian told me about Anna is true.

"We should look for a Russian."

I lie again. "I already signed a contract."

"You didn't?"

"Yep. It's done."

He groans. "I don't have time for this. You hired her, you better make sure you keep your eye on her at all times."

Oh, don't worry, big brother. I have every intention of keep my eyes on her as much as possible.

"Done." I hang up and go inside the building. I sit in the lobby, in a chair facing the elevator so I can see her when she gets off.

There is only one question I try to figure out while I wait for her. *How do I convince her to break up with her douchebag boyfriend?*

Anna

VIVIAN IS RUSHING OUT THE DOOR WHEN I ARRIVE.

"Do you always introduce people like that?" I accuse.

She winces. "Sorry. I'm running late. Did you get the job?"

My butterflies take off. "Ummm... I think so. He's waiting for me downstairs. He wants to take me to the building then his place to review blueprints, then dinner."

Vivian smirks. "His place? Dinner?"

"Now you're making me nervous. I was going to ask if he's a psycho I need to be worried about."

A crazy man who's sexy and totally out of my league.

"Not at all. Dmitri is an excellent catch. Women are always going after him. He's hot and successful. Plus, he has the sexy Russian accent thing going on."

I groan. "I'm not looking for a new boyfriend." I don't even know if Mitch and I are technically broken up. I've spoken to him a few times. He keeps apologizing and says he wants me back. I asked him to put the money back in my accounts, and he said he would when I come back.

The more time that passes, the more I realize I need to stay away. If I go back, he'll suck me back in. But I hate throwing away five years of my life. And no matter what he did to me, I still love him.

I wish I didn't. It would make it easier, especially when I try to sleep at night. But I do.

Vivian made an appointment for me to see her friend, who's a counselor. She works with women who have experienced domestic abuse. At first, I told Vivian that wasn't me, but over the last few weeks, I realize it is me. I am a victim.

And I hate it.

I originally went to the counselor to appease Vivian, but it was different than I thought it would be. I liked her friend, Paula, and have gone three times now. Vivian has been great, and Harper stayed in Chicago with Steven, so she is here, too. But Paula seems to understand how I feel, differently than my family or friends can. And I still can't discuss anything with Chase without him going berserk.

"Oh, and it sounds like it's a problem I'm not Russian?" I say.

Vivian shrugs. "I'll explain the dynamics to you later. He and his brothers are just trying to help out their people."

I already understand it and don't need Vivian to explain it. I have friends from many cultures, and I experienced similar things in New York. "He's going to be my boss."

"Mmm...not really. He's hiring you. It's not like you're his employee."

"Not technically, but still..."

Vivian puts her coat on. "If I were you, I'd wear jeans for the walk-through, then take several outfits to change, depending on where you're going to dinner."

"Seriously? I'm about to break out in hives now."

She snorts. "Don't forget shoes. Those black stilettos you just bought are good ones. Oh, you should take your new red dress!"

"Vivian—"

"Gotta go. Bye! Text me how it's going!"

"Vivian—"

She waves and leaves.

Is this really happening? I go into the bathroom and wince when I see my reflection. I have on no makeup and my hair is all messy.

I shower and shave, dry my hair, then get nervous when I stare at the clothes in my closet, wondering what to wear and pack.

Since Chase won't let me go back to New York to get my stuff, he issued me a credit card. I still have no access to my accounts. The bank said my funds were transferred, and there is nothing I can do. Apparently, I was a joint account holder on Mitch's credit card, and he revoked my privileges. I would apply for my own line of credit, but since I have no income coming in, I didn't want to commit fraud and lie on my application. I didn't want to take Chase's money, but I couldn't keep washing my one outfit every night. He even threatened to pick out my new wardrobe, so I caved and decided it was better to select my own clothes.

Vivian and Harper took me out and made me buy things for all sorts of occasions. It was a little overboard, but the retail therapy made me feel better, even if it was short lived.

I take Vivian's advice and put on jeans, a dressier black top, and ankle boots. I decide to wear my hair straight and keep my makeup more casual so I don't appear to be trying too hard.

This is work, I remind myself.

I pack a dressier outfit I could wear for dinner or to look more professional, and the red dress, plus two different pairs of shoes. At the last minute, I throw my hairbrush, curling iron, hairspray, and makeup in the bag.

My stomach has a million butterflies in it. Dmitri is waiting when I step off the elevator, and the flutters intensify.

He might be one of the hottest guys I've ever seen. He's got the sexy shaved-head look going on and is taller and more built than Mitch. And Vivian was right, his Russian accent will put any girl's panties in a twist. He has just a touch of a beard going on, amazing green eyes that morph between light and dark, and there's a hint of danger about him.

When I saw him on the day of Quinn and Jamison's wedding, he checked me out when I passed him on my way to the bathroom. I tried not to give him any attention and felt guilty for getting flutters since I was with Mitch. When I ran into him at the bar, he checked me out again. Today, his gaze dropped several times to my cleavage when we were in the booth. Then he scanned my body when I stood up.

I could be imagining things, since I haven't had sex in months. Mitch kept blowing me off and making comments about my weight. I hadn't gained any, but it might have me interpreting Dmitri's attention the wrong way.

If I can't keep Mitch, how would a guy like Dmitri even be interested in me?

The thought smacks me in the face. *This is work. Keep it professional.*

Dmitri rises when I step off the elevator, and his eyes travel the length of my body before meeting mine. I feel like his prey when he looks at me like that, but I reprimand myself.

Don't screw up your first job in Chicago.

He reaches for my bag and whistles. "You look nice, kotik. What's in this?"

Kotik. What does it mean?

He said he would tell me at dinner.

I don't know any Russian words. But my heart skips a beat whenever he calls me kotik. And my face feels hot again from him whistling and the way he's looking at me.

"Vivian said I should wear jeans. I wasn't sure what the attire was the rest of the day, so..." I release a nervous breath.

His lips twitch. "Okay. Let's go check the building out." He puts his hand on the small of my back and guides me outside to his car. Tingles race through my body at his touch. He slides into the seat next to me, and his woody, amber scent fills the small space.

My nerves increase, and I twist my fingers together. "How far is the building?"

"Not far. Chicago is smaller than New York. How long have you been here?"

"A couple months."

"Since the wedding?"

My mouth goes dry. I quietly reply, "A few days after."

Dmitri focuses on me.

"What?" I nervously ask.

"Why did you move to Chicago?"

"My brother made me."

"Why?"

My pulse increases, and I peer out the window. "Can we not talk about this?"

He doesn't answer right away. His fingers trace over my hand. "Did I get it wrong, earlier?"

"What?"

"Are you no longer with your boyfriend?"

"No...yes... I don't know. It's...it's complicated."

His jaw clenches.

"Why does it matter anyway?" I blurt out.

He tilts his head. "Is it not obvious to you?"

"What?"

"I'm interested in you."

My pulse beats in my neck. I inhale sharply. "As your designer."

He arches an eyebrow in amusement. "And other ways."

Oh God.

I turn toward the window and focus on the blur of the buildings passing by. I'm barely out of my relationship with Mitch. My things are still in the apartment we've shared for four years. Why would he, Mr. Sex on a Stick, be interested in me?

"Have I scared you, kotik?"

I turn to him. "What does that mean?"

His eyes drift over my body and back to my face. He licks his lips. "You want me to spell it out?"

"I don't know Russian," I blurt out, though he already knows this.

Amusement crosses his face again. I'm not sure what is so funny.

"I said I'd tell you at dinner what it meant. Speaking of which, what did you pack to wear?"

"Ummm..." I shake my head, suddenly feeling overwhelmed and embarrassed. The flames on my cheeks grow hotter.

Why did I bring such a fancy dress?

I shouldn't have listened to Vivian.

Why did I bring a bag?

He drags his finger over my cheek.

I close my eyes. No one has touched me in so long. Since Mitch kept ignoring my affection for him, I'm not sure if it feels good because it's attention or because it's Dmitri.

No, it's definitely him.

He lowers his voice. "These last few months, I wondered what happened to you."

I open my eyes. *He thought about me?*

"Why do you look surprised, my kotik?"

My kotik? He says it like I'm his.

My heart skips another beat.

The car stops, and he glances out the window. "We're here." He reaches to the seat across from us and grabs hard hats, steps out of the car, then reaches in to help me out.

He's a gentleman, too?

Mitch couldn't even open a door for me, much less help me out of the vehicle.

Why am I thinking about Mitch?

This is a huge professional opportunity. I need to keep it that way.

He puts the hat on me then leans into my ear. "It's a good thing you don't know Russian."

"Why?"

He steps back, checks me out slowly, then says, "My guess is the workers are going to say things to you that will make you blush."

I didn't think my face could burn any more, but it does. I'm not used to compliments. All Mitch did was tell me how fat he thought I was over the last year. I try to remember when a man last told me anything nice about my appearance, but I can't.

He grins. "Do you know Polish?"

"No. I only know English."

He wiggles his eyebrows. "There're only a few workers I need to worry about, then."

"I thought you only hired Russians?"

He shakes his head. "No. We don't totally discriminate." He winks and puts his hand on my back. He points to the building. "If you're as good as Vivian says you are and impress my brothers,

I'll make sure you get the next project we're working on. It makes this one look like peanuts."

My stomach flips. I've only worked on individual units. *What has Vivian gotten me involved in?*

This is past my skill level.

Is it?

Fake it until you make it.

I'm going to kill her.

We walk toward the fifteen-story building. Right now, it's just a shell with no windows or doors.

"What is this going to be?" I ask.

"Mid-range apartments. Three to four bedrooms each. We want two design concepts. One for the three-bedroom and one for the four-bedroom, to differentiate them."

Okay, so it's like designing two different units. I can do this.

He motions for me to go first through where the doors would be.

"This is the lobby area?"

"Yes. We want it to be a gathering place for residents."

"The entire floor?"

"Yes."

"Did your other designer create anything yet?"

Dmitri's face falls. In an irritated voice, he says, "No. We kept asking. She was supposed to present something today. We have nothing for any area."

I swallow hard. This is a huge project. I've never done anything this extensive. It excites and terrifies me.

"The hallways, elevators, and common bathrooms need to be designed as well," he informs me.

My chest tightens.

I turn and grab Dmitri's arm. "I'm sorry, but all my samples are in New York. I have swatches of every paint color imaginable, flooring, wallpaper, counters...everything. But nothing here."

"We order directly from the supplier, but we have showrooms here."

"I don't even know where they are in Chicago."

"We have accounts at several. I'll take you. Would it be better to look at the blueprints first or go to the showroom?"

"Probably the blueprints first so I can create a list."

"We will go tomorrow, then."

"If you tell me where it is, I can go myself. I don't want to waste your time." I usually bring samples to my clients for them to approve or choose from.

He spins me and steps so close to me, his body is flush to the back of mine.

My heart hammers faster.

He points over my shoulder. "See all this?"

"Yes."

"If this stays this way, I lose millions. We don't have enough time on this project right now. Anything I can do to help you and speed up the process is not a waste of my time."

I exhale. "Okay."

"I will also add you to the accounts when we are there so you can deal with them in the future without me present." He places his hand on the small of my back. "Let me show you a three- and four-bedroom unit."

I should tell him not to touch me and keep it professional, but I don't.

We go to the second floor and into both units. The men working all start talking in different languages, a few of them whistle, and Dmitri says something to them in Russian.

When we finish, I ask, "What about the roof?"

He raises his eyebrows. "The roof?"

"Are you doing anything with it? I designed one for a friend in New York, and it increased the value of each unit significantly."

"We've never done anything like that before. What kind of increase are we talking about?"

"Twelve percent."

"And the cost to develop it?"

"About two percent."

He whistles. "That's a decent profit."

"I'm sure Vivian would know if it would add extra value for you."

He grins. "Well, let's go look at the roof, kotik."

I still don't know what kotik means, but the more he calls me it, the more special I feel.

He probably uses the term for all women.

We go up to the roof. It's not the highest building in Chicago, but it still has great views, and you can see Lake Michigan.

"What would you do up here?" he asks.

"You're targeting families, right?"

"Yes."

I glance around at the large space. "Create a park with artificial grass." I point. "Make that half a sporting area, the middle part a playground, and this area over here, put in grills, places to read, gather, etc. I'd add glass so the view of Lake Michigan isn't obstructed and it's still safe."

Dmitri studies the bare space. "I like it. Let me talk to my brothers and a few real estate agents, including Vivian, to get their opinions on what it would do to the value of the units."

I step over to the edge. "I don't see any parks around."

"No. There aren't in this neighborhood."

"Well, talk to your people. See what they think."

His eyes twinkle. "You have any other ideas?"

"Not right now."

"Fair enough. Let's go to my place and through the blueprints?"

Nervous flutters flit in my stomach. His place. "Sure."

4

Dmitri

ANNA'S SMARTER THAN I EXPECTED. I DIDN'T THINK SHE WAS ALL looks and no brains, but she's already bringing fresh ideas to the table. I'm not sure if her roof idea will be profitable or not, but it's something my brothers and I never explored and our old designer never mentioned.

I wish she would tell me what the situation is with her ex-boyfriend—or tell me for sure he is her ex. My gut is saying she moved to Chicago to get away from him, but I can't be sure until she confirms it.

We get in the car, and she nervously twists her fingers in her lap.

"How old are you?" I ask.

"Thirty-two."

Good. She isn't as young as she looks.

I've dated my fair share of women in their twenties, but after a while, the difference in our maturity levels always shines through. So I made a pact with myself not to date any woman who isn't thirty or older, but I would have had to break it if she told me she was. I'm not sure what her boyfriend situation is, but I'm going to do everything in my power to make sure she dumps him so I get a fair shot.

"You look younger."

"Hmm," she mutters, as if she doesn't believe me.

"What's that about?"

"Tell that to my wrinkles."

I peer closer at her face, which seems to make her nervous. "Where?"

She scrunches her face and points to several spots.

"Everyone has lines when they do that."

"I didn't use to," she says and looks out the window.

I pull her chin back toward me. "You're a beautiful woman. I'm not sure what kind of crap your boyfriend or ex-boyfriend, whatever he is, has said to you, but he's a moron and full of shit."

She blinks hard and turns away again.

What has he done to you, my kotik?

"How old are you?" she murmurs.

"Forty-three."

She gapes at me. "Really?"

"Yep."

"I thought you weren't past thirty-eight."

"It's my lack of gray hair," I tease.

She glances at my head. "Shaved looks good on you."

It's the first time she's mentioned anything that could mean she's attracted to me, so I do a victory pump in my head. She's not told me to stop my advances toward her, but I wish I knew for sure if she was interested or not.

"How long have you been with your ex?" She hasn't confirmed it, but I'm going to call him that so she can start getting used to the term.

"Five years."

"He's around thirty-five?"

Her eyes widen. "How did you know his age?"

I shrug. "Guessed it. So before him, who did you date? Anyone serious?"

"Not really."

"And they were all close to your age?"

"Yes. Why are you asking?"

I tuck a lock of her hair behind her ear. "I wanted to know if you've been with a real man before. I figured you haven't."

Her face reddens. I've lost track of how many times she's made my dick twitch with her sexy little blush. She quietly asks, "What made you assume that?"

"Because if you had been with a real man, you wouldn't have stayed five years with your ex. And you wouldn't be grappling with whatever it is that is confusing you about him, right now."

She bites on her lip, and her eyes fill with tears. She turns and wipes her face.

What did that piece of shit do to her?

I can't stand not knowing. It's driving me nuts. I saw enough the day I met her about the type of person he is, and I'm sure I only saw a piece of his nastiness. And when he called her ass fat, she was embarrassed but not surprised, which meant it wasn't the first time he degraded her.

Any man who can't appreciate an ass like hers is a fool. If I could make a mold and set it on my coffee table to stare at, I would.

Time to change subjects so she doesn't get more upset.

"How long have you had your business?" I ask.

"Just a few years. I was starting to make a good name in New York."

And now she's moving here after working so hard to build her reputation. What did that fucker do to her?

"I can see why. You have good ideas."

"I haven't shown you anything yet."

"If the roof pans out to be profitable, I'm increasing your fee."

She tilts her head. "You don't even know my fee."

"Speaking of which, when we get to my place, we need to get your contract drawn up and signed."

She stays silent.

"Why are you staring at me like that?"

"I've not had a client ever push me to sign my contract before."

"Is there something in it I need to be cautious about?" I'll read it before I sign it, but I'd be surprised if it isn't similar to other designer contracts.

"No, of course not."

I put my head next to hers. "From now on, when you get a new client, you have them sign your contract before you give them ideas."

"But you've not seen my work."

"You could have pulled it up online and shown me."

She bites her lip.

"I know a lot of these builders. They will take advantage of you. You give them ideas, they will use them and find the cheapest person to implement them, cutting you out of the picture."

"I'm not the best at the pricing side of things. I just want to do the design part. I can run the numbers to stay within the budget, but I'm bad at charging. My brother, Chase, he's the one in the family with the business brain."

I hold her face next to mine. "There's nothing wrong with your brain. I will teach you."

"Teach me?"

"Yeah. How to deal with these builders in this city and not get ripped off."

"Are they that bad?"

"Some of them, yes. If you want a list of who you can trust and who to handle with caution, I'll give that to you as well."

She glances at my lips with her blue doe eyes.

She hasn't confirmed he's her ex yet.

One thing I won't be is any woman's piece on the side. I force myself to move away from her face. The car stops, and I glance out.

"We're here." I grab her bag and laptop.

"I can carry those," she says.

"No, my little kotik." I step out and reach for her hand. We stop at security, they give her a pass, and we get in the elevator.

"Are you from Russia, or do you only know how to speak the language?"

"My family immigrated when I was eight."

"Was that rough?"

"A bit. But I was a child. It was easier for my brothers and me than my parents."

"How many brothers do you have?"

The elevator dings and opens up into the penthouse.

Her eyes open wide. "Wow! Great view!"

The entire front of my house is glass, overlooking Lake Michigan and parts of Chicago. It's a windy day, and the white caps have picked up. The trees have changed colors and are vibrant red, orange, and yellow. It's still fairly light out, but it'll be getting dark soon.

"Thanks."

"So, how many brothers do you have?"

"Three. Maksim, Boris, and Sergey, in that order. I'm the second oldest."

"No sisters?"

"Nope. Is it just you and Chase?"

She shakes her head. "I have another brother, Nick, in New York. He's the oldest."

"No sisters?"

"No." She crosses her arms and taps her biceps, looking nervous again.

I pull out a chair at the table. "Have a seat."

She sits.

I set her laptop in front of her then take the chair next to hers. "First things first. Write up my contract."

She furrows her brows. "Umm..." She stares at the waves and fidgets.

"Anna, why aren't you tapping numbers on your computer?"

She puts her hands over her face.

I remove them.

"I'm not sure how to charge you. I've not done anything this big before. I've done a lot of individual projects but not an entire building. If you don't want to work with me, I understand. I should have told you earlier."

I point to her computer. "Pull your contract up. Let me see it."

She does, and I read through it. "You have a good contract."

Totally undercharging her services.

"Chase made me get it when he found out I wasn't using one."

I try not to shake my head so she doesn't feel belittled, but I'm glad her brother watched out for her. "Hold on a minute." I go into my office, pull out the contract I had with Lada, and hand it to her.

"What's this?"

"How Lada, the other designer, billed us."

She reads it and opens her mouth. "Wow. She charges a lot!"

"You're worth not a penny less."

She shakes her head. "You don't know that. You've still not seen my work."

"Sure, I do." I push her computer back to her. Change your rates to hers."

She hesitates.

I tease, "Do I need to fill your contract in for you?"

"No."

I tap the laptop. "Get typing, kotik. I'm going to pull the blueprints out while you finish."

"Ummm...are you sure—"

"Yep. Now, all I want to hear is your fingers hitting those keys. The sooner we get done, the closer we get to dinner."

And I get to see what you brought to wear on your sexy little body.

I take the blueprints out of the office then unroll them across the table. "You done?"

She nods.

"Email it to me." I pull my card out of my wallet. "Here."

She sends it, I pull it up on my phone, scan it over, sign, then send it back to her.

We spend the next few hours going through the blueprints. She makes a long list of items for tomorrow, and I shut the laptop. "Okay, what did you bring to wear for dinner?"

Her face turns red. "Vivian told me to bring a dress, but I also brought a skirt and top, depending on where we're going?"

"Put your dress on, kotik. I'm hungry, are you hungry?"

She scans my face and stares at my lips again. "Yeah."

"Good. I'm going to take a shower. Let me show you where you can get ready."

"How much time do I have?"

"As much as you want."

She tilts her head, as if she doesn't believe me, which makes me think her ex was always making her rush to get ready.

I lean into her ear. "Take all the time you want. I've got all night. And I'll probably still be hungry after dinner."

5

Anna

DMITRI LEADS ME TO A GUEST SUITE AND SETS MY BAG ON THE BED. He pauses, and my flutters take off. All day he's been looking at me with this confident expression. His gaze lingers on my different body parts as if he's undressing me. If anyone else did it, I'd think they were a sleazy pervert. I would be self-conscious about the size of my body, hearing Mitch call me fat. But Dmitri's eyes make me feel hot. He hasn't done anything inappropriate, but his expression tells me he wants to. And it makes me border-line desperate for him to do whatever he wants to me.

Even before Mitch stopped paying attention to me, he never looked at me the way Dmitri does. I've been trying to be professional and not squirm all day around him. And I can't stop staring at his lips. He's caught me several times, and a cocky expression forms on his face. But instead of kissing me, he always backs away.

Being at his house doesn't help my current attraction to him. Everything about it reeks sexy bachelor. Slate-gray walls, mixed with black leather furniture, dark woods, and soft light, seamlessly flow throughout the penthouse. The backdrop of the lake, with the waves crashing against the shore, only makes me wonder more what it would be like to have him crashing against me.

"Take your time, kotik." He winks and leaves.

I release the breath I was holding. The same view of the water is in the bedroom. Soft, Russian music comes across the surround sound, increasing my nerves and throbbing body parts simultaneously.

How much effort should I put in?

He's a client. Don't give him any reason to think there could be anything more.

I remove my dress from the bag, happy there aren't any wrinkles. I take out my shoes and stare at the makeup and curling iron.

Against my better judgment, I go all out. I look in his drawers and find a pack of razors, shaving cream, toothbrush, toothpaste. I tie my hair in a knot, take a shower, and even though I shaved earlier, I shave again.

When I finish my shower, I spend an hour on my hair and makeup, then slip my red dress and black stilettos on.

My phone rings.

"Hey, Vivian."

"How's it going with Dmitri?" Her question sounds innocent, but I know what she's really asking me.

"Fine. I got the job."

"Of course you did. You're brilliantly talented."

My family always tells me I am. Mitch never really raved about my skills and always dropped comments about it being a glorified hobby and taking time away from him. So I always thought my family was telling me that to be nice. But now that Dmitri hired me and made me charge what his designer was, I'm not sure what to think.

"Ummm...he made me change my rates," I blurt out.

Her voice lowers. "What do you mean?"

"He showed me his other designer's contract."

"She is always in demand. She's good." Her voice changes to worry. "But what did he make you do with your contract? You already are undercharging, and I've told you this several times."

"I feel guilty," I admit.

"Why? I'm not following?"

"He made me write in her rates."

Silence fills the line.

"Vivian? Are you still there?"

She clears her throat. "I only know Dmitri a little. He's been generous with my foundation, and we've done some real estate transactions before. One thing I know about him is if he can skin a snake to get out more blood, he will. But if he believes in you, he won't let anyone take advantage of you, including him. I've seen both sides of him."

My heart beats faster. "But, he's not seen my work yet."

"Then you said or did something to make him think you're worth it. And you are, Anna. So I wouldn't feel guilty or second-guess it. Your work is amazing. You're going to rock his project."

I stay quiet.

"Are you still there?" Vivian asks.

"Yes."

In a teasing tone, she says, "I was really calling to see if you were coming home tonight."

"What?"

"For dinner," she adds, but I know she's insinuating more.

"No. I just got ready. I probably should let you go so I don't keep him waiting."

"Are you wearing the red dress?"

"Yes."

"And you took the black stilettos?"

"Yes."

"Good. Where is he taking you?"

"I don't know, but you're making me nervous."

She laughs. "Okay. I won't wait up. Should I cover for you with Chase?"

I groan. "I'm not in high school."

"Yeah, but do you want fifty questions when you get home?"

"God, no."

"Okay, then let me do my wifely duty tonight."

"Too much info. Don't want to think about you and my brother."

She laughs. "Have fun. See you in the morning."

I hang up and assess myself in the full-length mirror then turn and stare at my ass, wishing it could magically get smaller.

The longer I look at my reflection, the more nervous I get.

Crap! I forgot a handbag.

I clutch my phone and take my wallet out of my purse. I open the door and step out.

The lights are dim, softly glowing around the ceiling's edge, intensifying the penthouse's provocativeness. Darkness has set in, and stars light up the night sky over the lake, along with lit-up buildings. A woman's voice seductively sings in Russian.

Dmitri is at the window with his back to me. The fabric of his black, long-sleeve shirt stretches across his shoulders, outlining his muscular physique, and is tucked into his belted black pants.

He's on the phone, speaking in Russian. His voice sounds angry. I've not heard it sound rough before except when he threatened Mitch at the bar, and even that was subdued compared to this. I take a few steps backward.

What am I doing here?

My shoes clatter on the wood, and he spins.

His eyes morph from dark to light then to confused. He says something else and hangs up. As he comes toward me, I take more steps back.

He freezes. "Anna, why are you retreating from me?"

My heart is pounding too fast. My lungs seize up. I try to catch my breath.

What is happening to me?

He holds his hands in the air in front of him. In a soft voice, he says, "Do you think I'm going to hurt you?"

I'm shaking, and I don't know why.

He slowly moves toward me and pulls me into his chest. He brushes his lips on my head. "Why are you scared, kotik?"

His arms and woodsy, amber scent calm me.

Get a grip.

"I'm fine," I reply, but it comes out shaky. This hasn't happened to me before. My anxiety turns to embarrassment and grows from his next question.

He tilts my chin so I can't avoid him. His green eyes darken, and his voice is stern. "Anna, what did he do to you?"

So much shame fills me. "Nothing."

"You lie to me." He says it softly, and as a fact, not a question.

I close my eyes, not wanting to look into his and hoping to stop the pooling tears in mine.

"Tell me it's over with him, and you aren't going back."

I open my eyes. "My stuff is still there."

His jaw clenches. "I see. But things can be replaced. You cannot, my beautiful kotik."

I glance into the darkness, not used to being called beautiful, or feeling safe, like I do in his arms, or the pulse in my body growing every second he holds me.

He kisses my forehead. "Let's go to dinner. We will talk more about this later."

I don't want to talk about it later. But something tells me there is no point arguing.

He reaches to take my hand, but I'm still clutching my phone and wallet.

"I... I forgot to bring a purse. My other one..."

He takes my phone out of my hand and slides it in his pocket. "Give me your ID. Leave the wallet."

I obey.

His lips brush the back of my hand and tingles race up my arm. He devours my body with his eyes, glances behind me to my ass, and pins his gaze to mine. "Looks like they made this dress just for you."

Butterflies take off in my stomach. For the first time, I notice a chest tattoo peeking out from under his shirt. I decide to be bold and trace what I can see with my finger. "What is this of?"

"It's Russian. It says, 'No past, no future.'"

I repeat it.

"Without our past, we cannot have our future. It shapes us and determines what we will and will not tolerate going forward. We can never forget the past lessons, or they will be repeated in our future."

I inhale deeply, letting it sink into my head.

He wraps his arm around my waist, and his palm sits on my ass cheek. He leans down to my ear. "I'm hungry, my kotik." His hand lightly squeezes my ass, making me think he's not hungry for food but me. And no man has ever made me feel that way before.

Dmitri leads me out of the penthouse and into his car, not taking his hand off my bottom until I slide onto the seat.

I instantly miss it. As self-conscious as Mitch has made me about my ass, I love the feel of his palm on it.

"I should have asked you earlier. Are you a picky eater?" he asks.

"Do I look like one?" I reply then regret it.

Why can't I be confident like I used to be? When I used to date, before Mitch, I never would have said anything like that.

His eyes darken. He swiftly pulls me onto his lap. "You know what I see, my kotik?"

I don't respond, embarrassed for my lack of self-confidence, and try to turn away, but he doesn't let me.

His fingers stroke my ass. "I see a blonde bombshell with a sexy ass..." He glides his finger up the side of my body and traces the top of my dress then around the fullness of my chest. "Voluptuous breasts..." His other hand slides between my legs, an inch from my sex. "And perfect thighs."

My lungs take in air in shorter breaths. My pulse beats faster in my neck. I squirm on his lap, squeezing my thighs against his warm hands, staring at his lips.

He leans into my ear. His breath is hot, and more flutters explode in every part of me. His deep voice and Russian accent get thicker. "I still haven't heard you say it."

"What?" I whisper, the scent of him making my blood pound harder.

"That you aren't going back to him."

I freeze, not sure why he keeps asking me or cares so much. I'm pretty sure he can have a different woman every night in his bed. Even Vivian said women are constantly throwing themselves at him.

His middle finger strokes so close to my slit, I'm sure he can feel the heat radiating through my panties. His lips brush against the skin under my ear, and he murmurs Russian.

I rock my hips on his lap and turn my face toward his so our mouths are only inches apart. "I don't know what you said."

He pins his eyes to my mouth and says some other things I can't comprehend, while caressing my ass cheek and thighs.

I close my eyes, enjoying the way words roll off his tongue, wanting him to kiss me more than I've ever wanted anyone to. The car comes to a halt, and he stops talking. I realize I'm panting. I open my eyes and his drill into mine, blazing hot, his face hardened.

Is he mad?

The driver opens the door, and Dmitri slides his hand off my thighs. He moves me off him, steps on the sidewalk, then reaches in to help me out.

There's a line around the corner of the restaurant, but he guides me to the front. A bouncer a bit smaller than Dmitri slaps hands with him and speaks in Russian then motions for us to go through.

Russian music plays, similar to the kind Dmitri put on while we got ready. The restaurant is dark, except for candles on the tables and dim lights around the ceiling. A hostess smiles at us. He dips down and kisses her cheek.

A tiny bit of jealousy shoots through me. It's an innocent gesture, but I don't like his lips on her. I don't know what they say, but she turns and smiles brighter at me.

I force myself to be polite, and she leads us through the restaurant. A woman is singing on stage, along with a three-person band. Her long gold dress glitters against the dark backdrop. Sex oozes from every word she sings.

The hostess escorts us to a booth. It's hidden from others but still has a view of the stage. Dmitri motions for me to slide in. I do, and he sits next to me.

"Anna, do you drink wine?"

I nod.

He says something to the hostess, and she smiles, then leaves. A waitress appears quickly with a red bottle, opens it, pours a few inches in a goblet, and hands it to Dmitri.

He puts it in front of me.

"I'm not a wine connoisseur," I admit. "I'm not picky."

His lips twitch. "I never said you were. And I want to know your opinion, kotik."

"Why?"

"Humor me. Drink. Tell me your thoughts."

I take a sip. The semi-sweet notes, full of blackberry and cherry, burst on my tongue. "It's delicious."

He glances at my lips, says something to the waitress, and she fills the rest of my glass and his. He turns, has another conversation I don't understand, and she disappears.

Food arrives quickly. One dish after another is set in front of us until the table is full. Dmitri has me try everything first, feeding me, grazing his hands the entire time on my thigh or back. I don't know what anything is. I've never had Russian food. He tells me the name of each item, but I don't remember any of it.

He makes me feel good about myself and I laugh throughout the night, and it's the first time in a long time I've genuinely felt happy. He never takes his gaze off me, often brushing his lips against my ear as he talks. By the time dinner is over, my body is throbbing and hot.

All I want is for him to kiss me. But he never does.

I've never met anyone and had sex with them right away, or even knew I wanted to. But I know I do with Dmitri. I'm burning for him, aching to have his hands all over me. And I see how much he wants me, in his eyes.

We leave the restaurant. He slides me on his lap and we stare at each other's lips. I think he's finally going to kiss me, but my phone rings, pulling me out of my trance. He yanks it out of his pocket then glances at it. His jaw clenches. He hands me the phone.

Mitch and my face light up the screen. It was taken a few months after we started dating, and we look happy in it.

I hit the button to ignore the call, and he calls again. I do the same thing, and text messages pop up. I turn off my phone. "Sorry," I say, but it sounds weak and pathetic, even to my own ears.

Dmitri says nothing, only scowls and turns toward the window.

I'm not sure how to get us back to where we were. I don't know why I had to bring my phone.

We go back to Dmitri's place. He avoids my eyes. I'm not sure what to do. When we get inside, he goes into the bedroom and brings my bag and purse out. His face is hard. Hurt and annoyance are in his eyes. "I'll take you home now, Anna." He hands me my license and wallet.

I step forward and put my hand on his cheek.

He stares at the ceiling.

"Dmitri," I quietly say.

He glances down. "I'm not playing this game, Anna."

"What game?" I ask, confused.

"Where I'm in second, and you go back and forth between us."

"I would never do that," I claim.

"No?"

"No."

"But you've not told me you aren't going back to him. And he still calls you."

"I told him not to anymore."

"But he still is."

"He's never listened."

"Then block him."

Mitch will be so pissed.

My heart pounds in my chest. I should pick up my phone, turn it on, and block Mitch. But I don't. I only stare at Dmitri with my insides quivering.

He shakes his head. "I want you in my bed. All night...until the morning sun is shining so bright, we're forced to get up. But until you tell me it's over and you aren't going back to him, it's not happening."

I'm not sure why I can't tell Dmitri it's over between Mitch and me or block Mitch out of my life forever. I know Mitch isn't who I should be with and don't want him anymore. Dmitri is who I want.

But he's full of fire, and mystery, and a bit of danger. And I'm barely out of my last relationship.

So I let my fear guide me instead of my heart. I say nothing and let him lead me out of his penthouse, into the car, then up to Chase and Vivian's.

The elevator opens, and I turn to him. We've said nothing since his place.

"I...ummm...it's not that I still want him," I say, unsure what I'm trying to tell him and why I'm stopping us being together.

He stays silent, staring at me.

"Ummm..." Tears well in my eyes.

He sighs, steps forward, and pulls me into his arms. "Go to sleep, kotik. I'll pick you up tomorrow to go to the showrooms."

I gaze up at him, wanting his lips on mine, and knowing I blew it.

He releases me, steps back, and motions for me to get off the elevator.

I do so hesitantly then watch the doors close, wondering how I manage to screw up everything in my life.

6

Dmitri

"WE AREN'T GETTING ANYWHERE," SERGEY SAYS, SPOTTING ME.

I lift the bar in the air, grunting. I've added more weight than I usually lift, trying to work some frustration over Anna out of my system.

It's not helping. I'm barely listening to Sergey, and I should be. The deadline we set for Lorenzo Rossi to sell us the land is quickly approaching. If we don't get it, we can't move forward with our plans for the surrounding land. The millions we've invested, we'll lose.

But all I can think about is Anna. I can't figure out why her ex has such ahold on her. I'm not positive about what he did to her, but I know he hurt her. Her things are still in New York, which means it would be easy for her to run back to him.

"Argh," I grunt, pushing the last rep up, barely getting through it.

Sergey grabs the bar and helps guide it onto the rack. "Not bad, old man. I thought you weren't going to be able to finish."

I snort. Sergey's ten years younger than me. Since I hit forty, he likes to remind me about his youth.

"Jesus, you trying to kill yourself?" Maksim asks, walking toward us with a towel around his neck and sweat dripping down it. Boris is next to him, just as sweaty.

"Needed to show you all who's boss," I claim, trying to avoid telling them any of my frustrations. "So, Lorenzo is trying to take us for more than our verbally agreed-upon price?"

"Enough that it doesn't make the project worth it," Maksim replies.

Boris wipes his face. "Someone should make him disappear."

Maksim whacks him in the chest with his towel. "Stop acting like a thug. And that won't get the property transferred to us."

"I knew we shouldn't have bought those lots without that piece. We were asking for trouble," Sergey mutters.

"Shoulda, coulda, woulda," Boris chides. "We did it. Now we deal with it."

"Unless we come up with a way to make Lorenzo come down on his price, we're screwed. Our land isn't worth the investment to clear it if we don't have his lot," Sergey continues.

Boris groans. "You want to tell us something we don't know, Einstein?"

"Enough," Maksim growls. "Dmitri, what's the situation with the East Bay development? Is that designer going to have a concrete plan for us so we can get these materials ordered?"

"What designer?" Boris asks.

Maksim raises his eyebrows at me. "Dmitri hired a new designer yesterday since Lada bailed."

Sergey's eyes light up. "Please tell me you hired that sassy mouthed Irena. I'll take over all the supervision if you did."

Boris scratches the corner of his lips. "You've got drool on your mouth."

"Did you see that woman's legs?"

"Like you would even have a chance. She'd eat you alive."

"Oh, there would be eating going on. But I'd be the one doing it."

Boris snorts.

Maksim groans.

I rise and grab my towel, wiping my face. "Sorry to be the dream breaker, but I hired someone else."

"Who?"

"An American," Maksim says in a deadpan voice.

"Are you crazy? That's a lot of money to let out of the community," Boris says.

"Is she hot?" Sergey asks.

Yeah. The hottest woman on earth.

"Show some respect." It comes out in a growl, and I didn't mean it to. I avoid their gazes.

"Tell me you didn't hire her to get some ass," Maksim mutters.

"Shut up. I don't need to hire anyone to get ass. She's super talented and has big ideas." I can back this up because I spent the night on her website, looking at her before-and-after photos. Vivian was right about her talent.

He crosses his arms and tilts his head. "Like what?"

"Like how to increase our profit."

"How?"

I pick up my water and down half the bottle. "She did a roof in New York. It increased the net profit by ten percent. Since we're targeting families, she had some great ideas and pointed out how there aren't any parks close to the building."

"Ten percent?" Maksim asks, and I can almost see him calculating the math in his head.

"It's a lot of zeros," I sarcastically say.

"No shit," he mumbles.

I drink the rest of my water and toss the bottle in the trash. "She may be American, but Lada never brought anything to us to increase the overall sales potential."

"We need to get some real estate agents to weigh in on that," Boris says.

"I'll handle it."

"And her?" Sergey asks.

"What about her?"

"You going to handle her, too?"

"Shut up." I take my towel and smack him with it. "Don't disrespect her."

Boris grunts. "So, you did hire her to get in her pants?"

I point at him and Sergey. "You two need to grow up. She came highly recommended and is talented. Shut your mouths about her, or we're going to have problems."

They both give me a smug look. I ignore them and go to the locker room, not into listening to them.

Maksim follows me.

"I don't want to hear your bullshit about her not being Russian." Maksim means well, and I understand giving opportunities to Russians in our community, but we're also American, and sometimes he forgets it. We fled Russia in the middle of the night, and we're a shining example of the American Dream. I strip off my clothes and walk naked to the shower.

The water is cold, but I step under it, hoping it helps get Anna off my mind.

"We need a plan B if we can't get Lorenzo to sell us his land. It's too much to lose. Even if it's something that makes the loss smaller."

I take a few pumps of the soap in the wall container. "It would have been smarter for us to have a plan B before we bought those pieces of land."

"We didn't know the mayor was going to sell the parcel to Lorenzo."

I grunt. "No, but we still should have been better prepared. It was cocky of us to do something like this." If we don't get the land, we won't go bankrupt, but it will hurt. And it will put a lot of our guys out of work—men who rely on our projects to feed their families.

Maksim steps in the space next to mine, and my other brothers come in the locker room.

I finish showering, dry off, and put on my clothes.

"Let's go to breakfast and figure out a plan B." Maksim comes out of the shower and opens his locker.

"Sorry, can't today."

"Why? What's more important than this?"

"East Bay."

"The foremen have it under control."

I sling my bag over my shoulder. "I'm taking Anna to the showrooms."

"Since when do we do the designer's job for them?"

I slam my locker, fed up with everything, my patience wearing thin. "She's new to Chicago. I need to add her to the accounts. If I'm with her, it will save time. I can place the order today, instead of dragging it out, since Lada screwed us so bad."

Maksim's icy blue eyes turn to slits. "Make sure you're keeping our priorities straight, little brother."

I step toward him. "I thought the twenty million we have wrapped up in East Bay is a priority?"

"You know what I'm getting at."

"Mind your own business." I step back.

"If she's under a contract with our firm, it is my business."

"Okay. You win."

He shifts on his feet. "What's that?"

I'm so over this entire conversation.

"I'll give her the address of the showrooms, have her go on her own, then drag numerous materials all over Chicago. She can present to all of us, and we can debate about it all. In the end, we'll go with whatever she advises us because that's what we always do with any of our designers. At the end of the week, I'm sure we'll know what we want and then we can order everything. It'll cost us a minimum of two hundred thousand for the time delay, but hey, at least you'll have your say."

He clenches his jaw.

"Yeah, I thought so. I'll send you the sheet on what I order today." I walk out of the locker room and slam the door on my way out.

I'm angry we're about to lose millions and Lada screwed us over. I'm happy Anna's on the project, and we're going to get some fresh ideas. I think it's been long overdue anyway. And I don't want to hear my brothers' opinions today.

I get in the car and realize I don't even have Anna's phone number. It's only seven in the morning, but I dial Vivian.

She picks up after one ring. "Morning."

"Sorry to bother you so early, but I didn't get Anna's cell number or tell her what time I would pick her up today."

"She's here. Do you want to talk to her?"

I debate. "Actually, would you have time this morning to meet? I have some things I want to run by you and get your opinion on."

"Sure. When do you want to come over?"

"I just left the gym, so whenever."

"Come over now. I'll tell Anna to get ready."

"Thanks, but tell her there is no rush. I don't want her to stress."

"All right. Coffee?"

"Sure."

"See you soon."

I hang up, and my stomach flips. I don't like where I left things with Anna last night. I wish it would have ended differently.

If only she wasn't still caught up on her ex.

If he really is her ex.

God, please let him be and stay her ex.

The car ride to Vivian's is short. I'm soon standing in her kitchen. Anna is nowhere to be seen, which doesn't calm my nerves.

"Sit." Vivian points to the table. She hands me a cup of coffee and takes a seat across from me.

Chase walks in and slaps my hand. "Dmitri. How are you?"

"Good. You?" I don't know Chase very well. I've only met him a few times. I'm aware of his business acumen as well as his friends he seems to be partnered with who have all moved to Chicago from New York.

"I'm good. I heard you hired Anna for one of your new builds."

"Yeah. She's saving our ass. My designer took off with no notice."

"Well, thanks for hiring her. Maybe growing her business here will give her the confidence she needs to leave her old life in New York behind without any second thoughts."

My stomach flips.

Vivian clears her throat and smiles. "So, what did you want to ask me about?"

"It's actually an idea Anna had yesterday. If we develop the roof on the East Bay project with an athletic area, park, and community gathering area, do you think we can get more for the units?"

Vivian takes a sip of water. "There is no park anywhere near that area."

"That's what Anna pointed out."

"If done right, I think you can get substantially more."

"How much more?"

She thinks for a moment. "Off the top of my head, ten to thirty percent."

"Thirty percent?"

She puts her hand in the air. "Don't get excited. That's the top end. But I would be surprised if you only get ten."

Don't get too excited. It's only one real estate agent's opinion. I need to talk to several.

"Okay. I've got another issue I need to pick your brain on."

"What's that?"

Chase sits next to Vivian with a cup of coffee.

"Are you aware we bought up the Five Fifty-two block?"

"Sure."

I tap my fingers on the table. "We've got an issue."

She raises her eyebrows.

"There's one lot we don't have. The mayor agreed to sell it to us. At the last minute, he gave it to Lorenzo Rossi for nothing. We agreed on a verbal price with Lorenzo, but he's been screwing us around and now wants so much it would make the project not worth it."

"The mob boss's, son?" Chase asks.

"Yeah. He claims he's '*legit*.'" I put my fingers in quotes.

"I'm sure he is," Chase sarcastically says.

I rub my hands on my face. The day has just begun, and I already feel exhausted from it. "I need a plan B. My brothers and I are going to lose millions if we can't get that lot, and we arrogantly bought the rest without any other ideas."

Vivian's eyes widen, which only makes my stomach drop more. She might understand property and developments better than my brothers and me.

Chase leans forward. "Whatever you do, don't get my sister involved with that man."

"Involved with who?" Anna's voice cuts in.

My blood pounds harder just from the sound of her voice. I glance toward her, and it only heats my veins further.

The woman can wear anything and make my adrenaline spin. Her navy pencil skirt and form-fitting, thin, cream sweater aren't holding my desire for her down. She glances nervously at me with her big, blue eyes, and I wink at her, forgetting her brother is in the room but not wanting her to feel strange around me after how we left things last night.

She blushes and addresses Chase, who seems oblivious about my attraction toward her, too focused on my negotiations with Lorenzo.

"Answer me," Anna says.

It's the first time I've heard her be assertive. I like it, and my dick twitches.

"Nothing you need to worry about," he says.

She puts her hand on her hip, pulling the material of her shirt tighter against her waist and breasts. I almost groan out loud. She's got the perfect little body, and it's driving me crazy.

She glares at Chase. "I'm not a child."

He rises and takes his cup to the sink. "Didn't say you were."

She follows him. "You're treating me like one." Her pencil skirt hugs each cheek of her round ass in perfection, teasing me further.

She's going to drive me insane all day.

"No, I just don't have to tell you everything."

"Fine. I'll go around you and ask Dmitri." She spins. Her eyes are full of fire, and her face is slightly red.

I reach my limit. I rise. "We need to get going, or we'll miss our appointments."

"I want to know who I'm not supposed to get involved with."

"Chill out, Anna," Chase mutters.

She turns and points at him.

Her ass, once again, grabs my attention.

"This is why I shouldn't live with you," she asserts.

"So, you'd rather be back in New York getting the shit beat out of you?"

"Chase!" Vivian reprimands him.

I knew that bastard ex of hers did something to her. But my desire to kill him only gets stronger with this new information.

Her face grows redder, and she picks up her purse, then avoids me, walking quickly toward the elevator.

"Anna, I'm sorry," Chase calls after her then mutters, "Shit."

He confirmed my suspicions, but I don't like what he just did. "Not cool. Your sister deserves a bit more respect, don't you think?"

He crosses his arms, and his face hardens.

I turn to Vivian and kiss her cheek. "Thanks for your advice and the coffee."

"Sure. I'll think about your other issue."

"Thanks." I join Anna at the elevator, but she avoids me.

It feels like forever when the doors finally open. We step inside, and she presses the lobby button.

The elevator moves down, but I hit the stop button. I spin and step toward her. She retreats to the wall.

I slide both hands in her hair. My lips brush against hers. "Tell me you aren't going back to him, my kotik."

A tear slips down her cheek. She closes her eyes and whispers, "I'm so embarrassed."

I kiss her tear. "Just say yes or no. Are you going back to him?"

Another tear falls. She opens her eyes. "No."

I nod. "Good." I press my lips to hers, and she gasps, then opens her mouth, sliding her tongue against mine.

Everything I thought about what it would be like to kiss her is wrong. I assumed it would take her a while to warm up to me. That I was the hungry one and my attraction for her was more one-sided, and I would need to show her how good we could be together. But she comes at me like a tiger pouncing on its prey, as if she could devour me through our kisses alone.

And my desire to consume every inch of her flesh grows more intense. Her lips alone are a delicious piece of chocolate, melting against mine to the point I don't know where I end and she begins.

Everything she gives me is raw and real. There's nothing indecisive in her kisses. She wants me, and I wonder who needs who more. And if tongues and lips could ruin a man, hers would be the bullet that destroys me.

Every second that passes, she lights me up to the point my body is humming against hers. When the alarm goes off, she's breathless and quivering in my arms. A man's voice tells me to press the button to unlock the elevator. I reach for it, hit it, then slide my tongue back in her mouth, palming her ass as my erection hardens against her stomach.

The doors open, and someone clears their throat. I take her hand and quickly guide her out to the car. The door is still open when I pull her on my lap.

She holds my head in her hands and smashes her lips to mine. My blood continues to spin in my veins.

"Stick to the agenda, boss?" my driver asks in Russian.

I barely hear him. "Mm-hmm."

He shuts the door and I dive further into the magnificent wonderland of Anna Monroe.

7

Anna

"YOUR SEXY LITTLE ASS IN THIS SKIRT IS DRIVING ME NUTS, MY kotik," he murmurs in my ear with his Russian accent, while squeezing my cheek with his palm. His hot breath sends more tingles down my spine, and I squirm on his lap, rubbing his erection with my outer thigh.

He groans, fists my hair, and presses his lips to mine.

Everything I thought I knew about a good kiss ceases to exist. His tongue creates chaos in my veins, flicking against mine fast and needy, then slower so I can catch my breath, then with more hunger than before.

His hand moves from my ass to my leg. He slides it up my skirt and between my thighs, stroking my skin with his thumb. It's an adrenaline injection straight to my sex without him even touching it, and I whimper.

"I want these thighs around my neck," he mumbles and inches his fingers closer to my wet panties.

"Yes," I whisper then glide my tongue urgently around his.

The car stops. I don't notice it until the door opens. Dmitri turns and barks out something in Russian to the driver, and he shuts the door.

Dmitri returns to kissing me. After a few minutes, he stops. Both our chests are heaving, trying to find air. He tucks a lock of my hair behind my ear then holds my cheek in his palm. "Kotik, tell me you aren't going to see or talk to him again."

I freeze. "I don't want to."

His eyes turn to slits. "Then don't."

"My stuff is still there."

"I'll buy you new stuff."

I tilt my head. "That's nice of you but not necessary. And it's my computer and samples for my business."

"You can get new samples, and your laptop is at my place."

"No. My brother bought that for me, since Mitch removed me from the bank account. But I have a lot of work stuff on my old one. I didn't have everything in the cloud."

Dmitri's eyes darken. "He stole your money?"

I look away, embarrassed by how stupid I was to let Mitch have total control over so many parts of my life. "I don't want to talk about this."

"Anna—"

Anger, which I've been feeling more lately toward Mitch, rears its ugly head. "I'm an idiot, okay? I'm a thirty-two-year-old woman who doesn't even have her own bank account or credit card. Everything I had, I gave him access to. I literally have nothing. The clothes on my back and credit card in my wallet are from my brother. And I don't want to ever see him again, but I want my computer and samples back."

And if the universe has to play a cruel joke on me, my phone rings. I already know from the song I made into the ringtone who it is.

Dmitri's face hardens. "Is that him?"

"Yes."

"Give me your phone."

"Why?"

"I'm going to tell that piece of shit to send your laptop and samples to you, or I'm going to come find him and break his legs."

I bite a smile.

"I'm not joking, Anna. He has it coming to him for ever laying a hand on you, not to mention stealing your money."

I turn away, full of shame again.

Dmitri makes me look at him. "What he did to you isn't anything for you to be embarrassed about."

The phone continues ringing. "Then why do I feel that way?"

"I'm not sure, kotik, but you shouldn't."

"You still haven't told me what kotik means," I blurt out, and the phone goes silent.

Dmitri glances down the length of my body then back into my eyes. "It means pussycat."

"Pussycat?"

His eyes grow hotter. "Yeah."

My stomach flutters. I quietly force myself to ask, "And are other women your pussycats?"

Amusement crosses his face. He drags his finger over my lips. "No. Only you."

I bite my smile again.

He kisses my forehead. "We should go inside, kotik. There's a lot to do today."

We get out of the car and go into the showroom. The materials are similar to the ones in New York. It doesn't take long for me to feel comfortable and fall into my designer mode.

While I look at things, Dmitri adds me to the account. Most materials will be ordered elsewhere, and I want to take things with me so I can piece them together. I soon have too many sample materials to carry.

Dmitri comes behind me and puts his arms around me. "How's it going, kotik?"

I sigh. "I have a stockpile of all this in New York. This is making me realize how much I need to replace." *And it's going to be expensive.* Some samples are free, but a lot of things I had to pay for.

"Don't stress. Get whatever you need."

I point to the counter. "I need a cart." They don't have those in showrooms.

"Hold on a minute." He leaves and comes back with a short, stocky man. He has brown hair and eyes and a round face. "Anna needs those things boxed, and her samples are all back in New York. She needs replacements."

He pushes his glasses over his nose. "You need books, too?"

I hesitate. I have all this stuff at home.

New York can't be your home anymore.

"Anna, get everything you need," Dmitri repeats.

You can't do this project without your samples. "Okay."

By the time we get through the four showrooms, Dmitri's trunk is full. We stop at a cafe for a late lunch. "Where are we taking everything, kotik? My place or your brother's house?"

My heart hammers in my chest. "I'm probably going to be working all night getting things together. I know you wanted to order materials today. I'm sorry I haven't given you any recommendations yet."

Dmitri picks up my hand and traces the lines in my palm. "It wasn't realistic of me to expect that. We have time."

"We do?"

He grins. "A few days, max."

"No pressure," I mumble.

He checks me out, and my body aches. I should be used to his ogling by now, but it only makes me hotter. He drags his finger down my arm to my elbow and back up, accelerating the pounding of my blood. "Why don't you work at my place?"

Heat flies into my cheeks. "I'm going to need a few days, not a few hours."

A smug expression fills his face. "I'll stop at Vivian's, and you can pack a bag."

I bite on my lip.

He moves his chair closer and puts his arm around me. "I want you in my bed. Do you want to be?"

"What if I disappoint you?" I blurt out then cover my face in embarrassment.

He removes my hands. "How would that be possible?"

I turn away.

In a low voice, he asks, "When did you last sleep with him?"

"Why?" I ask, focusing on the rain hitting the pavement outside.

"When I ask a question, I want answers. Just like if you ask me something, I will tell you."

"The beginning of the year. But I'm pretty sure he was with several women since then," I mutter.

"Your ex is a fool."

Maybe I'm bad in bed. It's the thought that's plagued me for almost a year. I tried so hard to please Mitch, but nothing worked. The more I tried, the more he rejected me.

Dmitri makes me look at him again. "You should not put up with that, kotik. A man who goes looking for other women when he has you and doesn't worship you, is not a real man. He's definitely not the one for you."

"What about your girlfriends?"

Dmitri scowls.

Why can't I shut my mouth?

"Let's get something straight. I am not your ex. I don't go looking for others when I am with a woman. Cowards cheat. I am not one."

"I'm sorry. I didn't mean..." I shut my eyes. *Why do I have to ruin everything?*

His lips brush against mine, and he parts my mouth open with his tongue.

I respond to him, kissing him back with everything I have until the waitress clears her throat and puts our food down. "Do you need anything else?"

He pulls away, doesn't look at her, and continues to stare at me while I try to catch my breath. "Thank you. We're good."

She walks away.

He murmurs in my ear, "Kiss me like that in my bed, and we won't have any issues, kotik."

Nerves flip in my stomach, mixing with the flutters I've had since meeting him yesterday.

"Tell me you'll pack a bag. Or come back with me, and you can work naked for the next few days."

"What if you get sick of me?"

Why am I fighting him?

Because I'm a chicken.

"What if you get sick of me?" he replies and raises his eyebrows.

Not possible, Mr. Sex on a Stick, Russian God.

His fingers move between my thighs. "Tell you what, let's try it out and see what happens. My guess is we're going to have a good time."

I squirm, and he smirks.

"Okay."

His lips twitch. "Yeah?"

I nod.

He leans into my ear. His finger grazes my slit. He says something in Russian, but I don't ask what it is. It sounds dirty hot.

"Am I going to be able to work, or are you going to distract me too much?"

The green in his eyes brightens. "I plan on a little bit of work...with a lot of distraction."

8

Dmitri

It's after four when Anna and I get to Chase and Vivian's. When the car pulls next to the curb, she says, "Do you have any phone calls you can make?"

"Is this your way of telling me to stay in the car?"

She releases a big breath. "Yes."

"Why don't you want me going with you?"

She hesitates then says, "My brother might be inside. He's been coming home from work early every day, claiming it's to make sure Vivian is okay, since she's pregnant, but she's not always home, so I know it's to check on me."

Does she want to hide us?

"Ah. I see. And what are you going to tell your brother when you leave and have a bag with you?"

She twists her fingers in her lap and looks slightly ill. "I'm not sure."

I put my hand over hers. "Kotik."

She looks up. Her blue eyes are full of worry. "Hmmm?"

"Let me go with you. I will talk to your brother."

"And say what?"

"What do you want me to tell him about us?"

"Ummm... I'm not sure. You're my boss. And I've never done anything like this before."

"You aren't my employee."

"No, but you're the one who hired me."

"I don't think we're breaking any HR rules," I tease, but it doesn't ease her worry.

She bites her lip.

"What did you mean you haven't done this before?"

She looks out the window.

I decide to make light of it, trying to ease her anxiety. I push her hair back then brush my lips on her neck, near her ear. "Spent the night at your boss's place?"

She shudders and closes her eyes. "Yes."

She's always been a good girl. The thought only increases the pounding in my veins to make her mine.

I move her chin so her lips are in front of mine. "Look at me, kotik."

She opens her eyes.

"You aren't a child, but I will handle your brother."

It only seems to make her more nervous.

"You don't want him to know about us?"

"Us..." She swallows hard. "What does that even mean?"

So this is what she's worried about.

"Did I not make it clear?"

"What?"

I slide my hand between her thighs and outline her panties with my finger. The heat from her sex adds to the torture I've felt since I laid eyes on her at the bar.

She gasps and holds her breath.

"I'm definitely trying to get in your panties, but it's not to throw you to the curb once I do." I kiss her jaw. "I'm planning on having you in my bed for a long time, kotik."

She furrows her brows. "I'm not sure if that's a good thing to say to my brother."

I chuckle then peck her on the lips. "I will handle your brother. You focus on packing. I'll speak to him if he's there."

She doesn't seem convinced.

I slide my finger under her wet panties and stroke her naked slit. It's the first time I've passed the barrier, and her mouth forms an O.

Jesus, she's so smooth. I need to get her to my place.

"Do I need to calm your nerves before we go?"

Her eyes widen, and her breasts rise and fall faster.

Someone blares on their horn, and she jumps. I pull my hand out. "On second thought, I don't want any distractions when I make you come." I open the door and step out then reach in for her. "Come on, my kotik." I pull her out and into my arms.

"Dmitri..."

As much as I don't want her stressed, she is. I slide my hands in her hair. "Do you want me to make your brother believe I'm not interested in you?" My jaw twitches.

She murmurs, "You seem upset at the thought."

Give her whatever she needs.

"I'm not into hiding. But if this is what you want, I'll do it. So I'll ask you one last time, do you want me to lie to your brother about us?"

She surprises me and slowly shakes her head. "No."

"That's good, kotik." I kiss her, and she kisses me back until my dick is aching again.

"But don't kiss me in front of my brother today."

I brush my lips on hers. "Understood." I take her hand, and we go inside. The penthouse is quiet, and she leads me to her suite, which is the size of an apartment.

Like my place, the penthouse has impressive Lake Michigan views but is decorated in a coastal design.

"Did you design this?" I ask.

"No. It was coastal when they bought it."

"It's nice. Different for the area."

"Yes." She points to a couch. "Have a seat. I'll hurry."

Why is she always worried about rushing?

"No need to hurry, kotik. Take your time." I walk to the window. It's a typical windy, fall day in Chicago. The white caps are rather large. Daylight is fading, and in a few hours, it'll be dark.

"Anna, are you—"

I spin.

Chase stands in the doorway. He folds his arms and furrows his eyebrows. "Dmitri. Where's Anna?"

"Packing."

His eyes turn to slits. "For what?"

"My place."

He doesn't move and continues staring at me. His voice is low when he finally asks, "Why is she packing for your place?"

"Two reasons. We're on a deadline. She's going to be working long hours to get me out of the jam my other designer put me in."

"And the second?"

My heart beats faster. "I like her. She likes me. We're together."

His face hardens. "Together?"

"Yes. I think you can figure out what that means."

"She just got out of a relationship."

"A pretty shitty one from the sounds of it. Which brings me to my next question."

"What's that?"

I step several feet in front of him. "Why has her stuff not been moved here?"

He scowls. "She's not stepping foot in her old place."

"No, she's not," I agree. "But she wants her laptop and samples. Why haven't you gotten them for her?"

He scrubs his hands over his face. "Don't come in here and act like I'm not doing everything I can for my sister."

"I didn't say that."

"Didn't you?"

"No. But she's adamant she needs her things. So I'm asking you, what's stopping you from getting them? You're a man of means. What is the situation?"

Chase sighs and points to the barstool. I sit and he takes the seat across from me. "Nothing is in her name. Not the lease, or her bank accounts, or whatever else he did with her money. I spoke with the neighbor who helped break up our fight and called the police. He said Mitch changed the locks. I talked to my friends, who are cops. She's not getting anything back unless she's invited into the apartment, and she's only going back in over my dead body."

"You beat him up?"

"Not enough." Chase scowls.

I nod in agreeance. I don't know anything about it, but he's not in a body bag, so it's not enough. "The cops were called?"

"Yeah. I walked in on him hitting my sister in the face."

Anger flares through my bones.

"When was this?"

"Several months ago."

"And that's why you made Anna move to Chicago?"

He points around the room. "Yes. I bought this so she would have a place to come far away from him."

"You knew he was beating her?"

Chase's face turns red. "No. Of course I didn't. But I've tried to get her to leave him for years."

I hold my hands in the air. "My bad. I shouldn't have asked that."

He sits back in his chair and folds his arms over his chest. His face hardens. "Don't fuck with her, Dmitri."

"I have no intention of hurting her."

"She isn't meant to be a plaything, either."

"I don't use women, and I'm sure as hell not going to start with your sister."

"No?"

"No." I should be insulted but can't be mad at the guy for assuming anything. I'm actually happy to see him looking out for Anna. "How long was he hurting her?"

Chase sighs. "I don't know. She won't talk to me about it. She told Vivian he assaulted her one other time about a year ago, but she wouldn't go into details. And she kept saying it was her fault."

Oh, my kotik.

I pull my business card out of my wallet and toss it in front of him. "My cell is on it. Send me the address in New York where she used to live."

He picks it up and taps it on the counter. "Why?"

"She wants her stuff. I'm going to get it for her."

"How?"

"Don't worry about it. Send it to me tonight."

He arches an eyebrow. "The cops are already involved. It's best if we stay away. Whatever she left, we can replace."

"Text me the address," I repeat.

"What address?" Anna asks.

I spin. "A property Chase said Vivian is looking at for her foundation, right?" I turn back to him.

He puts my card in his pocket and rises. "Yep."

I take Anna's bag out of her hand. "Are you ready?"

She nervously glances between us. "Yeah."

"See you later, Chase." I put my hand on Anna's back and steer her toward the door.

"When are you coming back?" Chase asks in an annoyed voice.

Anna freezes. "Ummm..."

I meet his challenging stare. He may be her brother and watching out for her, but I've made my intentions clear. I'm not having her worrying about what he thinks. "Not for a few days. We have a lot of work to do. It's a large project, and we need to get back on schedule. Is there something specific you need her back for?"

"No. Nothing is going on here," Anna chimes in with a stern voice.

That's my girl. You can speak for yourself.

"Good to know. You know where to find her if needed. Don't forget to send me the information."

Chase follows us through the penthouse. "Call me if you need a ride at any time, Anna."

I spin. "If she wishes to leave at any time, I will escort her home."

The elevator opens, and Vivian walks in. "Dmitri. Anna. Chase." She glances suspiciously between us. "What's going on?"

"I'm going to Dmitri's for a few days," Anna replies.

Vivian tries to hide her smirk. "Okay. Have fun."

"We'll see you both later," I say and lead Anna into the elevator. When the doors shut, I hit the button for the lobby, then the stop one. I drop the bag and tug Anna into me then kiss her.

She kisses me back until the alarm goes off. I hit the button, and she breathlessly asks, "What was that for?"

"You told me not to kiss you in front of your brother. You didn't say anything about the elevator."

Her lips twitch. "Thanks for coming up. That was easier for me than having to deal with him on my own."

I cup her cheek and stroke her jawline with my thumb. "A real man doesn't send his woman into an ambush."

"Was Chase that bad?"

"No. He's just being a big brother. If you were my sister, I'd lock you up."

She slowly says, "But you two are okay, right? You aren't fighting?"

I trace her lips. "We are fine. There's nothing to worry about, kotik."

We step out of the elevator, and I guide her to the car. The door shuts, and her phone rings. I recognize the ringtone, and her face falls.

"I'm sorry," she says.

"Block him."

"I can't. He'll destroy my stuff."

"You can't go back there."

She nods. "I know. But I have to figure out how to get my computer back. All my work is on it. Everything for my business is on the hard drive. I know I have to start over in Chicago, but I don't want to recreate everything I've done that I'm proud of."

I can't blame her for wanting her things, especially for her business. Chase will send the address, and I can take care of it for her. Then she can block him and never have to deal with him again.

She puts her hand on my biceps. "Please understand."

I pull her onto my lap. "Okay, kotik. I understand. But once you get it back, I want you to block him so he can't harass you anymore."

"I will. I promise." She leans forward and kisses me until we pull up to my place. I'm engrossed in her, but her phone rings again. She sighs and closes her eyes.

"Why don't you turn your phone off? Tell Vivian if they need to get a hold of you to call my cell."

She pulls it out of her purse, sends a text message, and turns it off. "Done." She leans back to my lips.

I almost forget about him, but I know that I'm not going to rest easy until he's out of her life for good. And Chase better send me his address sooner rather than later.

"I think we need a cart for my samples," she says and points to the window. My driver is pulling items from the trunk and stacking them on the sidewalk.

"My building has several. Let me go get one."

"Are you sure you want all this junk in your place?" she quietly asks, frowning at the growing pile.

He used to give her a hard time about her stuff. She doesn't have to tell me. I can tell by the anxiety on her face and how she's twisting her hands in her lap.

I turn her chin back to me. "As long as you come with all of it, you can bring whatever you need into my house. Don't ever question it."

She gives me a small smile and nods, but her expression when she turns back to the pile tells me I've not totally convinced her.

And I wonder how much damage he's done to her. I'm going to have to figure out how to undo it all, but I'm not sure where to even start.

9

Anna

MY SAMPLES HAVE TAKEN OVER DMITRI'S LIVING ROOM. AS I STARE at them, my stomach nervously flips.

All my work items were in the spare bedroom in New York. We never had guests nor used it before I started my business, but Mitch would get irritated whenever I had my stuff out. The room wasn't that large, and the queen-sized mattress filled most of the space. I had to work on the bed. I wanted to remove it and put a large table in the room, but Mitch wouldn't let me. The hours I spent leaning over my samples and drawing on my laptop didn't help my back, which already had issues sometimes from my large breasts.

Mitch couldn't stand anything left out and not in order, so I couldn't leave items out when I was in the middle of a project. Every night, I would make sure things were stacked perfectly in the closet so he wasn't upset. But he still would make comments about all the junk in our home.

Dmitri turns on the fireplace and takes the centerpiece off the dining room table, which butts up to the living room. He picks up my laptop. "Do you want this on the table or couch?"

"I can work in here on the floor so your table isn't full of my junk."

He crosses his arms. "Don't be ridiculous, Anna."

I point to everything. "This is creating a large mess, and it's stacked neatly right now."

He sets my laptop on the table, goes to the pile, and starts laying tile and wood pieces all over the floor.

"What are you doing?"

"You can't see what things are if they aren't spread out, can you?"

"I have a way to keep it neater."

He snorts. "Well, this seems like a better way to me."

"But then you're going to have a bigger mess."

"Are we having a party tonight I'm not aware of?"

"What?"

He spreads mini countertop slabs next to the flooring. "If you can't see it, you don't know it exists."

"Not true."

He moves the wallpaper and paint sample books several feet away from each other.

My chest tightens. "You need to stop."

He gives me a challenging stare. "Why?" He drops another book on the floor, and it lands with a thud.

I jump.

He steps in front of me.

I cringe and put my hands in the air, as if to block him.

His face drops and eyes widen. He lowers his voice. "Do you think I am going to hurt you, Anna?"

"I'm sorry. I don't know... I didn't mean..." I spin and put my hands over my face. My lungs feel smaller. I struggle to get enough oxygen.

Dmitri wraps his arms around me. His body is flush to my back. "You're shaking."

I keep trying to breathe.

He holds me tighter and puts his cheek against mine. "I would never lay a finger on any woman, especially not you."

I nod. *What is wrong with me?*

"I will not have you worrying about making a mess while you are here. You need space and light to work. If you need a table and chair, you will have it. If you need a second or tenth computer, I will provide it. If you tell me I need to go to the store and buy a roll of white paper and finger paints, I will."

I manage a laugh. "Finger paints?"

"If that is what you need, my little kotik, you shall have it. Are we clear?"

Stop screwing everything up.

"Yes. I'm sorry."

He kisses my cheek and spins me into him. "No apologies. Now, what about paper and pens? Pencils? What do you need?"

"Do you have those things here?"

He tilts his head. "I do. But if I didn't, it wouldn't matter. I would get them for you."

I'm not used to being supported in my work. It chokes me up a bit. After I calm my breathing, I reach up and pull his face to mine. "Thank you." I kiss him.

He palms my ass, and my lower body throbs. I'm getting used to his hand there. He holds my cheek often, and I like it. I'm not sure why he likes my ass so much, but it's nice not to feel self-conscious about it the way I did with Mitch. And nothing about Dmitri feels false, so I don't think he's pretending to like it.

Our kiss turns into a make-out session, and his erection digs into my stomach. He steps backward to the couch, sits, then straddles me on top of him.

"I thought we were under a tight deadline," I whisper as his lips move down my neck.

"We are," he mumbles and moves one hand up my shirt, shooting tingles down my spine. The other hand, he sticks down my pants so he's cupping my bare ass cheek.

Oh no! I didn't tell him.

Why does my life have to be one embarrassment after another?

I freeze.

His eyes fill with confusion. "Did I do something wrong, kotik?"

"No. Ummm... I ummm..." I sit back on his warm palm. He makes tiny circles on my cheek with his thumb.

"What is it?"

"I'm allergic to latex. I can't use normal condoms. I have to use lambskin."

He nods. "Okay. I can get some."

"But I'm clean and get the shot," I blurt out, and my cheeks go from hot to burning.

More heat flies into his eyes. "I'm clean and get a test every year. I had one last month. Do you want to see it?"

"No. I believe you. But what about the girls you've been with in the last month, since your test?"

"I haven't been with anyone in a while."

I gape at him.

"Why are you looking at me like that?"

"I just thought...well...you've really not been with anyone in a while?"

He drags his finger down my spine. "My forties made me picky in who I'm interested in. And I met this girl in a bar a couple months ago. It was only briefly, and she was with her dickhead boyfriend. I sort of kept comparing other women I met to her. It made it a little tricky to ask anyone else out."

My flutters take off. I try not to smile but fail. I probably look like a giddy schoolgirl. "Really?"

"Mm-hmm."

I brush my lips on his and say, "Do you want to skip the condoms, then?"

He arches an eyebrow. "Is this a trick question?"

I don't answer him. Instead, I slide my tongue back in his mouth and grind on his cock.

He unhooks my bra, and the doorbell rings. His hands freeze, and he groans. "That's one of my brothers."

"How do you know?"

"They're the only ones who have access. Security would have buzzed me if it was someone else. That's my warning they are in the elevator." He hooks my bra back together.

"You're pretty good at that," I tease.

A smug expression fills his face. "I have more skills than that, my kotik."

I bet you do.

"I should probably get off you if your brothers are here."

He squeezes my ass cheek and slides his hand out.

I rise and kneel next to the tile samples.

"What are you doing?"

I wince. "Looking busy, since I've never met your brothers and work for them."

He chuckles. "Fair enough." He rises and goes to the elevator.

A deep voice, similar to Dmitri's, says, "That motherfucker—"

"Watch your mouth. There's a lady present," Dmitri scolds.

"Oh. Sorry. Who..."

I hold up a piece of tile to the light, trying not to be an eaves-dropper.

"Anna, this is my brother, Maksim," Dmitri says. "This is Anna, our new designer."

"I can see that," he says, and I cringe inside.

This looks so bad. He's already upset I'm not Russian. Now I've taken over Dmitri's house with my work stuff.

It is what it is. At least there was notice so I'm not buck naked, straddling Dmitri right now.

I wish.

I put down the tile, smile, and spin, then hold out my hand. "It's nice to meet you."

He shakes it, his icy blue eyes drill into mine, and politely replies, "You as well. It looks like you got what you needed from the showrooms today?"

"Yes."

"Great." He turns to Dmitri. "Have the materials been ordered?"

"Not yet. We just got back. Anna needs time to put it all together."

An uncomfortable silence ensues. Neither Maksim nor Dmitri break their icy glare at the other.

"I'll have something together soon. I promise."

Dmitri breaks first, glancing at me. "There's no rush."

"If we don't order materials in the next forty-eight hours, we will lose big money every day," Maksim states in a deadpan voice.

"It's not Anna's fault Lada screwed us. She needs time to do her job," Dmitri insists.

"I'll have plans together to meet your deadline," I promise, not wanting to let anyone down or for them to lose money. But it's a huge project.

Dmitri says, "Anna—"

"Where did you say the pencil and paper was?"

He sighs. "In my office. The top desk drawer."

"It's okay for me to get it?"

"Yes, of course."

I smile. "Okay." I leave the room and go into the office, giving myself a pep talk.

I can do this. It's two units, the first-floor lobby and gathering area, common area bathrooms, hallways, and elevators.

Oh God. Why did I promise that?

What was I thinking?

Freaking out won't get things done. Better get to work.

I open the desk drawer, get the items I need, and go back to the living room.

"Triple? Who does he think we are?" Dmitri angrily barks.

"He also offered to buy our lots off us for what we paid, but the offer is only good for seventy-two hours. After that, he starts dropping the price," Maksim growls.

"Cocksucker is trying to railroad us."

"Boris isn't happy."

Dmitri's voice lowers. "He needs to keep his head about him. We don't need trouble with the Rossi family."

The hairs on my arm stand up. *The Italian mob? Why is Dmitri involved with them?*

I really don't know anything about him.

Maksim clears his throat and stares at me.

"Sorry. I-I didn't mean to interrupt."

Dmitri spins. Anger is in his eyes. It's not meant for me. I know that, but I don't like seeing it.

He's dangerous. I felt it from the start with him. *Am I going from one bad man to another?*

"You've done nothing to apologize for, kotik."

"Kotik?" Maksim says, raising his eyebrows and scowling at Dmitri.

Scorching heat crawls up my face. There's no way to deny to Maksim something is going on between Dmitri and me. I'm not sure if Dmitri wants to keep us a secret or not, but I didn't want his brothers to think he hired me to get in my pants.

Did he?

Why am I questioning everything all of a sudden?

He's doing something with the mob. Are his businesses legit, or is he a criminal?

My stomach flips. I turn and sit at the table, open my laptop, and try to concentrate.

I tell myself to focus. But it's impossible not to listen to the rest of the conversation.

"Any other news, or are you done?" Dmitri asks.

In a dry voice, Maksim replies, "That's it. I'll leave now."

Dmitri doesn't object, and Maksim disappears without saying another word.

I smell Dmitri before he touches me. His arms slide over mine, and he kisses my head. "Kotik, I'm sorry about my brother."

My pulse beats hard in my neck. *I don't know anything about Dmitri. My judgment isn't good. I stayed years with Mitch and shouldn't have.*

Why does his touch have to make me feel alive?

"You don't have anything to be sorry about." I move my arms away from his and put my hands on the keys, but I'm not sure what to type. The spreadsheet I created for my design jobs is on my other computer. I sigh and shut my laptop.

Dmitri sits next to me. "What's wrong?"

Why didn't I take my laptop when Chase told me to pack? Why did I walk away with nothing?

"I'm not sure what I was thinking."

Dmitri lowers his voice. "About what?"

My life. Us. What I'm doing.

My self-doubt and anxiety about everything surface. "I shouldn't have taken this job. All my spreadsheets are on my other computer. I've not done anything this extensive before."

"Take it a room at a time. You don't need to meet Maksim's deadline. It's unrealistic to expect you to deliver a quality product without proper time. I have a spreadsheet for ordering I usually use with Lada. Will it help to see it?"

"Maybe."

He assesses me, and I look away. "What else is going on here?"

"Nothing."

He turns my face to his. Hurt shows in his eyes. "You lie to me."

How does he always know when I'm lying to him?

"I realized I don't know anything about you," I blurt out.

A line forms between his eyebrows. "What do you want to know? I've been nothing but honest with you."

"I... I don't want to get involved in something worse than I was in before."

The green in his eyes darkens. His voice stays calm, but the anger can't be missed. "You think I'm worse than a man who beat you?"

I inhale sharply. The shame I always feel about Mitch and my situation fills me. But no matter what Dmitri is involved in, I don't believe he would hurt me.

I also never thought Mitch would. And then I stayed after he hurt me the first time.

"No. I don't mean that," I quietly reply.

"What exactly are you trying to say, Anna? Please, be clear." Disappointment and annoyance swirls with pain in his eyes.

What am I so poorly trying to communicate?

"Why are you involved with the mob?"

There. I put it out there.

He briefly closes his eyes, nodding. "Ahh. I see. We never discussed who your brother wanted you to stay away from this morning, did we?"

"Chase knows you're involved with the mafia?" I cry out.

Dmitri sits back in the chair and crosses his arms. "Anna, I want nothing to do with the Rossi family. My brothers and I bought pieces of land around a lot Lorenzo Rossi got control of. The mayor told us we could buy it from the city. At the last minute, he sold it under our noses to Lorenzo. We've been negotiating with him. If we don't get it, we're going to lose millions, and we have no plan B for our property, which is worth nothing if we don't develop it."

A mix of relief and regret fills me. "I'm sorry. I shouldn't have assumed anything."

Dmitri's jaw twitches. "What else do you want to ask me?"

"Nothing."

Something shifts in his expression. "Are you sure you don't want to ask me about my brothers and my role in the Russian mafia or anything like that?"

My stomach churns. "I didn't—"

"You didn't have to."

"Dmitri—"

"I've heard it all before, Anna. Save your breath," he mutters and turns toward the blackness of the night.

What have I done?

Why can't I shut my mouth? All I do is screw everything up.

He's been nothing but good to me.

I reach for his cheek, and he closes his eyes.

He covers my hand with his. "I'm sorry. You hit a nerve. It wasn't fair of me to accuse you."

My hand shakes.

Sadness fills his eyes. He tilts his head. "You are scared of me, aren't you?"

I rise and straddle him. "No."

"Then why are you trembling when you touch me?"

"I'm sorry. I'm trying not to screw up."

His eyes widen. "Anna, we're able to disagree. We can even argue at times."

My insides quiver. A tear falls down my cheek. I've done my best to be perfect for years even though it was never enough for Mitch. Everything with Dmitri feels like it could be real, but I feel like I'm going to ruin it before it even begins.

Dmitri wraps his arms around me. "I want to know what he did to you."

"I don't want to talk about it."

"Too bad. I need to know."

"Why? You heard my brother."

"Not that time. Before that."

My chest tightens, and the air thickens. I've never told anyone what happened the first time Mitch hurt me. I don't want to say it out loud. I know how it's going to sound, and I should have left then. But I didn't. He convinced me it was my fault but he would never do it again. He reminded me that everyone deserves second chances and I shouldn't throw out all the years we had together.

"This is only going to work between us if you're honest with me. And I want to know."

"Why?" I repeat.

"Just like you needed to know what I was involved in, I need to know the same about you."

I stay silent, and more tears fall.

"What are you afraid will happen if you tell me, kotik?"

"I don't know," I whisper.

He kisses me. "Nothing bad is going to happen to you if you tell me. Please. I need to know."

I keep my eyes shut. "He broke three of my ribs."

Dmitri strokes my hair. "How?"

I open my eyes. "It was my job to have dinner on the table by seven. My appointment ran over with my client. I... I didn't get home until seven thirty. The battery on my phone died. I couldn't answer Mitch's calls."

Dmitri's jaw clenches. "What happened when you got home?"

I look out the window and focus on the lights on the building. "He started screaming. I yelled back and told him to stop, but he wouldn't. I...he hadn't ever physically hurt me before. I went to the kitchen, and he grabbed the blue skillet...it was a Christmas gift from my mom and..." I get a flashback of the sound of my ribs cracking, and I clutch my side. Tears blur my vision.

"He hit you with it?"

I nod. "I don't know how many times. He hit the front of me, but he slammed it on my back when I crouched down. I lost air. I think I passed out. My neighbor called the police. When I woke up, I was in the hospital. They wanted me to press charges, but..." I put my hand over my face, ashamed, full of regret, and feeling broken.

"He convinced you not to? He promised he would never do it again?" Dmitri finishes for me.

I nod, unable to control my sobs.

Dmitri tightens his arms around me and holds my head against his chest, consoling me.

When I get my emotions under control, I sniffle and lift my head. "Please don't tell anyone. Can this just stay between us, please?"

He wipes my tears and nods. "I won't tell anyone. Your secret, and you, are always safe with me, my kotik."

It only makes me cry again, and he pulls me into his arms.

I don't know how he's dangerous. I know there's something about him that is. And I wonder how he can also make me feel so safe.

"I'm sorry. I don't know how my life got so messy."

He tucks a lock of my hair behind my ear. "Everyone's is. If they claim otherwise, they are a liar."

"Yours isn't."

"Sure, it is. I'm behind on a significant project and about to get my ass handed to me on another."

I take a shaky breath. "I need to get started. I want to meet the deadline."

"Anna, it's not realistic."

"Maybe not, but I want to try."

"It's not fair—"

"I want to try. I... I need to."

He hesitates then cups my cheeks and traces my jawline with his thumbs. "All right. But you have to let me help you."

"Okay."

We spend the next four hours choosing every piece needed for the three-bedroom unit. Dmitri's spreadsheet isn't as extensive as mine, but we use it, and it does move things along.

We work well together and laugh a lot. Everything I suggest he says he likes and approves. He orders sushi and gets it delivered. We eat while working, and when we get to the end, he looks at the spreadsheet. "Huh."

"Is that a good or a bad huh?"

Dmitri shuts the laptop, slides it down the table, and scoots his chair back. He grabs my waist and picks me up. He sets me on the table and leans into my ear. "You're fifteen percent under budget for that unit." He kisses behind my ear.

"Really?"

His hand moves down to my ass. "Yeah. And it's going to be nicer than what we normally do."

"It is?"

"Mm-hmm." His lips graze my collarbone. "I think it's time you got out of this skirt, kotik." He unzips the back.

Flutters race through my veins.

He still wants me. Even after what I told him.

"Your ass in this skirt has been torturing me all day," he murmurs and tugs it off me, along with my panties.

The cold wood feels good against my hot skin. I kiss the curve of his neck, and he slides his hands up my shirt, grazing my nipples. I whimper, and he glides his hand around me and unhooks my bra. He cups my breasts and groans. "Ass and breasts, and when you kiss me, you make me believe you want me. You're every man's dream."

My tarnished confidence soars to the sky. "I do want you." I pull his lips to mine, and our tongues swirl together in a kaleidoscope of perfection.

His hands move over every part of my body, as if they were meant to roam freely. There's no hesitation or awkwardness. Every trace of his fingers or tease of his knuckles or skim of his palm is with confidence.

I've never had anyone light me up by touching me before. Everything disappears except for him and how he makes me feel. The scent of his skin's been driving me crazy all day, yet it seems to get more intense the more he dotes on me.

He dips his head to my chest, and I kiss it, loving how he keeps it shaved, and I'm able to touch my lips to his skin while his mouth is devouring my breasts.

I used to love my body, but when Mitch started making comments about it, I became self-conscious and compared myself to other women. Dmitri mumbles Russian into my skin and sets my loins on fire. I don't know what he's saying, but it rolls out of his mouth and sounds sexy. And I'm naked, but he's fully clothed, which should make me nervous, but all I feel is a deep desire for him to consume me in any way he knows how.

He lifts his head and kisses me, deep and urgent. His hands slide on my thighs, then near my sex, but not on it.

I release the buttons on his shirt and push it over his shoulders. Tattoos cover his chest and right arm. I've never dated anyone with tattoos before. But the sight of his ripped flesh covered in ink turns me on more.

I pull him closer, and his hard pecs press into my breasts, warm and pulsing from his heartbeat.

He reaches behind him, yanks the chair, and sits. His mouth teases my inner thighs until I'm shaking and dripping on the table. Something in Russian fills the air, and he palms my ass and scoots me closer to the edge.

He throws my thighs over his shoulders. His mouth hits my pussy, and a deep, guttural groan vibrates against it.

I become his dinner. He goes slow, as if I'm a fine wine that should be savored, exploring every part of my sex with his mouth and fingers, until I'm barely on the wood and riding his face while he palms my ass.

"Oh...oh...oh..." I grip his head, squeezing my thighs around his neck. Tremors skyrocket through my body until I'm screaming out his name, not able to control my cries, which is different than any other time I've ever had sex.

He doesn't stop. His fingers grip my ass, and he holds my body as close to his face as possible.

I thought I knew what it was like to orgasm. I was wrong. Everything I had ever experienced before is a mere shadow of what he does to my body. And when he's done, I'm a quivering mess, desperate for his mouth on mine, wanting more from him.

He picks me up while kissing me, carrying me into his bedroom. At some point, he got rid of his pants. He's as naked as I am, and his cock is hard as steel.

I try to grip it, but my hand doesn't fit around his smooth shaft. I glance down and gasp at how large it is. *How will that fit in me?*

He sits on the edge of the bed. "I want to watch you, my kotik."

I don't know what he means. "What?"

"I want to squeeze your ass and watch your beautiful breasts bounce as you ride me." He slides me onto him.

"Oh God!" I cry out as the tip of his cock enters me.

"Take your time," he murmurs. He palms the back of my head and kisses me then maneuvers my hip with his other hand, letting me inch down him, syncing with the rhythm he sets for me.

"That's it, kotik. Oh fuck," he growls.

"You like it?" I breathe, barely able to talk.

"Fucking perfection," he mumbles then leans back on his elbows, watching me. I stare down at his stunning perfection of muscle and art, feeling hotter and hotter.

I should feel self-conscious, but the smoldering look in his eyes only grows hotter. I reach behind my neck and gather my hair, holding it to my head and rolling my hips on his cock. I close my eyes, enjoying the way his girth slides against my walls, filling me past the point I thought was possible.

He rolls his thumb on my clit slowly, as if to tease me, until I can't take it anymore and beg him. "Please...oh...please."

He gives me everything I want, and my moans compete with his Russian words. Heat, as I've never felt, consumes me as my sex clenches his cock, spasming. Adrenaline floods my veins.

Our bodies pellet with sweat. He sits up, palms my ass with one hand and my head with the other. "Such perfection," he mutters and kisses me for the rest of the time, until we're both shaking and crying out.

Pleasure continues to annihilate me, cycloning through every cell until I'm dizzy.

"Don't stop, kotik," he growls and grips my hip, ensuring we don't lose our momentum.

"Dmitri...oh God...oh..." I cry out as his cock swells inside me, and adrenaline pumps harder.

His groan ricochets through the air, and he shouts something in Russian.

I collapse against him, shaking, my chest heaving into his.

His arms hold me tight, and he murmurs things I don't understand in my ear.

I never want him to let me go. In his arms lies serenity. His body is a temple of safety, and I want to worship it over and over. Everything I thought I knew about sex and two people being together was wrong. And I wonder if what we just did was a fluke or reality.

10

Dmitri

OVER MY LIFETIME, MANY WOMEN HAVE BEEN IN MY ARMS. BUT NO one has ever felt as good in them as Anna. Not one of them has ever touched me and elicited such a deep craving for more.

And I finally understand what it means to have chemistry. Not just in regards to sex but at all times of the day.

We're still breathing hard when I slide under the covers with her. She rests her head on her fist. The front of her sexy body presses against my skin. Her face is flushed, making her blue eyes pop.

I can't keep my hands off her. It's like she's the gold standard of everything a man needs in a woman.

She's talented and smart. Every suggestion she made for our project, she put thought into. And it showed me how Lada screwing us over was the best thing that could have happened for our business.

It's clear we were comfortable with Lada, and she got lazy with us. Different materials we normally use I'd show Anna, and she would pull something else out just as high of quality but with a slightly cheaper cost. When you're dealing with one piece, it isn't a big deal. But because of the amount of space we're covering, it adds up to substantial savings.

And her design ideas are fresh. When we started the project, I imagined something similar to what Lada typically creates for us, but Anna's flair is different. And I'm genuinely excited about her concepts.

"You're really talented," I say while I palm her ass and trace her curves with my other hand. I steal a quick kiss and add, "And not just in the bedroom."

Her face flushes deeper. "Do you think your brothers will like it? It's different from what you showed me."

"They'll love it. You're saving us money, and it's fresh. We'd been asking Lada for something unique and cutting edge."

Anna's face brightens, but then she frowns. "I have a lobby design I did on my computer in New York. It would flow well with the overall aesthetics of the unit. I also had samples of the materials in my apartment and a different lighting book I loved. I didn't see those in the showrooms yesterday, but the costs would fit in your budget."

"I will get your computer and samples back, kotik." *If I have to go to New York and squeeze the life out of your ex myself, I will.* When she admitted to me what he did to her, it took everything I had to remain calm. But my insides were a raging furnace of anger.

She furrows her brows. "How?"

"Don't worry about it. But I will."

My answer doesn't appease her. "Dmitri?"

I try to kiss her, but she pulls away.

"Don't do that to me."

"Do what?"

"Treat me how my brother would."

I drag my finger over her breast. "I don't think I treat you anything like your brother would."

She sits up. Her face hardens. "I'm not a child you need to protect."

"I didn't say that, kotik."

She gets out of bed and glances around the room.

"What are you doing?"

There's no sexier ass in the world than hers.

She doesn't answer and leaves the room.

I follow her. "Anna?"

She snags my shirt off the ground and puts it on, fastening only a few buttons. She sits on the floor, grabs a wallpaper book, and quietly says, "I've got a lot of work to do."

I throw on my boxers, sit next to her, and rub my hand on her back.

She closes her eyes.

"This isn't worth getting into a fight over."

She turns to me and angrily replies, "You said, and I quote, 'When I ask a question, I want answers. Just like if you ask me something, I will tell you.' I guess your statement is only true when it's convenient for you."

I groan. She's right. I demanded full disclosure from her and told her I'd give it to her in return. "Listen to me, kotik. Some things are meant to stay secret for a reason. The less you know about certain things, the better."

She turns to me. "You got upset with me when I asked you about your dealings with the Rossi family. You accused me of thinking you were in the Russian mafia, which I didn't even consider, by the way. But now you say things like this, and I don't know what to think."

"So now I'm part of the Russian mob?"

"No. But you're acting shady."

"Shady?"

"Yeah. And I don't want you to do something for me that is going to land you in jail or worse."

I pull her onto my lap. "I'm not going to do anything of the sort."

I know how to cover my tracks at all times.

She tilts her head. "Then why won't you tell me?"

"I'm debating in my head which course of action to take. Can you trust me?"

She sighs. Humiliation fills her face. "I'm tired of being a stupid girl."

I palm her head. "You are nothing of the sort."

"I am. I trusted Mitch with everything. I never asked questions so he wouldn't get mad. And I don't want to live like that anymore."

"I'm not him."

The statement hangs in the air, and her expression makes my stomach flip.

"You think I'm like him?"

"No! But I don't want to be in the dark about things that concern my life. And if you don't want to tell me something when I ask about it, then you have that in common with him."

It's a slap in the face. But I can't blame her for feeling this way.

She shuts her eyes and quietly says, "I shouldn't be with someone who I can't be on an equal level with."

Panic grips me. "We are."

"Not if you're going to hide things from me."

"Some things a man should be able to do for his woman without disclosing. If it is to take care of you and protect you—"

"I'm not a child," she harshly insists.

"I'm aware of that."

She scrunches her face and looks away.

"Why is it wrong for me to want to fix your problem for you?"

She pins me with her eyes. "That's not the issue we're discussing, Dmitri."

"It feels like it."

She takes a deep breath.

"I'm not a man who's going to sit back and let anyone hurt you. And no one is going to steal from you then hold it over your head to try and manipulate you."

"That's my fault. I gave him control over everything."

"When are you going to see that none of this is your fault? He chose to hurt you and take advantage of your trust. That's on him, not you."

She traces my chest tattoo. "No past, no future. You live by this motto. It's inked on your body for all to see. If anyone should understand why I shouldn't make the same mistakes again, it's you."

"I'm a mistake?" I growl.

She slides her hands around my neck. "No. But keeping me in the dark is what he did. And I allowed it."

"I'm not him," I repeat.

"I know you aren't."

"I don't think you do."

"You are nothing like him. But I don't want to make the same mistakes."

I try to understand where she is coming from and why she's telling me this. But it feels like she's putting me in the same box as her ex.

"So, you're never going to trust me, then?"

"You aren't listening to what I'm telling you."

I move her off my lap. "I am. But I also know what kind of man I am. I'm not going to change. I take care of my woman. I give her my trust, and I expect hers in return. I'm not sure how this will work between us if you can't do that."

She bites on her lip and tilts her head.

I put my hand on her cheek. "I don't want to keep going around about this. As much as I want you, kotik, I'm a forty-three-year-old man. I'm not a boy. I won't change. My job is to take care of you how I see fit, and if I can't, this won't work between us. It's the one thing I know I can't compromise on. I'm sorry."

"Dmitri—"

To torture myself, I kiss her. "You are beautiful and talented. Everything about you is rare and unique. But if I can't be the man I know how to be, then we're living in a lie. And neither of us deserves that."

Her blue eyes glisten. I get up and leave the room, not able to look at her anymore, worried I'm going to cave. If I do, we'll only draw out the inevitable and hurt ourselves worse.

When I get into the bedroom, I stare at the fireplace. When I glance at the bed, it mocks me. I wonder how so much can go wrong in a matter of minutes.

But I know myself. I can't be in a relationship if there isn't trust. If I'm not allowed to make decisions on her behalf to help her, we'll both end up miserable.

And no matter what she says, her lack of trust in me is due to him. I'm not going to change my core beliefs to make up for his mistakes.

I can't stare at the bed any longer, and the pain of seeing her is too much. So I go into the bathroom, turn on the shower, and lean my forearm against the cold tile. The hot water streams down my body as I grapple with my thoughts.

Am I being unfair?

No, I know myself. Trust is everything.

Maybe she needs more time?

We're setting ourselves up for heartache. It's a point I can't bend on.

She's your dream woman.

I'm always going to want to take care of her, and she's not going to let me.

Her arms slide around my waist and her body presses against my back.

I exhale and put my arm over hers. "Kotik—"

She kisses my back, and I close my eyes. "Don't let me go," she whispers.

It's so quiet, I question if I heard it. I spin and cup her cheeks. "I don't want to. You're everything I could ever want."

Her eyes fill with tears. "Then, don't toss me to the side."

"I'm not. I'm letting you go before I hurt you."

"It's too late. You're hurting me right now."

I palm her ass, tugging her closer to me, and hold her head so she can't avoid my eyes. "If we can't trust each other, what do we have? Hmm?"

"I never said I don't trust you."

"Anna—"

"Tell me what you want from me."

The steam gets thicker. The blue in her eyes flickers against the gray air.

"I want permission to take care of you how I see fit. I need your trust, and to know you believe in your heart, I'm not him. No matter what, I would never do anything to hurt you."

Tears drip down her cheeks. Her lip quivers.

"In return, you get my trust. You get to decide how to take care of me. And I won't question anything. I'll know everything you do comes from in here." I press my hand over her heart.

She nods. "Okay."

"Yes? You give me permission?"

"Yes."

I brush my lips against hers and put her hand over my heart. "Good. I give you my full trust."

She parts her lips, and our tongues flick with a new hunger. Before, I wanted to make her mine. Now, she is. And I'll give every good piece of me I have to her.

I pick her up and turn so her back is against the wall, entering her in one fluid movement.

Her cry echoes against the walls, followed by her sweet whimpers as I thrust into her. She digs her nails into my shoulder.

"My trust is with you until you don't want it anymore," I tell her, giving her full permission to wreck me someday but knowing she needs to see the power of what I'm giving her. "Do you understand?"

"Yes," she whimpers. Her mouth forms an O, and she arches her back, pressing her breasts into me.

Then I make it clear what her permission means to me. "No one will hurt you, my kotik. If they do, they will receive my wrath. And I will not give you the details. Not because I don't trust you but because it's better if you do not know. This is part of how I protect you."

She struggles to keep her eyes open and loudly moans. Her walls spasm around my cock and body trembles against mine.

I push her wet hair off her forehead. "I want to hear you agree to my terms. I can't have you in all ways and not this."

Her heady eyes and flushed face are so beautiful. She doesn't know it or the power she holds over me. And as much as I want her as mine, I want to be hers, too. To know she's claiming me and no one else.

"Tell me," I growl.

"I agree," she blurts out.

I kiss her, pounding into her quicker, muffling her cries of ecstasy.

"What do you want from me in return? Tell me," I murmur in her ear.

"You...oh God... Dmitri... I only...like this...always wanting me..." Her tear-filled blue eyes kill me.

She believes I will lose interest in her, and that she is not sustainable perfection.

I kiss her and hold her chin. "There isn't any other woman on earth like you. Every part of you is extraordinary. And I am not a fool. I will never tire of worshiping you. Do you understand?"

"Promise me," she whispers and closes her eyes.

"Open your eyes, kotik."

She obeys, and tears fall.

"I promise you."

She nods.

I dip down and suck on the curve of her neck.

Her hot breath hits my head. Her nails dig into my shoulders harder, and her pussy convulses on my shaft so violently, it sends me into my own euphoric spiral.

I can't hear my voice over hers, our sounds fill the air, along with the water hitting the floor. I crash into her, releasing my seed so deep, she screams and combusts further in my arms.

I dry her off and take her to bed.

"I have work to do." Her blue eyes are bloodshot.

"It's late, my kotik. Sleep first. Later we will work on the next piece."

"I want to meet the deadline," she says, her voice full of determination. But I also sense she needs this to prove to herself she is capable of what I already know she is.

"It took us four hours to do the first unit. Some of the pieces will be the same for the other. But let's assume each area takes another four hours. We have the lobby, elevator, common bathrooms, and hallways."

"Yes. There's still a lot."

"If it's four hours for each area, which I don't think it will be, we need twenty hours."

She stares at me, debating.

"Trust me, my kotik. Sleep now, work later. When you wake up, you will be refreshed."

It's a small test. Can she trust me enough to follow my wishes that are in her best interest?

She yawns. "Will you set the alarm?"

I stroke her cheek. "Yes. Now get your sexy ass under the covers."

She bites her smile and obeys.

I pull her into my arms. "Close your eyes."

She does and is asleep within minutes.

I pick up my phone on the table and set the alarm. Then I look at my messages.

Nothing from Chase.

I internally groan, knowing I'm going to need to sit him down and have another chat. I kiss Anna on the forehead. She's mine, and I'm hers. From now on, if I need something concerning her, he's going to give it to me and not question it. I know he has her best interest at heart, but it's no longer his call.

Chase will give me her old address. And everything that Anna's ex is holding over her head, or stole from her, he's going to turn over to me. I'm coming for him. She may not have been mine when he hurt her, but he's still going to feel my wrath.

He has no idea who I am or what I'm capable of. But he's going to learn quickly. I may avoid the Russian mafia at all costs and try to forget about them, but everything I've learned about paybacks is due to my past with them. I'm an Ivanov. One thing people in Chicago already know is you don't mess with my brothers or me. That includes our women.

11

Anna

THE ALARM DOESN'T RING. DMITRI'S LIPS WAKE ME. THEY ARE ON my breasts, and his hard erection is digging into my thigh.

My sex pulses, and tingles explode everywhere his mouth touches. I slide my hands on his head. "What time is it?"

He looks up. A smug expression and his green eyes make me squirm. He says something in Russian.

He's so dirty hot.

He could be telling me he wants to go to church, for all I know. But every word rolling out of his mouth makes my loins burn.

I've never had a man pay so much attention to my different body parts. When Dmitri focuses on me, he doesn't just touch me and go on to the next part. He consumes every piece of me until I don't think I can handle it anymore.

I slide my hand down his muscular back, and he pulls away. He smirks and flips me on my stomach before I know what's happening.

Both of his hands palm my ass, and his shaft grazes the back of my thigh.

"Ummm..."

"Shhh. Let me enjoy your ass for a minute, kotik."

I look behind me, not sure what he means, and he dips down and kisses my ass cheeks the way he did my breasts.

It's another new thing no one has done before. I never thought I would be comfortable with anyone's face near my ass, but the sensations rolling through my body tell me I was wrong.

He slides his hand under my stomach, pulls me up on my knees, and kisses the hole of my sex. Then he dips his tongue deep inside me.

"Oh...holy...oh...." I cry out.

He grunts and massages my cheeks while rolling his tongue around my walls.

I clench his tongue, and he groans, gliding his hand around me, then circling my clit and inner pussy faster. I come almost instantly, arching my back and muffling my cries into the pillow.

His lips travel up my tingling spine until he gets to my ear. The heat of his flesh covers the back of my body. He puts his forearms on both sides of my shoulders, and he slides his cock into me. "Morning, my sexy little kotik."

"Good morning," I breathe. "Oh...oh..." I cry out as he pounds deeper in me.

"Give me your sexy lips," he growls.

I turn my head and whimper in his mouth as his cock continues to wreak havoc on me. The taste of my orgasm is fresh on his tongue, and he flicks it in my mouth.

He fills me to the point I wonder if he'll split me in two. Everything about him feels larger.

Is it bigger in the morning?

I've never had sex in the morning before. Mitch was a fanatic about getting out of bed and showering. He said sleep made your body dirty.

If that's true, I suddenly love dirt.

Dmitri moves one hand to my clit and his other to my breasts. He manipulates every nerve ending I have.

My body breaks out in a sweat. "You're so good," I moan and don't realize it until it's out.

"Your sexy little body turns me on, kotik," he murmurs in my ear and sucks on my lobe.

His "sexy little body" comments make me do an internal happy dance. I want him to love my body. *I* want to love my body again. Mitch didn't. But Dmitri seems to be enthralled with every inch of me.

He speaks in Russian, thrusts harder, and I fly over the edge, every part of me exploding under his touch.

When he comes, I skyrocket again, losing the control to hold myself up and collapsing on the bed while he groans my name in my ear.

I roll over and pull his head to my face, sliding my tongue into his mouth. I'm still breathing hard, and so is he, but we match each other's intensity.

"I knew you were meant to be in my bed," he cockily states.

"Do you normally wake up like that?"

He arches an eyebrow. "With my dick hard as a rock and dying to be inside you?"

Heat floods my cheeks.

He kisses my neck. "Or my tongue craving your sweet pussy?"

I bite on my smile, not sure how to answer him.

The alarm rings. He reaches over, glances at it, and his face falls.

"What's wrong?"

"Nothing." He kisses me again then rolls off me. He rises and pulls a T-shirt out of his drawer. "Put this on."

"I did pack clothes."

He grins. "I think this will be a panty-free morning."

"You're sure about yourself," I tease.

He smirks then puts the neck over my head. I slide my arms through, and my stomach grumbles. "What do you eat for breakfast, kotik?"

"Nothing."

"Why not?"

"Too many calories," I mumble and walk out of the room.

He follows me. "Well, we're going to change that. You can't starve yourself."

I spin. "I'll gain weight if I start eating breakfast. I've already blown my week with your dinners."

"How?"

"My macros. They're all off. And I can't lose weight, no matter what I try, so any increase is going to make me gain."

"And what does your macro count look like?"

"Why do you want to know?"

"I work out and lift. I'm not ignorant about this stuff. What's your ratio?"

I groan. "Are you going to monitor what goes in my mouth, too?"

His eyes turn to slits. "Is that what he did?"

I don't answer and sit at the table.

"One, you don't need to lose weight. You could add thirty pounds and you'd still look amazing. Two, if you don't eat enough, you can't lose. It'll backfire, and your metabolism will drop. Three, I plan on giving you several more workouts today, so I'm pretty sure you'll work off any extra calories."

I open my laptop and ignore him, but I'm looking forward to his "workouts."

He sits next to me. "What's your ratio?"

"Are you going to bug me all day about this?"

He grins. "Yep."

I shake my head, get up and fish my phone out of my purse, and turn it on. I ignore all the text messages and missed calls from Mitch and pull up my app. "Here."

He scrolls through my info and mumbles, "This is ridiculous."

"What?"

"You're starving yourself. A child eats more than this."

I try to take my phone back, but he rises.

"Give it back."

"No. I'm going to program this to what you should be eating to maintain your weight. You're thin enough."

"You're annoying me now."

He leans down. "I'm also making breakfast, and you're going to eat it."

"I just need coffee." My stomach growls again.

He smirks. "I'll make you coffee. But you won't be able to resist my food."

"Are you a gourmet cook, too?"

"You can tell me when you taste my breakfast."

I roll my eyes.

He sits down again. "Do you feel dizzy a lot?"

"During sex with you?" I tease.

"Normally, I'd appreciate your comment, but I'm serious."

I don't answer him. I am starving all day long, get headaches, and am sometimes shaky. I usually only eat a lean protein serving for dinner.

"I thought so. This changes today, kotik," he quietly states.

"I don't want to gain weight."

"If you eat right, you won't. But you're damaging yourself eating this way. How long have you been following this plan?"

I glance out the window. The waves on the lake are rougher than yesterday, and the white caps are sizable. "I don't want to talk about this."

"How long?" he sternly repeats.

I stay quiet.

He turns my chin. "Tell me."

"The last three months. I keep lowering my calories and elimi-nating things so I can lose. But nothing budges," I admit.

"Because it doesn't need to. And you're starving yourself."

"I'm not."

"Yes, you are."

I take a deep breath, exhausted with this conversation, and my stomach rumbles again.

"One week," Dmitri says.

"For what?"

"You eat the macro count I put in your phone for one week. Three meals a day and a few snacks."

"No way. I'll gain a ton of weight."

"No. You'll probably drop a couple of pounds of water weight."

"It's not possible."

He grunts. "I'll make you a bet."

I put my arms and head on the table. "You're impossible," I moan.

"I think you're scared, since you know I'm right."

"Fine. But when I gain ten pounds in a week, and can't fit into any of my clothes, I'm blaming you."

"You can stay in the house naked."

I elbow him. "Not funny."

"You won't gain. No more starving yourself." He kisses my forehead. "I'm going to make breakfast."

I'm going to kill him if I gain weight.

I rise and go into his bathroom. I take off the T-shirt and step on the scale. I'm the same as always.

At least I didn't gain weight from the last two nights.

I go back to the main room and pick out pieces for the four-bedroom unit. The smell of eggs and bacon hits my nose, and my stomach growls louder.

Dmitri sets a cup of coffee down and kisses my head. "Those look good together. I wouldn't have thought of pairing those."

"It's a bit edgier. Kind of risky," I reply, picking up the countertop slab and looking closer at it. "I'm still not sure if I even like it or not."

Dmitri kisses me on the lips. "Eat some breakfast. It'll clear up the fog in your head."

"You're annoying." *And so freaking hot, I'm ready for my next round of exercise.*

He checks out my body in his predatory way. "Don't be too annoyed. I think you might just fall in love with me." He winks and goes into the kitchen.

My heart hammers in my chest. *That's definitely a possibility.*

1 2

Dmitri

"Let's take a break." I rub my face. Anna's designed all the areas except the hallway and common bathrooms on the main level. I've been inputting her choices into the system and making sure everything aligns with our budgets. So far, she's saving us a lot of money. And her ideas are of high quality.

It's past four. Chase still hasn't sent me a text, and I need to speak with him. I don't want to do it over the phone.

I hand her my cell. "Call Vivian and see if Chase and her are home."

"Why?"

"Let's get out of here for a while."

"But I only have two things left."

"Yes. And against all the odds, you're going to meet the deadline."

"You're helping."

"Shh. I won't tell anyone," I tease.

She rises off the floor and straddles me. Her blue eyes drill into mine. "Thank you."

"You're saving our asses, remember?"

She strokes the side of my head. "Can we go somewhere besides Chase and Vivian's?"

Maybe it's better if she isn't anywhere in the vicinity when I speak with her brother.

"Sure. Is there another place you want to go?"

"Where would you be if you weren't here with me?"

"It depends. Possibly on a job site."

"Okay. What would you be doing tonight?"

I glance at my phone to remember what day it is. "Thursday nights, I watch Boris fight."

"Fight?"

"Yes. We own a boxing ring."

Her eyes light up. "And people can watch?"

"Sure. But it's typically the fighters' close friends or family."

"Great. Let's go!"

"You want to go watch a fight?"

"Yes. Why wouldn't I?"

"Do you normally watch boxing?"

She shrugs. "When the big fights are on television."

"It's a *hole in the wall* gym. There isn't anything fancy about it."

She rises. "Awesome. I can wear jeans, then?"

"I don't know. Are you going to wear the pair you wore the other day?"

"No. I need to wash them, so I left them at Chase's. Why?"

I stand and squeeze her ass. "Because your ass was hot as hell in them."

She smirks. "I guess it's your lucky day, then. I have a second pair and brought them with me."

I groan. "You're killing me, kotik."

"How much time do I have to get ready?"

"Plenty. It starts at seven."

She bites on her lip, and her eyes travel down my body. "I have to shower."

"Is that an invitation?"

She shrugs, and I pick her up and throw her over my shoulder. She screams and laughs until I put her down in the bathroom. Neither of us are wearing a lot of clothes, but we shed them quickly.

After our shower, it doesn't take long for me to get ready. "I have a few phone calls to make. Take your time." I kiss her and go to the living room and sit on the couch.

I call Vivian.

"Hey, Dmitri."

"Hey, how are you feeling?"

"Great. Everything okay with Anna?"

"Yeah. She's great. Hey, could you send me Chase's phone number?"

"Sure. He just got back from a workout and is in the shower. Do you want me to have him call you?"

"No, that's okay. Can you tell him I'm still waiting for the information we discussed?"

"Sure. What about?"

"He will know what I'm referring to."

She hesitates. "Does this have to do with Anna?"

"Yeah."

"Ah. I see. Are you two having a pissing match over who gets to make decisions for her?"

"Ouch."

"Mm-hmm. I thought so."

I sigh. "Do you think you can help me out?"

"Nope. She can make her own. You two should both realize that."

"You have it wrong. This isn't about that. I agree with you, I promise."

Vivian sighs. "I'll give him the message, but I hope you two don't create a bunch of stress for Anna."

"It's not my intention. Please send me his number."

"Will do."

"Thanks." I hang up, and Anna's phone rings. It's been on since earlier today. It's her ex. I know it from the ringtone. I grab it and send it to voicemail, refraining from answering it.

He starts sending her a chain of texts. Each one makes my blood boil hotter.

"Stop ignoring me. This game you're playing is over. Get your ass back to New York."

"I've got paperwork to add you back to the accounts. Come home and sign them."

"I said I was sorry. It won't happen again. Now stop letting your brother rule your life and come home."

"I bought you tickets for the design show. It's next week. You know how much they cost, so get back here."

I turn the phone off and pace the penthouse, staring out into the Chicago night.

This needs to end. He needs to understand she's finished with him.

"Penny for your thoughts?" Anna says.

I turn. "Wow." I scan her body. She's wearing jeans, a hot-pink top with the shoulders cut out, and her black ankle boots. Her hair is straight, and she has natural-looking makeup on. I pull her into me. "You look amazing."

She bites on her pink lip. "Thanks."

I kiss her then glance at the time. "We should get going."

We leave and get into the car.

"So you're really close with your brothers?" she asks.

"Yeah."

"What are they like?"

"You met Maksim. Unfortunately, I'd like to say it was a bad day, but that's him."

She tilts her head and smiles. "I guess I'll get to stick it to him when I finish the project before his deadline?"

I trace her fingers, which are resting on her leg. "You have the right attitude."

"What about your other brothers?"

"They're more laid back than either Maksim or me, but they are also younger. Unless you get Boris in the ring or piss him off."

"So, Boris is who I want in a dark alley with me?"

I snort. "That's a good way to describe him. But you could take any of my brothers or me into that situation and you would be protected."

She crawls on my lap, straddling me. She takes a deep breath then asks, "You're dangerous, aren't you?"

My pulse pounds between my ears. "I would never hurt you."

She shakes her head. "That isn't what I'm asking. I trust you, remember?"

I put my hand on her cheek. "What's dangerous mean to you, kotik?"

"I'm not sure."

My heart races. "What could I do that would make you run from me?"

She covers my hand on her cheek and closes her eyes. "I can't be positive anymore."

"Why not?"

Her brows furrow. "I think I'm confused."

My thumb strokes her jaw. "About what?"

"Everything I used to believe."

"And what do you no longer believe?"

"That if you try hard enough, you can make anything work. But you can't."

I stay silent, knowing she's talking about her ex. I hate hearing what she used to do and feel for a person who couldn't appreciate her.

She continues, "If you do what you're supposed to, everything will work in your favor. But that's a lie."

"What else?"

"Things are black or white. But in reality, they are gray."

She's always been a good girl, innocent in many ways. And he tried to destroy her.

"You know what I think?" I ask.

"What?"

"I think the person you're with is a determining factor on whether trying hard enough can work or not. But if you have to try too hard, it was never meant to be."

"Harper told me to stop trying. I should have listened to her."

"Do I get to meet your friend soon?"

She smiles. "Do you want to?"

"Yes."

"Okay."

I trace her lips. "There are black-and-white things, but sometimes you have to mix in the gray. And if you're doing something that isn't working in your favor, then maybe the thing you wanted was never supposed to be the right thing for you."

She stares out the window.

I shouldn't broach the topic. I already know the answer. It only serves to put a knife of jealousy through my heart. I quietly ask, "You loved him for a long time, didn't you?"

Shame fills her eyes. She nods.

"What about him did you love?"

She scrunches her face. "I don't know. I thought I knew, but the more time I spend away from him... I don't know."

I swallow the lump in my throat and ask the question that has been plaguing me. "Do you still love him?"

"No." She says it with confidence.

Relief fills me, but I also see something else in her expression. "You're confused about what love is? You wonder how you know what it is if you could be so wrong about him?"

She slowly nods. "How do you know that?"

"I read it on your face. And I know what it's like to question pieces of you that you believed in and thought you knew."

She kisses my forehead. "And that is the dangerous part of you? The parts you questioned?"

Don't lie to her.

"Yes," I admit.

"And they are gray, not black-and-white?"

"Yes."

"They are things you would not want me to know, in fear I would leave you?"

"No. It's not fear you would leave me."

"Then what is it?"

"Fear you would never be able to love me." It's something I've never admitted to anyone before. I didn't plan on confessing it, but lying to her seems unfair after she gave me her trust last night.

She pauses for a moment. "I promised you I'd trust you fully. You said you gave me yours in return. Does trust not include my ability to handle whatever it is?"

"It isn't about your ability. Some things are so dark, they threaten to destroy everything."

I'm not sure how I expect her to react. She leans into my lips. Before she kisses me, she says, "Then I won't ask you any more questions about this tonight."

13

Anna

SEVERAL WEEKS AGO, I WOULD HAVE NEVER BELIEVED THIS IS MY life. The project I'm working on, side by side with Dmitri, shows me what I'm capable of. He believes in me and keeps telling me how talented I am. And I realize how much Mitch's belittlement of my business was another way he held me back and in his control.

If I had known what it was like to be with a real man, one who not only accepted me for who I am but also was attracted to all of me, I wouldn't have stayed with Mitch. I can see how low my self-esteem dropped from the years I spent with him and how he played a role in making me think I wasn't worthy of anything else.

Everything Dmitri does makes me feel good about who I am and what I have to offer the world. I haven't known him for long, and everything is moving fast. I'm sure the smart thing would be to slow down, get to know him better, and then give him my trust.

But I don't know how. Dmitri's an all-or-nothing person. He's patient with me, but he requires the same things Mitch did. But it doesn't resemble anything Mitch and I had.

Both men demanded my loyalty, respect, and trust. Unlike Mitch, Dmitri returns every bit of what I give him but tenfold.

Maybe I should run and not let another man control any aspect of my life. Perhaps the intensity of what is going on between Dmitri and me can't last, and I'm fooling myself, setting myself up for the biggest letdown yet. But I can't fathom how to let go of him or not give myself freely to him.

And I know he's dangerous. I don't know how, but I've felt it since I met him in the bar. He claims if I know, I'll never be able to love him, but what could be so dark it would reverse every feeling I have for him?

I could push him to tell me his secrets, but I kiss him, wanting him to feel worthy of my love, like how he's made me feel these last few days. Before I met him, I assumed I was unlovable, and no man could want me with my body or career.

Dmitri's changed all of it. He's not a man who should experience anything less than the burning desire I have for him. I'm not sure if his longing for me to be his is less or more than my need for him to be mine. And I want him to feel, in the depths of his core, my insatiable desire for him and only him.

My lower body throbs. I can't help it and circle my sex on his growing erection. We have clothes on, but my panties are wet. I reach for his belt, and the car stops.

He grabs my hand. "If you want to watch the fight, we don't have time."

"Okay," I murmur and continue kissing him.

He dips his hand in my pants, sliding into my sex.

I whimper. "I thought we didn't have time?"

"I don't need a lot of time to give you what you need, kotik." He rubs his fingers on my clit.

"I...oh... I... Dmitri...oh God!" I cry out, as adrenaline shoots through my body.

He murmurs, "That's my girl. Have another." He repeats his actions, sending me soaring again. His lips muffle my cries. "Are you sure you want to go inside?"

I smile against his lips and pant, "No. Yes. No."

He chuckles and kisses my hand. "We can leave whenever you want."

I take a deep breath. "Should I be nervous about meeting your brothers?"

"No."

"Even though I'm not Russian?"

His lips twitch. "They've had time to get over it. Besides, it's only about helping our people survive. It isn't personal. But all my brothers date women of all ethnicities, including American."

"They do?"

"Yes. We're American, too."

"What about the fact you're my boss?"

His eyes twinkle. "I told you, I don't think we need to worry about HR."

"Are your brothers going to think differently?"

Dmitri snorts. "All they care about is making sure you get the job done. Beyond that, it's not their business. Besides, none of them are saints."

"Meaning?"

He slides his hand in my hair. "If we see something we want, we go after it. That's how my parents raised us. None of us sit back when we see a woman we want."

"Do you normally date women you work with?"

Amusement crosses his face. "I haven't before. My brothers have." He leans closer. "You're my one and only, kotik."

It shouldn't matter who he's been with in the past, but I have to bite back my smile. I like being his one and only.

He opens the door. "It's now or never. Last chance to stay in the car."

"Don't tempt me," I tease and slide off his lap.

As always, he reaches in for me. My heart flutters. His chivalry makes me feel special. My brother and his friends all hold doors open and do nice things for their wives, but I've not been on the receiving end from someone I dated in years.

Something about Dmitri is different. Almost old world. Maybe it's the Russian culture in him or his sexy accent, making me feel that way. I'm not sure, but he pulls me out of the vehicle. His hand slides to my ass, and he tugs me into his body.

I never imagined a man's hand on my ass would feel so electric. Or I would be comfortable walking around in public that way. But nothing about Dmitri's palm on my cheek feels derogatory. He's showing the world I'm his, and I don't want him to remove it.

It's dark out. The neighborhood we're in doesn't look the best. Boarded-up buildings and bars on windows line both sides of the street. Another man gets out of the front of the car. He's bigger than Dmitri and has a scowl on his face. He's one of the scariest men I've ever laid eyes on.

I shudder and lean closer to Dmitri. "You brought two drivers?"

Dmitri palms my ass harder. "That is not a driver. Viktor is a bodyguard."

Viktor steps behind us. I peek behind Dmitri's shoulder. Viktor's eyes are slits, and he scours the street around us.

"Why do we need a bodyguard?" I ask.

"You don't ever come down here without me, kotik. This is not a good neighborhood."

You don't need to worry about that.

Another man stands near the door, wearing all black. He's as wide as a refrigerator, but I'm pretty sure it's all muscle. His neck is thicker than anyone's I've ever seen.

Steroids anyone?

"Boss." He nods and opens the door.

"Leo." Dmitri motions for me to go through. "After you, kotik."

I'm suddenly nervous. I hesitate, and Dmitri pats my ass.

I step into the stairwell of brown walls and worn carpet. Sweat-filled air becomes thicker the closer I get to the top. Russian and Irish male voices echo in my ears.

There is one open room and two small offices. A wall of windows faces the main area. Several dozen men are punching bags or working with trainers. A ring with a black-and-white rope sits in the middle of the space. The dark mat has the same letters and design as Dmitri's chest tattoo.

No past, no future.

Dmitri resumes his position next to me, places his hand on my ass, and guides me toward the offices. As we walk through the gym, fighters and trainers glance at us. Some nod. Others exchange greetings with Dmitri. But he moves us across the room quickly.

A man in a black T-shirt and jeans stands in the office with his face toward the brick. His clothes fit his body like Dmitri's. The fabric stretches over each muscle. He pushes his hand through his dark hair, and his back muscles pop out. He's speaking Russian aggressively into the phone.

Dmitri knocks three times on the open door, and he spins.

His face is red, and he shakes it at Dmitri. He quickly glances at me and raises his eyebrows.

Nervous butterflies fill my stomach. I assume he's one of his brothers. I see parts of Dmitri in the shape of his eyes and lips.

He says something else, which I would think is a threat by the tone, then hangs up.

Dmitri's body stiffens, and he gruffly says something to his brother in Russian.

His brother responds.

I need to learn Russian.

They go back and forth then Dmitri turns to me. "I apologize, Anna. Forgive us for being rude. This is my brother, Sergey."

Sergey steps forward. His accent isn't as thick as Dmitri's when he speaks English. "Anna, our new designer?"

"Yes."

He smirks at Dmitri then leans down, kisses my cheek, and says, "I've heard a lot of good things about your work."

"Really?" I ask in surprise.

"Yes."

"Wait until you see what Anna has put together. It's fresh and cutting edge," Dmitri boasts.

Sergey smiles. "Can't wait."

Dmitri releases his arm from around me and goes to a fridge. "Anna, you want a bottle of water?"

"Sure."

He takes out two. He opens one and puts the cap back on then hands it to me. "Boris getting ready?"

"Yeah. Maksim is taping his ankle."

Dmitri looks out the window. "Killian looks ready."

"Is that who he's fighting?" I ask.

Dmitri nods then places his hand on my ass and pulls me to the window. "See the guy in green shorts on the corner bag?"

"Yeah."

"He and Boris have gone head-to-head since they were kids."

"Who wins?"

"Both of them. It depends on the year."

"Do they hate each other?"

Dmitri snorts. "Nope. They're pretty good friends."

"Really?"

"Anna, are you into boxing?" Sergey asks.

I spin. "I usually watch the fights when they are on television. But it's usually in a bar. I've never been to a live one before."

"So, the sight of blood or violence isn't going to make you squirm?"

The only thing making me squirm is Dmitri's hand.

"No. I can handle it."

Sergey nods his head, as if impressed. "All right. I won't get out the blindfold."

"Ha, ha."

Dmitri slides his fingers over the curve of my ass cheek, and tingles race down my legs. "Let's grab a seat, kotik."

"I've got another call to make. It was nice meeting you, Anna," Sergey says.

"You, too."

Dmitri steers me to the metal chairs in front of the ring. He introduces me to several men, both Russian and Irish. They all seem to know each other well. I try to remember their names, but it's hard with his hand caressing my ass and the look he keeps giving me.

He introduces me to everyone as, "This is my Anna. She just moved here from New York and is an amazing interior designer." Pride shines in his eyes when he says it.

My face is scorching hot from his praise, but he only tugs me closer to him.

Maksim comes out of the locker room with Boris. I know it's him before Dmitri tells me because he is a cross between the three brothers. If I pinned their pictures on a wall, I could take each of their features and match them. Boris has Maksim's lips but Dmitri's nose and Sergey's forehead. Together, the four brothers could fill a fitness magazine with all their different ripped body parts and sexy good looks. And they all carry the air of danger Dmitri does.

I'm not sure why I'm not scared of any of them. I should be after what I've been through with Mitch. He showed me people can be more than they let on, which means if the Ivanov brothers appear dangerous, it's probably more intense than anything I could ever imagine. But I'm not intimidated.

Instead of sitting, we stand. The three brothers surround me while Boris fights. All I feel is a wall of protection. Maksim is friendlier than he was in the penthouse, especially when I tell him I will meet his deadline and come in under budget. Sergey likes to joke, but he also has an edge about him.

Boris doesn't come near me until after the fight is over. His eyes glow the entire time in the ring, as if he could stare death in the eye and not flinch. He and Killian are both bloody by the time the fight is over. Round after round, they knock punches into each other, until the very last minute. Boris swings and lands a hard fist into Killian's cheek, knocking him down.

Half the men in the room cheer. It's loud, and I suddenly realize more people came in. I just never noticed. I was in the bubble of the Ivanov brothers.

And something about their protection makes me feel powerful. I don't know how or why, but it does. I've grown up in a goody-two-shoes environment. Besides Mitch, I have never been around anyone who even hinted at danger.

I'm in a gym full of screaming men who could all crush me in a second. There are no other women besides me. Viktor is near the staircase, leaning against the wall, a reminder anything could happen.

But I am Dmitri's Anna. So nothing will.

It's a cocky thought. I'm never arrogant. But the blood pumping through my veins from the victory of the fight and new sense of security gives me a confidence I'm not used to.

A new thought springs into my mind. *Maybe that's more dangerous than the Ivanov brothers.*

14

Dmitri

"You've impressed me. Not just by meeting the timeline but the concepts as well. Thank you for getting us out of the jam Lada left us in," Maksim says.

Anna beams. "I'm glad you like everything."

"I do."

"We all do," Boris says.

"Anna, you want another coffee?" Sergey asks and rises.

"No, thanks."

"Actually, we need to leave. I've got an appointment," I say, stand, and hold Anna's coat for her.

"What for?" Maksim asks.

I give him my shut-up stare. "For the gym." I'm meeting with Chase today. He doesn't know it, but it's been several days, and he hasn't texted me Mitch's address. My patience is wearing thin. I've also been working and enjoying Anna, so I've not left her side, but time is ticking. Mitch's calls and text messages are only getting worse. I'm not sure if Anna has even turned her phone on, but I'll look when she's getting ready. His current threats involve coming to Chicago.

Let him attempt it. He'll never leave and end up in Lake Michigan with an anchor around his neck.

Maksim's expression changes. "Anna, if we want to develop the roof, how quickly can you put some plans together for us?"

"I'll have to research the equipment and some different regulations on what materials are allowed on the top of buildings." She pauses then winces. "Maybe a week?"

I'm about to jump in, but Boris beats me to it. "We aren't in any rush. You could take a month, and we would be in good shape."

"I don't need a month."

"Let's set a month deadline, then. No need to stress. If you finish sooner, great, if not, no worries."

She smiles and glances at Maksim.

He nods. "I'm good with that."

"Okay."

I slide her coat over her arms. We say our goodbyes, leave Maksim's place, and I guide her out to my car.

"Are you sure you don't want me to take a cab home? It seems silly for you to take one instead," Anna comments.

I snort. "I will not have you in a cab."

Anna's lips twitch. "I won't melt in a cab."

"I have a driver. My brothers have drivers. Your brother has a driver. I do not want you in a cab with someone I do not know driving you. It is not safe."

She tilts her head. "Why? Since when?"

Since you are mine.

Don't lie to her. She gave you her trust.

I glance at my watch then reach for her cheek. "Like most men who have money, I have enemies, my kotik. Viktor will watch over you at your lunch. But no one will know he is focused on you."

She sits straighter and quietly says, "I see. Do I need to worry when I am not with you?"

"No, I don't want you to worry. But I will not put you in any situation where a stranger is driving you, or something could happen."

She stays silent, and her blue eyes never leave mine.

My stomach flips. "Tell me what you are thinking right now, please."

"Is this how it will always be?"

I cringe inside. "Possibly."

She glances out the window.

"Anna—"

"What if I'm with a friend? Say Harper and I want to go shopping after lunch. Do I tell Viktor? Do I have to text you and ask permission so you know my every move?" Her face is slightly red, but her voice is calm. I'm not sure if she's angry or not.

My pulse increases. She's asking a fair question. And I've not thought that far ahead. I curse myself. I don't want to worry Anna, but I also don't want her to be unaware. I pull her onto my lap. "Do you remember how I told you we were trying to buy a piece of property for our development from Lorenzo Rossi?"

Her eyes darken. "Yes."

"It's not going so well. It has morphed from him selling us his one plot, to us giving him the seven pieces we have for practically nothing. It makes me nervous. He hasn't made any threats, but I don't want him to ever catch any of us off guard."

"You think he'd hurt me?"

"I want to be proactive with your safety."

She taps her fingers on her thigh.

"Are you angry with me?" I ask.

She shakes her head. "No."

"Why not?"

"Honesty doesn't anger me, Dmitri. Lies and keeping me in the dark does."

She still doesn't know who I really am.

She can't ever find out.

I will protect her from it all.

"Go wherever you want with Harper today. You will probably need to explain who Viktor is to her when you get in the car. He will stay out of your way until it is time to leave."

"What about you?"

"What about me?"

She strokes my cheek. "If I have your car and bodyguard, how will you stay safe?"

"I know how to protect myself, kotik. You don't need to worry about my safety."

She traces her finger over my biceps. "Do you have a gun, Dmitri?"

"Not on me."

"But you have one?"

"Yes. It's in my safe."

She takes a deep breath. "Do you have your knife on you?"

"How do you know I own a knife?"

"It was on the dresser."

"Ahh. I see."

"Is it on you?"

"Where are you going with this?"

"Can you answer my question?"

I slide my hand in my jacket and pull out the Russian pocket knife my father gave me on my eighteenth birthday. "Yes."

She touches the stainless steel. "Am I correct that if you had to slit a man's throat with this, you would know how to? You would not hesitate?"

My blood pounds harder in my veins and my chest tightens. "Yes. You are correct."

She runs her hand on the side of my head and nods. "Okay. You will take the cab. I get the car. Viktor will watch over me."

"You don't seem surprised at my revelation."

"No."

"You don't want to run from me?"

"No. You are a dangerous man. I already know this. Thank you for being honest. But do you think Viktor could smile so he doesn't scare Harper?"

I can't help the grin forming on my face. "I'm not sure he's ever smiled before."

She softly laughs then leans into my lips. "I have a more important question."

"What's that?"

"My project is over. Am I going back to Chase's or staying with you tonight?"

I push my hand through her hair. "I want you with me. But it's your choice. Do you want to stay?"

Please say yes.

"Mmm. If I stay, how are you going to kiss me?"

I don't hesitate and slide my tongue in her mouth so fast, she gasps then repositions her body on mine. She gives it back to me as good as I'm giving it to her while circling her hips on my lap until my erection is rock hard.

The car stops. She pulls back and breathlessly says, "Okay. I'll stay."

I squeeze her ass. "You're evil to leave me like this, kotik."

She bites on her lip, and I kiss her on the forehead. I move her off my lap, get out, then escort her into the restaurant. Harper is already waiting. Anna introduces us, and I stay with them until the hostess says their table is ready.

I'm not far from Chase's office building, so I walk the few blocks. The fall air feels good, cooling off the heat created by Anna and the conversation I was nervous about having with her.

She handled it better than I could have wished. And I didn't expect her to ask about my weapons. But she's smart, so I shouldn't underestimate what she might think about me.

Maybe I should tell her.

I can't. It's too much.

I'm so lost in my thoughts, I almost miss Chase's building. Security rings his office. I half expect him to turn me away with some excuse, since I don't have an appointment, but I also don't think he's stupid.

Security hands me a badge, gives me directions to his office, and I hop on the elevator. It opens on the twentieth floor, and I go down several hallways until I'm in front of the correct suite.

As soon as I get inside, I'm escorted to Chase's private office. He's standing with his hands in his pockets, staring outside the window overlooking the river. "Proper etiquette is to schedule an appointment."

"I believe we threw protocol out when you didn't send me the information I requested."

He spins and scowls. "Is my sister coming back soon?"

"That's her choice. She isn't my hostage."

"No? Kind of feels that way."

I take a deep breath and sit in the chair across from his desk. "Why would you ever think that?"

He crosses his arms. "She's been gone for three days. Her phone only rings to voice mail."

I point to his chair. "Why don't you sit down, and we can discuss the reason it's turned off."

He glares for several moments at me.

"We can do this all day. I have nothing else on my schedule."

He exhales and pulls out his chair. "Why can't I get ahold of my sister?"

"She texted Vivian to call my phone if you wanted to speak with her."

"I shouldn't have to go through you to talk with Anna."

"Instead of assuming I'm a controlling bastard who is hiding your sister from you, why don't you ask me why her phone was off."

He sighs. "Why?"

"He won't stop harassing her."

"I told her to block him."

"Me, too. But she wants her things."

"She can buy new stuff," Chase insists.

"Once again, we think alike. But she has proprietary information on her computer she wants."

"She needs to get over it. Whatever is in New York is staying there."

"She has a right to her things. And she's really talented—"

"I know she is," he defensively barks.

Stay calm. He means well.

I push my fingertips together and let the silence linger for a bit before speaking again. "We both want what is best for Anna."

"I've spoken to my attorneys and police buddies several times. It's not a black-and-white situation. Anna can't go back there, and he's not going to send her things to her."

"No, she isn't stepping foot there. But she deserves her things, and he needs to be dealt with."

"Stay out of this. You're asking for trouble."

"He's threatening to come to Chicago to get her," I bark.

The color drains from Chase's face. "What?"

"You heard me. He's only getting more enraged. Now, I asked you politely for his address several days ago. I understand your concerns, but I will handle this going forward."

His eyes turn to slits. "What are you going to do?"

"It's best if you don't know. Probably better you didn't text it to me." I shove the pad of paper and pen on his desk at him.

He hesitates, writes down the address, but holds it before handing it to me. "My sister has been through a lot."

"I know. She's told me everything."

"Everything?"

"Yes."

"Did she tell you what he did to her a year ago?"

"Yes. And no offense, but she doesn't want you or anyone to know, so please don't ask me the details."

Chase's face hardens. "I already know."

"How?"

"I own an ambulance company and know lots of staff members at all the hospitals in New York City. If you do enough digging, you can find out all sorts of things."

I rise. "If you know, then you shouldn't have a problem with me taking care of him." I hold my hand out for the address.

Chase rises, too. "That depends."

"On what?"

"What are you involved in?"

"I would never lay a finger on your sister."

"That's not what I asked."

Silence fills the air. The ticking of the clock on the wall seems to get louder.

Chase steps closer. "She doesn't need to go from one dangerous situation to another."

I'm serious about her. Lying to him is only going to make things worse.

"She's protected at all times. Right now, she's at lunch with Harper. My bodyguard is watching them. I've instructed her to only ride in my car, my brothers', or yours. She understands and agreed to this."

He clenches his jaw, and his face turns red with anger.

"It is what it is, Chase. And I will get her a new phone, so you don't have to call mine. But Anna is with me because she wants to be. If she ever decides she doesn't want me, it will be her choice to leave. And I would never do anything to force her to stay. But I don't have any plans of letting her go, so it's best if we work together."

His scowl only deepens. He shakes his head and hands me the paper. "Let me know when he's taken care of."

15

Anna

"Guess what?" Harper sings.

"What?"

She whips two envelopes out of her purse. "Surprise!"

"What are those?"

"Steven booked us makeovers!"

"Really? Why?"

"His property management firm just took over this salon. There was an issue with their plumbing. The old firm didn't take care of it. Steven promised her he would step in and get the issue fixed. The owner was so happy she gave him these, and he knew we were getting together today, so he booked us appointments!"

"Wow. Steven needs to get some extra love for this one," I tease Harper.

"Oh, don't worry, I already took care of him." She winks.

I laugh. "How's your job with Cindy going?"

"It's awesome. We just did these really sexy boudoir shoots for several models. But I don't want to talk about me. Now that I met the sexy Russian, I understand why Vivian said you hadn't been home in several days." She wiggles her eyebrows.

My face grows hot.

"Well? Don't hold back!"

"Harper!"

"Oh no you don't! I want details!"

"He's great," I say.

She folds her arms and smirks.

I lean in and lower my voice. "Fine. I really like him."

She claps her hands. "Okay...and..."

"He's...nice. And super supportive of my career."

"He's nice? Anna!"

I look around to make sure no one else can hear and scoot closer. "He's a stud, okay? I've had so many O's, I'm not sure what the next letter in the alphabet is anymore."

"Go, Dmitri!"

"Shhh."

"Oh, come on. You've been with douchebag for years. It's about time you got some spicy action."

The waitress puts our salmon salads down and refills our water. "Do you need anything else?"

"No. We're good." Harper smiles.

"Thank you," I say.

The waitress leaves.

Harper picks up her fork. "Not to rush, but we have a half hour to get to the salon."

"Okay." I take a bite of my salad.

"Glad to see you're eating," Harper says.

I groan. "Dmitri is all over me about it."

"What do you mean?"

"He claims I'm starving myself and damaging my body and has me eating a ridiculous number of calories. We have a bet, and I agreed to do it for one week. I told him I'm going to gain a ton of weight."

Harper puts her fork down. "I thought you stopped that?"

Embarrassment fills my face. I forgot about the little white lie I told Harper.

Okay, it was a flat-out big mistruth.

"I'm sorry. I lied."

"Why?"

I sigh. "I couldn't lose anything. The weight just stayed where it was."

"Because you don't need to. Your body is perfect the way it is."

"Well, it won't be after I eat a week's worth of Dmitri's calories."

She takes a sip of water. "What does he say about your body?"

My face burns.

"Thought so." She points at me. "You need to stop this crazy obsession you have over food. You didn't have a problem with your body image until Mitch. And we've already established the fact he's a complete asshat, so you should realize how utterly ridiculous any notion of your body not being beautiful is."

"I'm trying. It's not easy to turn his voice off," I admit.

Harper puts her hand on my arm. "Please tell me you aren't still talking to him."

"I'm not. But he won't stop calling and texting me. I keep my phone off, but when I turn it on, it's insane." I've only looked at my phone a few times since I've been with Dmitri nonstop. But whenever I do, I cringe and my stomach flips. Mitch's text messages are getting worse, and I haven't listened to any of his voice mails. I'm too scared to know what's in the messages, and I don't want to have anything to do with him anymore.

"Why aren't you blocking him?"

"I want my stuff."

"You can get new stuff." She puts a forkful of salmon in her mouth.

"It's not that simple. I have things on my laptop for work. I was stupid and didn't put everything in the cloud. I barely survived Dmitri's project without it."

"But you did. Over time, it will work itself out, and you won't miss it."

I drink some water, trying to control my anger. I'm so tired of everyone telling me to forget about my computer. The programs and information I have on it aren't replaceable. I worked hard for those things, and they'll make my business run smoother.

"Don't get mad at me," Harper gently says.

"You don't understand."

She puts her hand on mine. "I'm sorry. But I don't want you anywhere near Mitch."

"He texted he's coming to Chicago if I don't go back," I blurt out.

Harper's eyes turn to slits. "He's got some massive balls if he does that. Your brother will kill him."

"I think Dmitri would first." My conversation with Dmitri earlier in the car and the vision of his knife come to my mind.

She nods. "Yeah. I can see that. He's got that bad boy danger flair about him."

I stay quiet. *Guess this is a good time to tell her.*

"So, ummm..."

She takes another bite and raises her eyebrows.

I glance behind me. Viktor is sitting by the door where people usually sit to wait. His ever-present scowl is on his face. People are standing around, keeping their distance from him.

He does look like he just got out of a long stint at the federal penitentiary.

"See the scary looking guy over there? Near the hostess stand?"

Harper looks around my head. "Yeah. Why is he staring at us?"

"He's sort of our bodyguard."

"Sort of?"

"His job is to look out for us today."

"Is this a gift from your boyfriend?" she sarcastically asks.

I stare at her.

"You aren't joking?"

"No."

Her eyes widen. "Is this in case Mitch tries anything?"

Well, that's easier than the truth.

I tell another white lie. "Yes. Dmitri's overprotective. I told him it isn't necessary—"

"Bravo! Good for him. I like this new man of yours. Although, I'd love to watch him kick the crap out of Mitch."

"He has a boxing gym—"

"A real one?"

"Yeah. We went to watch his brother fight the other night."

"Like a knock 'em out, blood bath real one?"

"Yes."

"That's awesome! I want to go. When's the next one?"

"Ummm... I'm not sure. I think he said Boris only fights Killian once a year."

"Boris and Killian?"

"Yes. Boris is his brother."

She grins. "So it was Russia against Ireland?"

"Why do you look so excited?"

"Jeez, girl. Your life is way more exciting than it used to be. And not just because of the O's, although I'm happy to hear he's made you forget the alphabet. I hope you realize this and don't ditch him to go back to dingleberry dumb, piece of—"

Harper's phone belts out a rap song. She digs in her purse while the entire restaurant stares at us. "Sorry." She winces, finally finds it, and turns it off. "Time to go. Make sure you make up for not eating all this. I'm sure Dmitri is making you work off lots of extra calories."

I elbow her. "Harper!"

"What? Steven can burn my calories off all he wants. I'm not complaining. You shouldn't, either."

"I'm not."

She laughs, throws cash on the table, and finishes her water. "Ready?"

"Yep. Let me introduce you to Viktor."

"Ooh. Does he have a sexy Russian accent, too?"

"I don't think he talks."

"What?"

"You'll see."

We go to the front of the restaurant, and Viktor rises. Several people move farther away from him.

"Viktor, this is Harper. Harper, meet Viktor."

Harper sticks out her hand, and his lips barely turn up into a smile, then he grunts and pushes the door open, holding it for us to walk through.

Harper puts her hand to her mouth, trying not to laugh. I grab her other arm and lead her to the car. We get in, and she whispers, "Where did Dmitri find him?"

I shrug.

"I'd like to see Mitch try something with Viktor around."

Viktor isn't to protect me from Mitch. He's for the Italian mob.

Don't tell her. She'll flip.

"Let's not talk about Mitch anymore."

She tilts her head next to my face. "Agreed. Let's talk about you and Dmitri. He called you *kotik* when he left. What does that mean?"

Heat crawls up my face.

Harper's eyes light up. "Oh. Something dirty?"

"Ummm...no..."

She waits with a smirk on her face.

I take a bottle of water from the holder and drink half of it.

"Anna? What does it mean?"

"Pussycat."

She gapes at me. "Really?"

"Mm-hmm."

She pats my thigh. "That's hot."

"It's a Russian thing..."

"Oh, I'm sure it is. What else is a Russian thing?"

"You're killing me, Harper."

She grills me for the rest of the ride. We get to the salon, and Viktor gets out of the car and opens our door.

"Ummm...you can stay in the car. We're just going in there." I point to the building.

He shakes his head and points for us to walk.

Harper tilts her head up. "Viktor, can you tell me what time it is?"

He glances at his watch. In a thick Russian accent, he replies, "Twelve thirty."

She pats his arm. "Thank you."

We spin and go into the salon. As soon as we get several feet away from him, she whispers, "Viktor needs a good woman. He's got the sexy accent going on, too!"

I elbow her. "Shh."

"What?" She glances behind her then quickly turns her head back. "Some chicks dig the whole scary danger thing. I bet he gets a ton of ass."

"Harper!" But I can't help but wonder if I'm one of those chicks. Mitch was dangerous. Dmitri is dangerous. He still hasn't revealed anything else since the night we went to the boxing match, but I'm not oblivious to it.

But Dmitri wouldn't hurt me. Mitch did, and no one would ever say he was dangerous. Until he beat me up, I never considered him to be a threat. There's a big difference.

So what does that say about me?

A woman shoves a clipboard at me, pulling me out of my trance. "When you complete this, please bring it back."

"Thank you." I take the seat next to Harper, and we fill out the disclosure forms. "What are we having done today?"

"Hair, manicure, pedicure. Then we're going to the new store several shops down."

"Which one?"

"I forget the name, but Quinn and Piper were raving about it. They said Charlotte found it. And I just got my first paycheck, so I'm celebrating."

"I'm happy you got your job. I know you were stressing about money. I can't wait to get my first check. I'll be able to pay Chase back."

"You know he isn't going to take it."

"I don't like him paying for my stuff."

"Tell me about it. Preaching to the choir, girl."

I sigh. "I need to get a bank account opened, too."

"Can't believe Mitch took your money. He has no limit to his slimeball ways, does he?"

"It's my fault. I gave him control over everything."

"No, it isn't your fault. Even after Ian stole all my money, I would still have Steven manage my stuff in a heartbeat. He deals in numbers all day long, and that stuff gives me a headache. Mitch manages money for people. It made sense you trusted him. So don't beat yourself up."

"Would you really give Steven control after Ian stole everything before you even got divorced?"

She smiles. "Yep. I trust him. He's not Ian. No matter what happened between Steven and me, he would never hurt me like that. I know this about him. I'm sure most women would call me stupid. But I don't want my future to be dictated by the past. And it's not fair to hold Steven accountable for Ian's dirty actions."

"I guess that's a good point."

We fill out our forms, and she takes them to the counter, then comes back. "Say you and Dmitri got married. Would you really not share accounts with him?"

I shrug my shoulders. "I'm not sure. I haven't thought about it."

"Okay, but if you trusted him, wouldn't you let him?"

"I do trust him. I've just not had time to think about any of this. Can we change the subject?"

"Okay."

"And we just started dating, so don't go planning any weddings anytime soon."

She raises her eyebrows.

"Why are you looking at me like that?"

"That man looked at you like you were a prize possession he adores. And you've never looked at anyone you've dated like you look at him."

"Like what?"

"Gaga eyes. You two are in love. You're getting married someday. I can tell."

I groan. "Harper, we just met."

"So? What does that have to do with it? Dmitri doesn't seem to me like a man who doesn't know what he wants."

"Want and love are two different things."

"Are they?"

"Harper? Anna? Please follow me," a woman with pink hair and a big smile says.

We get up, and I'm relieved to end the conversation. She has us sit in pedicure chairs next to each other. We spend the next few hours getting our feet and hands pampered and then we go into the salon portion of the building. By the time we get there, we've had several glasses of champagne, and I'm feeling pretty tipsy.

"Looks like you're here for the Fall Makeover?"

"Yep! Bring it on," I say.

"Great. Is it okay if I turn your chair so you don't see anything until the end?"

"Sure."

Harper is in the seat next to me, and we spend the next few hours laughing more and eating the cheese and crackers they serve us with more champagne.

"Holy smokes! You look hot!" Harper exclaims when the stylist turns the dryer off.

Excitement builds, and the stylist spins the chair. My mouth drops open. I stare at my reflection.

My hair is dark, with several highlights around my face. Even my eyebrows were dyed darker.

I turn to Harper.

"What do you think?" she says. "Amazing, isn't it?"

"I'm not blonde!"

"No! But you look awesome!"

I turn back to the mirror. I've never been anything but blonde. A few years ago, I wanted to experiment with hair colors, but Mitch didn't want me to.

Dmitri likes my blonde hair. What is he going to think?

"Why do you look upset? Your blue eyes pop like crazy with that color! She did a great job," Harper says.

I look at the stylist. "I'm sorry. I just... I've never been anything but blonde."

"Did they not tell you at the front desk what the Fall Makeover is?"

"No."

"Yes, she did. When we first came in, before she handed us the clipboards," Harper says.

"Oh. I must have been distracted," I mutter and stare at myself some more.

It's not bad. Actually, it's kind of nice. I do look good.

But what if Dmitri hates it?

Then he isn't as awesome as I think he is.

My stomach flips, but I smile and turn to the stylist. "I love it. Thank you."

She smiles. "Awesome. I was worried for a minute. It looks soooooo good on you!"

"It does," Harper insists.

"Oh my gosh! I'm sorry! You look great too!" Her hair has the same highlights as mine, but her hair is already darker, so it isn't as drastic as my color.

She bats her eyes and puts her hand under her chin. "Watch out, Steven Sinclair. There's going to be a new girl in your bed tonight."

"Harper." I laugh.

She rises and hands her glass to her stylist. "Thank you, ladies. We hate to run, but it's getting late, and we need to get to the new shop down the street before it closes. Our men have needs."

"Oh. Are you going to Delivery?" my stylist asks.

Harper snaps. "Yes! Thank you. I couldn't remember the name."

"They have amazing stuff."

"Great!" Harper slaps cash on both their chairs and grabs my hand. She leads me out, and Viktor stands.

His face has the same stony expression as always.

"We're going four stores down. Don't wait up," Harper teases and pulls me out the door and down the street. When I glance back, Viktor is only several feet behind us.

We go into Delivery, and I gape. It's got every kind of lingerie you could ever imagine, from bondage to sweetheart.

"Mmm...too innocent. I think we need that section." Harper points to a more risqué area.

"This is more like it," she mutters and holds a dark berry-colored set up to my body. It's mesh and what I would consider classy dirty hot. "This is meant for you. It matches your nails and is perfect with your new hair."

"Okay. But you have to buy it for me. I'll pay you back when I get my check. I don't want my brother buying my lingerie."

She wrinkles her nose. "Gotcha."

We spend an hour in the shop, get several outfits each, and get into the car. When Harper gets dropped off, Viktor hands me his phone.

"Hello?"

"Kotik, are you having fun with Harper?"

"We just dropped her off, but I had a great day."

"Good. I can't wait to hear about it, but I'm not going to be home for another hour. Do you want me to grab something for dinner?"

"Sure."

"Okay. I called security and told them to give you full access. Do you have your ID card on you?"

Full access? Already?

My insides go giddy. "Yes."

"Great. It should only take a few minutes for them to get your fingerprints."

"All right."

"They will give you the elevator code, too. Make yourself at home. I'll see you soon, kotik."

"Bye." I hand the phone back to Viktor. He grunts, shuts my door, and the car lowers with the weight of him settling in the front seat.

We aren't far from Dmitri's. When we get there, it only takes security a few minutes to give me clearance, and I punch in the code for the elevator.

It's already dark, and the lights of the city twinkle from every room. I turn on the surround sound and the Russian music Dmitri often plays comes on. I still don't know what they are saying, but the woman's voice oozes sex. I find a bottle of red wine, the opener, and two glasses, and put them on the table next to the leather couch. There are candles in the main room and a fireplace. I light them and keep the dimmers on around the ceiling.

I go into the bedroom and take a quick shower. I redo my makeup, choosing colors I normally wouldn't because of my new hair color. I stare at my reflection, trying to get used to it.

I feel like a different person.

Please don't hate it.

I shouldn't put so much stock into what a man thinks about my hair, but I love the fact Dmitri thinks I'm beautiful. As much as I wish I didn't care, I do.

I remove all the tags off the deep-berry lingerie, put it on, then go out to the living room.

He should be home any minute.

The last time I attempted to wear lingerie, Mitch left me in the hotel room all by myself until I caught him with that waitress on his lap.

Dmitri isn't Mitch.

I open the bottle of wine, pour two glasses, then lay on the leather couch in a sexy pose with the drink in my hand.

I shouldn't be nervous, but I am. The hotel room scene with me waiting for hours won't leave my head.

The elevator dings, and my stomach flutters intensify. When it opens, Dmitri's Russian words fly into my ears before I see him.

He comes around the corner, stops mid-sentence, and heat flares in his eyes. Every part of my body, he checks out, as if I'm a rare piece of artwork, lingering on my breasts, sex, and thighs.

He says something quickly in Russian, tosses his phone on the chair, drops the food bags, and leans over me. "Kotik, you changed your hair."

I nod.

"You're one of the rare women who can wear any color and look sexy as hell."

"You like it?" I whisper in relief.

He brushes his lips to mine. "You look amazing." He traces his finger over my nipple. "And you got this for me?"

"Mm-hmm."

His eyes fill with more fire. His lips twitch. "Then let me take full advantage of my gift."

16

Dmitri

IF HEAVEN WERE SERVED ON A SILVER PLATTER, IT WOULD BE RIGHT now, here in this moment.

I've never given a woman full access to my home. I've dated several for months, two of them for years, yet no one had access to my place. I didn't think twice about calling security to add Anna.

My day consisted of one fire after another since my meeting with Chase, which didn't go exactly how I hoped it would. It could have ended worse, but it wasn't the discussion I wished for. And I didn't expect him to question me on my affairs.

To say my day was stressful is an understatement, and all I wanted was to see Anna. But it wasn't just a want. It was an ache like I had never felt before. To talk to her, hold her, and wrap myself into the world of us no one else is privy to.

And here she is, glowing like an angel on my couch. She has a new hairstyle, different makeup, and an outfit that accentuates every part of her perky little body.

And she bought it for me.

Most women can't pull off different hair colors and still hold my attention. I can't decide if she's more gorgeous as a blonde or with darker hair. And neither can my body, which is growing hotter each second just staring at her.

"Are you going to kiss me?" she teases.

I drag my finger down the curves of her body. "You're stunning, my kotik."

She bites her lip.

I stroke the thin material over her sex. "I've got a confession to make."

"What is it?"

"I got a little panicky you might have changed your mind and not come back tonight."

She squirms under my touch. "Why?"

"I don't know. Maybe you had time to think about what we talked about in the car?"

She opens her legs wider. "I did think about you."

"Yeah?"

"Mm-hmm. All day." She lets a long breath out.

I slide my finger under the mesh and stroke the top of her skin. "And?"

Her eyes close briefly. She tilts her hips up. "I wondered if you would change your mind and want some alone time tonight."

"I don't think that's possible. I'm finding it quite hard to concentrate on anything, since you're all I can think about." I grasp both sides of her panties and pull them outward so they rip. "Oops. I owe you a new pair, kotik."

She smiles. "It's good I bought several outfits, then. In case you don't have time to go anytime soon."

I slide my hands on her thighs then caress the inside of them, close to her sex. "I have a new favorite reason to come home."

"So you like lingerie?"

I lunge up her body. "No, kotik. I meant you." I kiss her, and she parts her lips hungrily, kissing me as she always does. I'm hers, and she's mine. No matter what my insecurities were earlier, she takes them all away.

I'm a bad man. She's a good woman. Together we're perfection. If I could wrap us in it and tie up the bow to permanently stay in this state, I would.

"I missed you," she whispers between kisses.

"I know. Me, too."

Her hands unfasten my shirt then slide over my chest. She pushes it off me and pulls me closer to her.

"You had fun with Harper?"

"Yeah. What did you do?" She flicks her tongue back in my mouth and reaches for my pants, pulling my belt off in a quick motion.

"Work. Nothing worth talking about. You've got skills, kotik," I tease then suck on the curve of her neck.

"Glad you appreciate them." She shoves my pants down to mid-thigh.

"More than you know." My erection presses onto her mound and stomach. I lower the strap of her top. "I love you in this. You keep surprising me. I think you can't get any sexier, but you do."

She lightly grazes her fingernails on my head, sending zings down my spine. "I want to be, for you."

I groan. "You are, kotik. God, so much." I pull her breast out of the mesh cup, lick it, then suck on it, listening to her whimpers until she arches her back and shudders

I reach down and slip two of my fingers into her sex, slowly pumping in and out of her.

"Dmitri! Oh...oh..."

In Russian, I blurt out, "You make me crazy, kotik. I'm a selfish man to let you come anywhere near me. But I can't help myself. You're an obsession, stoking a fire every second of the day within me."

Her skin heats, competing with my scorching flesh, and beads of sweat pop out on our skin.

The woman singing in Russian belts out the word love, and I catch my breath. I must be losing my mind, because I almost tell her in English, I love her. But it's too soon. She'd freak for sure. And I don't want her to feel like she has to say it back.

It should terrify me. But I suppose it happened the moment I saw her in the bar. The magnetic pull I felt toward her, I hadn't experienced before. And I couldn't forget her face. I never stopped wondering if she was okay, or beating myself up for not following her that night.

So I refrain from revealing my thoughts in English and lean into her ear. I tell her in Russian instead, swirling my thumb over her clit and continuing to slide my other fingers in and out of her pussy.

Her body convulses, and her eyes roll as she cries out my name. I murmur in Russian, "You're my beautiful perfection. And I love every part of you."

"Yes...oh God...yes..." She digs her nails into my shoulder blade, and it's a sweet pain that makes my cock throb.

I move to feast on her other breast and pull my fingers out of her. I drag them across her lips, and she sucks them into her mouth as I edge my tongue around her nipple.

Her moans enhance the song, crooning into the air. I push my face between both breasts, breathing a few seconds into her cleavage, inhaling her skin's sweet scent.

She takes her foot and puts it on the crotch of my pants and pushes them to my ankles. Her smooth legs wrap around my hips. She slides her hand over my ass. "I need you," she whispers. "Please."

It's irony. No one could need anyone more than I need her. I look up, and her sparkling blue eyes are the most gorgeous things I've ever seen. And she desperately craves me. It's so potent, my heart stirs.

I slide up, put my elbows on each side of her, and palm her head. In English, I say, "I need you, my kotik. Like the air I breathe, all day long."

She nods and digs her nails into my ass cheeks.

I slide in her tight, wet heat. Her moan mixes with my groan, and I'm finally fully wrapped in our perfection.

I inch into her, slowly at first, letting her body accept all of me until I can't sink into her anymore.

"So full...oh..." she whispers. "So...oh God...how can this be so good?"

"I know, kotik." The heat swirls, boiling my blood, raising my adrenaline until it's sitting on the surface of my cells and ready to explode.

"Don't stop...oh...please don't stop," she begs, closes her eyes, and arches her back. Her pebbled nipples slide across my skin.

I ravage her mouth, consuming every part of her possible until we're both shaking, sweating, and crying out incoherent things.

We come together, limbs and tongues wrapped around the other, bodies that have merged into one.

She's my everything. And I'll be the man she needs and craves, fighting the darkness so it never comes close enough to destroy us.

17

Anna

THE ALARM GOES OFF AND WAKES ME UP. DMITRI SNATCHES IT AND turns it off, but I slide onto his chest and kiss him.

He wraps his arms around me and flicks his tongue in my mouth until I'm breathless and straddling him.

He groans. "I have to go, kotik."

"Now?"

"Yes. My flight takes off soon."

"Flight? Where are you going?"

"I've got a work trip. I'm going to be gone for a few days. I think it might be best for you to go to your brother's. You can stay here, but you'll be alone, and you haven't seen your family in a few days."

I sit up. "Why didn't you tell me you were going out of town?"

He raises his eyebrows and cockily smiles. "You had a gift for me last night. It was only fair for me to show you how grateful I was."

I tilt my head. "Dmitri—"

"Please don't be upset. I wasn't thinking about anything but us last night."

I shouldn't be mad at him. All night, he only focused on me. He ignored phone calls. At one point, his brothers rang the bell, and he told them to go away. "Okay."

He pecks my lips. "I got you something, too."

"What?"

"A new phone."

"Why? My other one works fine."

"You can't use it. You aren't comfortable blocking him right now. I don't want to call Viktor to talk to you or your brother if you choose to stay there. And your family shouldn't have to call me to contact you, either."

I slide back on him. "Did my brother call you?"

"No, he did not call me."

I quietly ask, "Why are you pushing my brother on me?"

He puts his hands in the air. "I'm not. But I don't want him to think I stole you and am keeping you hostage here."

I snort. "He probably would."

Dmitri kisses me again. "I'm going to be late if I don't get moving. Stay here or at your brother's. But at least go visit him and Vivian."

"Can you tell me why you're pushing them on me?" I repeat.

He sighs. "Family is important. Yours is just as crucial as mine. One is not more important than the other. We are together, and both of our families need to be in our lives."

I freeze. All Mitch did was try to eliminate my family from my life. He made me feel guilty whenever I had an event or just wanted to see them. I used to visit my parents during the workday so it didn't inconvenience him, or I didn't have to argue about it.

I pop up on my knees and kiss Dmitri. "Thank you."

"For what?"

"Everything. But mostly just being you."

He opens his mouth to say something but shuts it.

"What were you going to say?"

He smiles. "Nothing. Just let me know where you are at. My number is programmed in your new phone."

I wiggle my eyebrows. "Did you put any sexy photos on there?"

An amused expression fills his face. "No. But I can if you wish."

I drag my finger down his chest and stop above his cock. "Maybe I'll surprise you with some pictures."

He groans. "Don't tease me, kotik."

Hmmm.

I roll off him. "Are you showering?"

"Of course." He rises.

"Do you want company?"

His eyes twinkle. "Is this a trick question?"

I follow him into the bathroom. We have an intense shower session. After, I sit on the bed, with a towel around my head and another around my body, while he packs.

"So, where are you going?"

He avoids my eyes. "To the east coast."

To the... My stomach flips. "You're going to New York?"

His face hardens, and he pauses but finally says, "Yes."

"Dmitri—"

"I have business there."

"That involves me?"

He folds a black T-shirt and sets it on top of the pile. He looks up. "I'm getting your stuff back. Unless he has destroyed it, which will create more consequences for him, everything in that apartment that belongs to you will be moved here."

"I don't want anything except for my computer and samples. Everything else can stay in the past."

"Then that is what I will bring back to you."

"How?"

He closes his eyes, and when he opens them, the green has turned to an almost-hunter shade. He steps forward and pushes his hands in my hair. "This is one of those times I will not share with you what I am doing. It is for your safety."

"Are you going to kill him?" I blurt out.

Something passes in his eyes. A chill races through my spine.

"No," he says without inflection.

Then why do you look like you're going to?

"Dmitri, I..." I look away, my stomach flips. Mitch is not a good person. I've grown to only feel hatred toward him. But I do not want his death to be due to me.

Dmitri tilts my head toward him. "I just told you I am not killing him. Your eyes tell me you don't believe me."

"But you would? If I told you to?"

He says nothing, and goose bumps pop out on my skin.

"And you want to?" I whisper.

"Of course I do. But you would hate me if I did, wouldn't you?"

Could I ever hate him? Would I still want his arms wrapped around me if he killed Mitch?

"You don't need to answer, kotik. Your expression tells me everything I need to know. I give you my word. He will still be alive when I finish with him. And you will have your things back, assuming he was not stupid enough to destroy them."

I release a breath. I try to speak, but I'm not sure what to say. *Is my laptop really this important?*

"Are you going to do something that will put you in jail?"

"I will not be in jail from dealing with Mitch. He is a coward. You do not need to worry about this."

I release a breath.

Dmitri's face softens. "Is this too much for you? Getting a bigger glimpse of me and what I am capable of?"

This is the point I would expect myself to run. To tell him it is and to stay away from me. Instead, I surprise myself and ask, "If I told you not to go, would you listen to me?"

"I am sorry, kotik. When a man hurts you, he pays the consequences. Nothing I do to him will ever make up for what he did or be enough. Even death would not absolve him from his actions. But if you told me you did not want me to go, I would still have to. He chose to assault you. When you made it clear to him that he needed to stop harassing you, he only continued making threats. If right now you broke my heart and said you never wanted to see me again, I would still need to make sure he understands he is to never intimidate or contact you again."

There's so much in his statement, but I can only respond to one thing. "Your heart would be broken?"

Sadness fills his eyes. He nods.

Tears fill mine. "Mine would be, too."

He inhales sharply and brushes his thumb on my cheek. "You are not going to run from me?"

I lace my fingers around his head. "No." I pull him down and kiss him.

His alarm rings again. He groans. "I have to go."

"Will you call me?"

"Yes. Your new phone is on the table in the kitchen."

"Okay."

He scans my face.

"What?"

"You are welcome to stay here, but I do think it's best if you go to your brother's. Visit with your family. Stay busy while I am gone. Viktor will keep an eye on you, no matter where you go."

"At my brother's?"

"Yes. He will stay outside their unit. My driver will take you wherever you want to go. Your brother knows about this."

"You spoke to my brother? I thought you said you didn't call him?"

"I didn't. I saw him."

"When?"

"Yesterday. Kotik, I have to go, or I will miss my flight."

We kiss for several minutes, and when he walks toward the elevator, I want to beg him to stay. But I know in my heart, there is no stopping him. He's made it clear he is going to deal with Mitch, no matter what my wishes are.

I'm not sure what I want to happen to Mitch. But I do want him to stop harassing me. I don't want to worry about him showing up in Chicago. And I never want to see him again.

"When will you be back?" I ask as he steps in the elevator.

He spins. "I'm not sure. Few days. I will let you know when I find out for sure." He hits the elevator button and the doors close.

I sit on the couch, trying to gather my thoughts. Part of me worries about what he's going to do. Another side of me says Mitch is going to get what's coming to him. It's these thoughts that make me wonder who I'm becoming. Or was this always part of me and I was just so worried about being perfect all the time and not upsetting Mitch, I didn't really know who I was?

I get changed and fix myself up, trying new makeup colors to coordinate with my hair, and go into my closet. Most of my clothes look better with my blonde hair.

I need to go shopping as soon as I get paid.

I go out to the table to learn how to operate my new phone. The cell has my name engraved on it and four different metallic-colored cases. Silver, yellow gold, rose gold, and black pewter.

I open the envelope that says Kotik on it and pull out a check and note.

Kotik,

I wasn't sure what case you wanted. If you don't like this phone, I'll get you a new one when I get back. Here's your first check. Did you set up your bank account yet? If not, there's cash in my safe. It's in my closet, and the code is 89695432. Take whatever you need.

I'll miss you.

XOXO

Dmitri

P.S. - I programmed the driver's number into your cell.

I REREAD THE NOTE, STUNNED HE GAVE ME THE CODE TO HIS SAFE. I look at my check, which is the biggest check I've ever gotten. I stuff it and the letter back in the envelope.

I need to get my bank account set up.

Then I'm going shopping.

But first, I need to talk to my brother.

I'm not sure what he and Dmitri spoke about, but I want to know.

I glance at the time. It's still early in the morning, and I know Vivian and he will be home. I pack a few outfits, grab my laptop, so I can work on the roof project while Dmitri is gone, and my new phone, along with the envelope. I text the driver, and he says he's ten minutes away.

Everything is so much closer in Chicago.

I didn't think I would like this city compared to New York, but it's quickly growing on me. I sit and look around Dmitri's, and it hits me that his place feels like home. *He* feels like home. He hasn't even been gone for an hour and I miss him already.

I pick up my cell and call him.

"Kotik, everything okay?" His voice is filled with worry.

"Yeah. I wanted to say thank you for the phone. And the check."

"You earned every penny of it."

"Thank you."

There's a muffled noise.

"Is one of your brothers with you?"

"Yes."

"Which one?"

"Boris."

"Why?"

He is quiet for a moment. "So I keep my patience."

My stomach flips. "Oh. Ummm..."

"Kotik, no more questions about this trip."

I take a deep breath. "Okay. You'll let me know when you're coming home?"

"As soon as I know."

"But it will be a few days?"

"Yes."

"Okay. I will stay at my brother's, unless he gets on my nerves."

He chuckles. "Brothers will do that. But his place is big. It seems like you have your own space. I'm sure it comes with a lock."

"Good point."

There are more muffled sounds.

"Anna, I need to go. I'll call you later, okay?"

"Okay. Ummm...stay safe."

"Don't worry, kotik. I know what I am doing. I have to go now."

"Okay. Bye."

"Bye, beautiful." He hangs up.

The driver texts he's downstairs. Viktor is waiting for me when I step off the elevator. His typical scowl is on his face.

"Morning," I say and smile.

He grunts, and his lips turn slightly up.

Well, that's an improvement.

I get in the car and text Dmitri. "Victor almost smiled. I think I'm growing on him."

I take out my other phone, ignore all the missed voice messages from Mitch and text messages, and program Harper, Vivian, Chase, and the rest of my family's numbers into my new phone. I send all of them a message.

"It's Anna. This is my new number. Please delete the old one."

"I want to talk to you," comes back from Chase.

"Then get me a cup of coffee ready. I'm on my way." I send it, and the car parks in front of his building. Viktor opens my door.

"Do you drink coffee?" I ask.

"Yes."

"Great. I need some backup."

He raises his eyebrow.

"I'm assuming you can sit next to me and have a cup?"

"If that is what you wish."

"Oh, I do."

I'm not sure how my brother and Dmitri's conversation went, but I have a feeling my brother is going to give me an earful. And I'm done worrying about what he thinks.

This is my new life. I'm with Dmitri. It's time he gets used to it.

I go into the penthouse with Viktor. Chase and Vivian's eyes widen.

"This is Viktor, my bodyguard. This is my brother, Chase, and his wife, Vivian." I point to a chair next to my brother. "Have a seat, and I'll get you some coffee. Sugar? Cream?"

Victor shifts and says in his thick, Russian accent, "Black."

"Of course it is. Okay, coming right up," I chirp.

He sits next to Chase.

I bring two cups of coffee over to the table.

Vivian clears her throat. Her lips twitch. "You switched your hair. It looks amazing on you."

"Thanks."

Chase stares at me.

I sit down across from him. "You wanted to talk to me?"

"Is he meant to intimidate me?" He glances at Viktor. "No offense."

Victor keeps his scowl on his face and drinks his coffee.

"What are you doing, Anna?" Chase asks.

"Don't you mean, what am I doing with Dmitri?"

Chase's face hardens. "Can we talk privately?"

"This is private. You don't hide things from Vivian, do you?"

Chase glares at me.

"Anna," Vivian softly says.

I sigh. *Time to get it over with. The fun is over.* I turn to her. "Be nice to Viktor. He grows on you after a while."

She winks. "Got it."

Chase and I go into his office. The moment the door shuts, he says, "I don't think you understand what you're getting involved in."

I angrily ask, "What do you think I'm involved in? Hmm?"

"He's dangerous, Anna."

"Not to me. Or you. But to anyone who wants to hurt me, yes. And you know what? I'm okay with it." I laugh. "Actually, I'm more than okay with it. It's nice having someone who wants me and will go to any length to protect me instead of harming me."

"There are plenty of guys who won't hit you."

"You think that's all I went through? I sat on pins and needles every day, allowing him to degrade me and make me feel like I wasn't worth anything."

Chase's face hardens. "He's an asshole. But Dmitri is involved in things—"

"What things?"

Chase crosses his arms and tilts his head. "Not good things."

"Tell me. What is he involved in that is so bad? Hmm?"

He stays silent.

"You can't. You don't know."

"Anna—"

"No, Chase. I know more than you do about him. The only thing you need to understand is he treats me well. Let me rephrase. He treats me like I'm the most important person on earth. I'm his priority. And I'm only here because, even though I'm sure you had your say yesterday, he still wants me to have my family in my life. So get on board. I'm not leaving him. And if you make me choose, I'll pick him."

"You just met him."

"Doesn't matter. He's the one."

His eyes turn to slits. "The one?"

"Yes."

"You just got out of a five-year relationship."

"Yep. And it taught me everything I don't want."

Chase grabs my shoulders. "Anna, listen to me. You shouldn't have to have a bodyguard following you around. Be smart."

"You're such a hypocrite."

His head jerks back, and he releases me. "How am I a hypocrite?"

"Ms. Thursday?"

His face falls.

"Yeah. I remember Vivian having a bodyguard and then your 'friend' kidnapped and almost killed her and you."

He clenches his jaw.

"Stop being two-faced." I take a deep breath. "Now, do you want me to stay here while Dmitri is gone or no?"

"Gone?"

"You know where he is."

His eyes widen. "He told you?"

"Not everything. He won't tell me anything that would put me in danger. But I know you saw him yesterday. He's on his way to New York. I'm not stupid."

Chase stays silent.

"Do you want me to stay or go?"

"Of course I want you to stay."

"Okay. I will. But one more thing."

He raises his eyebrows. "What?"

"We're never having this conversation again. You'll accept Dmitri and welcome him into our family." I don't stay for an answer. I know my brother. He can stew over it, but his final decision will be to do what I ask.

I go into the kitchen.

"Everything okay?" Vivian nervously asks.

"Yeah. I'm going to be staying for a few days."

"Good. I've missed seeing you."

"I want to go shopping later. Do you have to work today, or do you want to go with me?"

"I'm free. I'd love to go."

"Okay. I'm going to do some work for a while. Want to grab lunch first? I'm craving a cheeseburger. I haven't had one in years."

Vivian smiles. "Yes."

"Great." I tap Viktor on the shoulder. "Let's go, big guy. I'll put some coffee on in my part of the Monroe mansion."

18

Dmitri

BORIS HANDS ME THE PICTURES OF ANNA I GOT FROM THE POLICE and hospital files. Chase may have contacts in New York, but so do I. Once I knew where Mitch lived, I made a call to get everything from both incidents. It's the first time seeing the photos, and my stomach pitches so hard, I swallow down bile. My beautiful Anna is unrecognizable. Bruises and blood cover her face and body. I wonder how she survived. Her ribs on the X-rays are cracked into pieces.

How did she hide it from her family?

She must have been in excruciating pain.

Boris scowls. "Her brother didn't kill him?"

I give him the pictures of Mitch and Chase that the police took the night he brought Anna to Chicago.

Boris glances at everything and whistles. "Bet the police had a hard time breaking those two up."

"What do you need me to arrange, Dmitri?" Tolik Ivanov, one of our cousins who lives in New York City, strokes his black beard that hangs to the bottom of his neck. We're in his apartment overlooking Manhattan. He's who I called yesterday. Within hours, he messaged me. He got everything I wanted without any issues.

I brought Boris so I don't kill Mitch. I know if I cross that line, Anna won't be able to forgive me. So as much as I want to rip him to shreds and watch the last drop of blood leave his body, I won't do it.

Boris has more patience than I do. He is a fighter in the ring and a master at torture outside of it. He can control his rage or let it spiral when appropriate. I have a more challenging time. It's a flaw I have, and I know it. So I brought Boris because Anna means too much to me to screw this up.

"I need movers who can keep their mouth shut. Everything goes. Her samples get packaged and shipped overnight to my place. I'll take her laptop. Anything else in the apartment gets removed and donated to a family in need. I don't want one piece of silverware or tube of toothpaste left in his place, except for the blue skillet."

"The blue skillet?"

"Yes."

"When do you need this completed?"

"Tomorrow. Ten o'clock, I want everything gone but the blue skillet."

"Consider it done."

"Thanks." I put everything back into the folders. We slap hands and leave.

Boris and I get into the car waiting for us outside Tolik's building. I glance at my watch. It's close to noon in Chicago. I call Anna.

"Hi," she answers.

"Hey. What are you doing?"

"Vivian and I went to this new burger place. I'm about to bite into a greasy cheeseburger."

I smile, happy she's eating. "You're going to make my stomach growl."

"I'll let you know if it's any good."

"Okay. I spoke with Maksim earlier. He wants to know if you can meet tomorrow. There's a friend of ours. He's a developer and has been looking for a new designer since Lada was his as well. Maksim recommended you, and our friend wants to meet you."

"Really?"

"Yeah, why do you sound surprised?"

"Ummm... I'm not Russian."

I chuckle. "I think we're past that now."

"Okay. So how do I know what he looks like?"

"Maksim will pick you up and take you to the meeting. Probably lunch. I'll send you Maksim's number so you can arrange it."

"Wow. I'm feeling a little special here," she teases.

"You are special," I say firmly.

She quiets. "So are you."

My other line beeps. "Sergey is calling. I should take this."

"Okay. My cheeseburger is getting cold anyway."

"Enjoy. I'll send you Maksim's number."

"Thanks. Bye."

"Bye." I switch over. "Sergey, what's the situation?"

"Lorenzo just sent us a new offer. Another ten percent drop from his last one on all seven of the lots."

"Motherfucker."

"Yeah. Do you think it's time to do something about this?"

"No. Stay back. We don't need a war with his family if we can avoid it."

"It feels like he's pushing for one."

"Yeah, well, let's not jump the gun. Prepare but don't pull the trigger."

Sergey sighs loudly. "This isn't going to end well. I think waiting is a mistake."

"Do not make any moves," I reinforce. "Do I need Maksim to come slap you in the head a few times?"

"Shut up."

"Then stop being arrogant."

"Fine. When are you back?"

"Hopefully, tomorrow night."

"All right."

I hang up and shake my head at Boris. "Another ten percent drop."

Boris clenches his fists then cracks his knuckles. "He's looking for trouble."

I nod. "But we don't need it."

"His father has severe legal issues going on right now. Even with his connections, it's going to be hard for him to get out of going to prison." The governor and his mistress recently had a televised conversation recorded and streamed via YouTube about how the governor received illegal funds from Lorenzo Rossi's father. He skimmed money from the union workers' pension fund. "Lorenzo's going to take over. This isn't good. Dealing with this sooner rather than later is best."

"Maksim and I both agree we need to wait. You and Sergey need to cool it."

Boris looks out the window. "He's messing with the wrong family."

"Agreed. But we wait."

The car pulls up to a high-rise and parks. We don't wait for the driver to open the door, getting out ourselves. When we get to security, we give them our licenses and get badges to go through.

Another thing Tolik did was get us an appointment. We're at the finance company Mitch works for. Our meeting is with the CEO, president, and the rest of their investment team. It usually would take weeks to get them all together, but when we sent copies of a few of our current investment statements, along with our real estate holding portfolio, and told them we're meeting today or interviewing another firm, they made it happen.

But we aren't here to invest. They have another reality coming.

A red-haired woman greets us when we walk in and shakes our hands. "I'm Robin. Can I get you something to drink?"

"No, thank you." If I have anything, I might cough it up. Boris, on the other hand, orders a latte and checks her out, causing her to blush.

She leaves to get his drink.

"Seriously? We aren't here to get you a date."

He shrugs. "She's a sexy woman."

"Can we stay focused?"

"Don't worry. I'm on."

Within a few minutes, she comes back, hands Boris his drink, and shows us to a conference room. He reaches for the door before she opens it, and she nervously says, "Thanks."

He checks her out again until she's so red, I want to offer her some water. "No problem."

I want to knock him on the head for flirting, but there is no time. He opens the door. The wall across from us is all glass, and the brilliance of the city creates a spectacular backdrop. An over-sized, expensive mahogany conference table with two dozen chairs around it is situated in the center of the room. A wall with a big screen TV and counter with coffee and mugs completes the setting. The room is already full of suits.

We take our seats after introductions and handshakes. The CEO, Robert Dwinton, sits in his chair with a greedy smile on his face. "We're happy you've decided to discuss—"

I hold up my hand. "We are on limited time. If you don't mind, I would like to show you something?"

"Of course."

I slide a folder across the table. It has a press release, along with the pictures and records Tolik gave us.

He opens the folder, and his face drains. He looks at me. "What is this?"

"Your employee almost killed this woman. Not once but twice. Is this the type of person you employ at this firm?"

He shakes his head. "No, sir."

"I also believe that you have accounts at your firm worth several billion dollars of friends of ours. Here are their names." I slide another folder of the people who know our family and have their money here.

The room is so silent, you could hear a pin drop. Boris cracks his knuckles, and the weasel next to Robert squirms.

"Here's what is going to happen. You will fire this employee in the next hour. There is no severance and no recommendation. But before you do, he will restore the money he stole, which is invested in this firm, back to this woman."

"What money?"

I point to the only woman in the room, sitting several seats away. She is taking notes on her laptop. "Please pull up his personal accounts. I believe if you audit them, you will find it came from a joint checking account. This money was from this woman's paycheck. I'm assuming you will not find her name on the account, either."

"This is a big accusation," Robert says.

I nod. "Yes. And I'm sure the media outlet will love this part of the story. A beautiful, hardworking designer not only gets beaten but stolen from by an advisor in your firm. Imagine the PR nightmare you will have."

"There are laws we have to follow."

"Yes. And laws that can also hold you accountable for this wrong-doing. Don't you have a fiduciary duty to monitor the assets in your firm?" I raise my eyebrows at him.

He swallows hard. "We will look into this."

"Today. The assets all get transferred in her name today. The entire account."

"Some of it could be his money. He could sue us as well."

"Consider it interest. And I don't care if he sues you. You failed to do your due diligence and manage your employee."

I rise, and Boris follows. I slap a business card on the table. "You have until five o'clock to contact this firm to transfer her assets. In the next sixty minutes, he gets terminated as stipulated, or these families pull their money. We also send this press release to all the news outlets. Any questions?"

Wide eyes stare back at us. "Great. It was nice meeting you. Have a nice day."

Boris holds up his cup. "Thanks for the latte."

We leave the conference room. Boris grabs Robin's card off her desk and winks at her on the way out. As soon as the elevator door shuts, I slap his head.

"What the fuck is that for?" he growls.

"You aren't here to get some ass."

"You're the one in the relationship, not me. And until tomorrow, I'm free. So sit in the hotel if you want, but I'm hitting the town. And that redhead looked like the perfect woman to do it with."

I jab him in the chest. "You better be ready at seven tomorrow. Workout, breakfast, then we finish this and get back to Chicago. I don't need you with a hangover or off your game."

"Have you ever known me to not deliver?"

"No. But this is too important to screw up."

"Don't worry. I know my role."

I shouldn't worry. Boris has never let me down. But today was only the beginning of Mitch discovering my wrath. He's going to wallow in self-pity all night, but tomorrow he's going to learn how I really handle my business.

And there won't be any deadlines to meet.

19

Anna

MAKSIM COMES UP TO MY BROTHER'S PENTHOUSE. WHEN I COME into the main room, he's talking to Vivian.

"Anna, you changed your hair. It looks nice."

I didn't expect a compliment from him and freeze for a moment. "Ummm...thanks. What are you doing up here?"

"Picking Vivian's real estate brain."

She smiles. "I think it's a great idea. The foundation would be grateful for your help in developing it."

Maksim smiles, which I haven't seen him do very often, and his eyes twinkle. "Great. Should we get Chicago's newest, up-and-coming designer to donate her time to the project?"

Vivian laughs. "I think I can twist her arm."

I wave my hand between them. "Hello? I'm in the room."

"I'll tell you in the car. We should go, or we'll be late," Maksim replies.

"Alrighty, then. I'll see you later."

Vivian waves. "Bye."

Viktor rises and says to Vivian, "Thanks for the coffee."

"Anytime."

The three of us leave, and when we get in the car, I turn to Maksim. "So, what were you discussing?"

"Vivian has a piece of land that was donated to the foundation to develop. Her friend, I think she said her name is Charlotte, approached her about it. They want to build a new orphanage. The current one is falling apart. She contacted me a few weeks ago to build it. She has some grant money for materials, but we will supply the labor for free and oversee it."

"Wow. That's generous."

He shrugs. "So what do you think? Do you want to donate the design work?"

"Sure."

He tilts his head. "Just sure? You don't want to know any more details?"

"Do I need to?"

"You know you don't get paid, correct?"

I draw in a dramatic breath of air. "Is that what donate means?"

He chuckles. "Fair enough."

"Did you just laugh?"

"Yeah. Why?"

I raise my eyebrows.

His phone rings. "Excuse me." He answers it and starts speaking in Russian.

As soon as Dmitri returns, he needs to start teaching me Russian.

I turn to the window, trying not to read into anything, but Maksim sounds angry on the call. When he hangs up, his face is red.

"Everything okay?" I ask.

"Yes, nothing you need to worry about. Should we talk about Sacha before we get to lunch?"

"Please."

"He's very cheap until you prove yourself. You must not give him any ideas until you are under contract with him. Once you do one job for him and earn his trust, he will be loyal and not attempt to undercut you. Until then, if I tell you to stop talking, please listen."

"You're staying for the meeting?"

"Yes, of course."

"I'm sure I can handle it."

"No offense, but I know him well. I will not let him pull any of his tricks on you."

"Okay. Thank you."

"Of course. You must be careful in this city. Now, did you bring your contract as I told you to?"

"Yes, it's in my bag."

"Good. Once the contract is on the table, he will try to lower your fee. Do not fall for his game. Stick to your price. He will threaten to walk away. Let him. If he does, he will call later today and attempt to lowball you again. You do not allow him to change anything on your contract. He will then call you tomorrow and tell you he will sign."

"Wow. How do you know all this?"

"I have known Sacha since we were in school. He is set in his ways and very predictable."

I tap my hand on my thigh, slightly nervous.

Maksim grabs it. "You cannot fidget. It shows weakness. Be confident at all times."

I blow out a big breath. *Confident. Okay. I can do this.*

"If I clear my throat, you excuse yourself and go to the restroom."

"Why?"

"Do not worry about why. Just do it."

"How long do I stay in the bathroom?"

Maksim furrows his eyebrows. "Normal time."

I tilt my head.

"What?" he asks.

"What does 'normal time' mean?" I put my fingers in quotes.

"You know. However long it takes you women do what you do in the ladies' room."

"Do I put on fresh lipstick?"

"Whatever you want. Just go to the restroom."

Okay. This is a different kind of business meeting than I planned, but I'll go with it.

"Oh, I got a lot done on the roof design yesterday. I think I can have something for you by next week. If I didn't have to research so much, it wouldn't take as long."

He nods. "Great. I spoke with several real estate agents. They are all confirming what Vivian thinks."

"Awesome."

"Whatever you do, do not tell Sacha anything about a roof design or anything else to increase his profit until you are under contract."

My stomach flips. "Is this guy that bad?"

Maksim taps his fingertips together. "Not once you get to know him. But at first, yes. Plus, you are not Russian."

"I can't do anything about that." I smirk. "You should get over it."

Amusement crosses his face. "I am over it. And we will use it to our advantage today."

"How?"

"You'll see."

The car parks in front of the restaurant. It's the same Russian restaurant Dmitri took me to.

Maksim smiles. "Are you ready?"

"Yes. Dmitri brought me here. But I don't remember the names of anything he ordered. He didn't tell me the English names."

"Was there anything you didn't like?"

"No. Everything was great."

He nods. "Do not worry. I will order for you."

The driver opens the car door. Maksim steps out and reaches in to help me out, the same way Dmitri does, but once I'm on the sidewalk, he releases my hand. He places his hand on my upper back and guides me inside.

He kisses the hostess's cheek. Her name is Mila, and Maksim introduces us. We exchange greetings, and she leads us to a table.

Sacha is already there. He's only a little taller than me. He's bald, but it's not the sexy shaved look Dmitri has going on. He's got wire-rimmed glasses that slide down his nose, and he pushes them back up often with his stubby fingers. His face and body are pudgy.

Sacha reminds me of an accountant I knew in New York. But that's where the similarities end.

From the beginning, he tries to intimidate me. "She's not Russian," he says to Maksim, as if I'm not sitting in front of him.

"No. She's not. Which is how you know she's better than Lada, or I wouldn't have caved and hired her."

He peers at me through the tiny slits of his eyes, and I sit up straighter. He turns to Maksim and speaks Russian.

In a stern voice, Maksim says, "No Russian. Anna only speaks English. That is how we will converse during our lunch today."

The waitress comes over, and Maksim speaks quickly to her in Russian.

Or maybe we'll speak some Russian.

When he finishes, he turns to me. "I apologize. Galina only knows Russian."

I smile. "No worries."

Sacha sits back and crosses his arms. "Okay, Anna. I have a new, ten-story building going up in three months. Tell me how you're going to help me."

"I'm reliable, can meet deadlines, and stay within your budget."

"Anna did the impossible and saved us from losing big money. She met a deadline no other designer would have, saved us a gross of eleven percent overall, and also gave us an idea that will probably add another ten- to thirty-percent profit to our bottom line."

Sacha leans in. "And what is your idea?"

Maksim shakes his finger and tsks him. "Anna will not be giving you any ideas until she is under contract with you."

Sacha's face reddens. "I need to understand what she can bring to the table if I am going to take a chance on her."

Maksim confidently laughs. "I am vouching for her. Her rates are the same as Lada's, so she is within your budget."

Sacha shakes his head. "Lada is well known. Her reputation is pristine. She has earned the rate she charges."

My stomach twists. I'm still not used to the fees Dmitri insisted I charge.

Maksim turns to me. "Please take out your contract."

I pull it out, and he hands it to Sacha. "Lada left everyone in a lurch. Her style was stale. Anna's is fresh and edgy. The last project you had didn't do as well. It was a design issue. You know it, and so do I. We have all been pretending for the last few years that Lada is the best out there, but she isn't. Anna is. And this isn't her first project. She has a business and reputation in New York."

"Not in our community. I checked, and now I know why no one heard of her."

That's because I never did full buildings in New York.

This is so over my head.

But I did design an entire building here. That has to count for something.

"Ahh. Yes. But she is in our community here. She is our designer, and you can either be up and coming or stay behind. It's your choice, but Anna is not lowering her rates."

The waitress comes to our table with several dishes for everyone to share. I recognize a few of the items from when Dmitri and I ate dinner here.

Maksim motions to the food. "Anna, please go first."

I put a few items from each dish on my plate. Maksim and Sacha follow. When everyone's plates are full, we all take a few bites.

"Anna's rates are also going up soon. As her contract states, she's willing to lock you in at this rate for the next two years." Maksim takes a sip of his water.

I almost choke on my food. I'm not even used to the rates I'm charging now, and they are going up?

"She just got here, and she's already raising her rates?" Sacha says.

Maksim sighs in frustration. "She is not a new designer. She is highly educated, worked a decade under the top designer in New York City before opening her own business. She has talent."

How does Maksim know all this?

"Who did you work for?" Sacha asks.

"Claudette Mercier."

Sacha attempts to cover his gape. "The French designer?"

"Yes. I can give you a letter of recommendation if you like. She is very supportive of my career and business. She also has her cell number on it if you would like to speak with her."

Sacha swallows hard and glances at Maksim.

Maksim taps the contract. "I'll advise you to sign Anna, at this rate, while you can. We have other meetings this week scheduled. As you know, Lada left a big void for all of us."

"Plus, we have the foundation project," I interject.

Maksim's eyes light up. "Ah, yes. I forgot about that. Thank you for reminding me."

Sacha puts his fork down. "What foundation project?"

"The Vivian Caras Foundation is building an orphanage. Anna has volunteered to create the design."

Sacha nods. "That is a good foundation. Vivian does remarkable things for the community."

"Yes. Vivian is the one who recommended we hire Anna to get us out of our jam."

Sacha takes another bite of food and stares at me.

I try not to be anything but confident under his gaze, but it's difficult. I wish his mother would have taught him it's rude to stare.

I finish chewing, swallow, then wash it down with water. I dab my napkin on my lips and put it back on my lap. "Could you tell me a little about your project? Maksim hasn't told me much, and neither have you. Before I promise you what I can do, I need to know about it."

Sacha hesitantly tells me about the condo project. I ask many questions, and by the time we finish lunch, his eyes are full of excitement. I can tell how much his project means to him, which is something I love about my job.

Maksim glances at his watch. "We need to get going. We have another meeting today." They are the first words he's said in the last thirty minutes.

I try not to look surprised.

"With who?" Sacha says.

Maksim smiles and wags his finger. "Now, you know I can't tell you that."

Silence fills the table. It becomes uncomfortable.

Maksim finally rises. "We really must go, Anna." He holds out his hand to help me out of the booth.

I smile at Sacha. "It was nice meeting you. I enjoyed hearing about your project."

Maksim holds my jacket, and I slip into it.

Sacha says, "You're twenty percent too high. Drop your fee, and I'll sign right now."

Maksim presses his hand on my back.

My stomach flips. I would be happy taking a twenty percent cut. It's still more than I got in New York.

Maksim will kill you.

I smile. "Thank you so much for your time, but I can't do that. If you change your mind and I've not committed to another project, I'd love to work with you. My cell number is on the last page."

Maksim shakes his head at Sacha. "You're going to regret letting this one get away."

Maksim spins me, and Sacha says, "Ten percent. That's the best I can do."

Maksim tightens his grip on my arm.

I can't believe I'm turning this down. I take a deep breath. "I'm sorry. I can't reduce my fee. I wish you lots of luck."

"We must go, Anna. We will be late." Maksim steers me toward the door.

Am I seriously walking away from this?

As soon as we step outside, Sacha's voice calls out, "Fine. Full price."

I freeze.

Maksim spins me.

"Here." Sacha holds out my contract with his name on it and a pen for me to sign.

Maksim turns. "Use my back to sign. Then we need to go."

Adrenaline pumps through my veins. I scribble my name. "I'll make copies and send you one. Is email okay?"

Sacha hands me his card. "Yes. Please send it today. And I will send you times for us to get together and go through more details and any ideas you may have?"

"Perfect."

"Anna, time to go," Maksim says.

I shake Sacha's hand, and Maksim whisks me into the car.

When the door shuts, I gape at him.

"You did good, Anna. A little bit of training, and you'll do just fine on your own someday soon."

"How did you know all that stuff about me?"

Arrogance fills Maksim's face. It reminds me of Dmitri's expression at times. "It's my job to know about everybody."

20

Dmitri

"Everything is out?" I ask as the moving van pulls away from the building.

"All but the blue skillet and the kitchen chair," Tolik confirms. "Where should I put the laptop?"

"Go wait in the car. Nothing can happen to it."

He strokes his beard then itches his cheek. "Right." He pats me on the back, and I watch him get into the black sedan at the curb.

I walk into the building and put on my black gloves before I push the elevator button. There's no reason for them. When I finish this job, Mitch would be a bigger fool than I think he is if he attempted any legal action. But years of covering my tracks on anything remotely sketchy is ingrained in who I am.

I don't want to be here. It brings me no pleasure to do what I'm about to do. I'm only here because he hurt her. I wish he hadn't. But he did. So now it's time for him to pay the consequences.

Only a few hours to go, and I can be on my way back to Chicago. Anna and I can put this behind us and move forward with our lives.

Yesterday, forty minutes after we left, I received a phone call from the CEO. He terminated Mitch as stipulated. At four thirty, I received another call from our investment firm in Chicago. I had set an account up for Anna before I left. It's up to her what she does with it or if she wants to keep it there. But it was necessary to move the money from Mitch's firm to her control.

"Dmitri, we've received the paperwork. There's a transfer in place and should be complete in the next three business days," Vera confirmed.

"Thank you. I'll be in touch."

Boris and I had dinner then he went out. I spent the evening video chatting with Anna, missing her touch, and avoiding any topic about New York or why I was here. She avoided anything about her brother. But neither of us pushed the other one, and I was happy to hear she was at his place.

Family is everything to me. I understand Chase's concern. I'm grateful he showed up in New York when he did to take her out of the situation she was in. And Vivian and I have known each other for years, working on community issues together. We've not been close, but she's someone I would drop anything to help. She's a good person, and I wouldn't want anything to come between her and Anna, especially me.

Maksim and Anna should be in their lunch meeting right now. I have faith Maksim will help Anna close the deal, but I'm also on pins and needles. I want her to get it so she can keep building her business and confidence. I know she'll bring life to Sacha's project, and it'll help build her reputation in the Chicago market.

The elevator opens, and I take a deep breath, calming my nerves. I've never had to do something like this before for my woman. There have been other reasons. They all revolved around people I cared about but not like Anna, nor someone I was even merely dating.

You can't kill him.

My biggest fear is I won't be able to control myself, and once I get started and look into his eyes, I'll forget my boundary I promised Anna I wouldn't cross. I'm sure if she knew the extent of what I was going to do today, she wouldn't approve of it, either, but it's more forgivable than death.

I open the door to the apartment, step in and lock it, just in case. Boris is standing at the window and turns. "About time you got here."

"Where is he?"

"In the kitchen. Thought it was appropriate since that's where he first assaulted her."

The blood boils hotter in my veins, and the escalation of rage only grows.

Boris points to me. He's wearing identical black gloves to mine. "There is a line not to be crossed. Unless you've changed your mind?" He cocks his head and raises his eyebrows in hope.

I step toward him. "Do not ask me that again. No matter what, it is not to be broken."

He sighs, unhappy I won't let him go further, but nods. One thing my brothers and I despise more than anything else in this world is a man who hurts a woman or child. It's the sign of a coward, and none of us have respect or tolerance for those types of men. And there is a part of Boris that enjoys what we are about to do. While I don't deny it gives me gratification to serve some sort of justice upon those who have done the unspeakable, I'm not like Boris. And that's why I brought him instead of my other brothers. He has a craving for it, and it needs to be fed. It's why he still boxes. But this side of him, no amount of time in the ring can quench. So any situation we have, Boris is always a part of it.

"Let's get this over with. I'm ready to be home with Anna."

Boris's face changes. I've seen it too many times to count. It's almost a serenity that fills his expression. There's a calmness about him. Most men act like lunatics in these situations. Boris is cool as a cucumber. It's the total opposite of his demeanor in the ring.

I walk through the empty apartment and go into the kitchen. Mitch has a gag in his mouth. He's tied to the only remaining thing besides the skillet. Even his underwear and toiletries got packed and removed from the premises.

His eyes widen when I step into the room. He attempts to try and get out of the chair, and it rocks from side to side.

Boris steps forward and leans down to his ear. "Shhh," he coos then drags his finger down Mitch's cheek.

Mitch shuts his eyes and starts to cry.

I haven't even touched him yet, and he's bawling like a baby. Fucking coward.

I don't know why I'm surprised. It always happens. Cowards are all alike. But for some reason, I can't ever get used to it.

I step forward and bark, "Open your eyes."

He obeys while sobbing.

"Do you remember me? Hmm?"

His lip trembles, and he shakes his head.

Figures. Arrogant asshole thought he was better than everyone else.

"That's okay. I know who you are. And I know what you did to her."

He tries to scream, but it's muffled from the gag. I flip my knife open and shut a few times. Boris meets my eyes.

Better let him do it. He enjoys it more, and I have the skillet.

I nod, permitting him to take over for a moment.

Boris rips out his knife and puts the flat part of the blade on Mitch's cheek.

"You like to beat women?" I ask.

He tries to deny it, sobbing some more.

"She's told you not to call her anymore. But you still call. Why? Hmmm?" I step closer and crouch in front of him. His entire body shakes, and Boris turns the knife so the thin part of the blade is against his cheek. "When a woman tells you to stop calling her, you stop."

He tries to nod, and the blade nicks him. Blood wells on his cheek.

"You continue to threaten her. You claim you're coming to find her. You steal her money and personal possessions. Well, how does it feel to have everything you value taken away from you? Hmmm?"

More tears fall.

"I'm going to remove this gag for a moment. If you scream, my brother will cut your tongue out. He'll enjoy every second of it."

Mitch glances up at Boris, who looks down at him, smiling, itching to do what I just suggested. Then he pisses his pants.

That was quick. Normally happens a little further in.

"You just pissed yourself," Boris tells him calmly, as if he could go change his pants.

"Are you ready? Remember, the minute you scream, your tongue goes." He whimpers, and I slowly pull the gag off his mouth.

"Tell me what you want from me," he demands, but his voice cracks.

Boris pets his head, and Mitch squeezes his eyes shut. The blade of his knife digs deeper into the skin on his cheek. Blood drips off his chin.

"You will never contact her again. You will never threaten her again. You won't even say her name again. If you do, I'm coming after you. Next time, I won't be so nice." I point at Boris. "I won't allow him to be nice, either."

Hatred flares in Mitch's eyes. He wants to tell me to fuck off. I can see it. And I push him to the point where he does.

"She's mine. She'll never be yours again."

"Fuck you," he mumbles.

Unlike Boris, I don't stay calm. I take my hand and slap his cheek that doesn't have the blade against it, crushing his face into the sharp metal's edge.

He screams in pain. But it's okay. We already know his neighbors aren't home. But I put the rag back in his mouth. He chokes, but I secure it with a new piece of tape.

"No one can hear you. And just like she screamed for you to stop, but you didn't, I'm not going to, either."

He looks at me with a mix of fear and confusion.

I rise and pick up the skillet then turn, tracing the edge with my finger. "Remember this?"

Mitch's eyes tell me everything, and my stomach flips. It's a cast-iron skillet. It's heavy. It probably took two hands for her to pick it up when something was in it, maybe even when it was empty. And he battered her with it, as if she was a fly he needed to swat and kill. But he also bruised her where no one would see it.

I nod to Boris.

He smiles and licks his lips. He takes the rope on the counter, laces it under Mitch's armpits, then ties a knot in the back. He threads the end through the twelve-inch eyelet hook he installed earlier.

I release Mitch's legs, and he attempts to kick me, so I slap him again. He cries, but I know it's nothing compared to how he's about to sob.

Boris releases the rope around the chair but leaves his hands tied behind his back. Mitch stands, which only helps put him in the position we want him in faster. Boris pulls on the rope until Mitch is dangling on his tiptoes and shaking from fear.

I step closer. "When you broke her ribs, you didn't fracture them. You split them apart. It's only fair I do the same to you, don't you think?"

He tries to scream again, and Boris steps behind him and leans into his ear, petting his head. "Shhh."

It makes Mitch freak out more. His body flails everywhere, but Boris has the rope tight in his hand.

I glance at Boris, and he steps back, tightening the rope even more so Mitch can't move as much.

I step several feet back and hold the skillet like a baseball bat. Then I swing it as hard as I can into his rib cage.

A cracking sound fills the air.

That's what it sounded like when he mercilessly battered Anna.

How loud did she cry or beg for him to stop before she passed out?

Mitch wails behind the gag.

Boris smiles and nods for me to go again.

I repeat my actions and then Boris releases the rope. Mitch falls to the floor, face-first, and I beat on his back, just like he did to my Anna.

I'm not sure how many times I hit him, but Boris stops me. He takes the skillet out of my hand and sets it on the counter. "Time to go."

Mitch sobs quietly. I'm sure his body is in shock. He's slumped to the floor. But I turn him over and lean into his ear. "If you ever attempt to come near her again, I will finish you off. Then I will come after everyone in your family. That includes your parents, your sisters, and your brother. If you discuss what happened today with anyone, or attempt any legal ramifications, my other brothers will complete what I just threatened."

I rise, and Boris and I leave the apartment. We get in the car waiting at the curb.

"How did it go?" Tolik asks.

I remove my gloves and put them in my bag. "Watch him over the next thirty days. I want a report on every move he makes and then we'll reassess."

My gut says he isn't going to attempt to contact Anna ever again or try anything legally, but you can never be too careful.

"Will do," Tolik replies.

I grab the computer off Tolik's lap and put it in my bag. We get to the airport and on the private plane. Boris cleans his knife in the seat next to me. "We should have killed him."

"She wouldn't have forgiven me. I know her. She didn't have to say it."

Boris shuts his knife. His gray eyes darken. "We need to take care of Lorenzo. This isn't going to go away."

"We have time. The last thing we need is a war with the Rossi family."

"We quietly do it. You know this."

"We wait. Now, I'm done talking about this."

He sighs and pulls out his phone.

I pull out mine. There's a text from Maksim that Sacha signed a contract with Anna. I text her. "I'm on my way home. Can I take you out tonight to celebrate your contract?"

"What if I want to stay in and celebrate?"

"Even better."

2 1

Anna

DMITRI MOVES MY HAIR AND KISSES THE BACK OF MY SHOULDER.

"Mmm."

"Morning." He pretzels his limbs around me.

I snuggle my backside into him farther. "Morning. You're so nice and warm."

His fingers graze over my outer thighs, moving to the insides and near my sex. His lips brush my ear. "If you're cold, I can fix that."

I turn into him and pull his lips to mine. "Mmm. Can we stay in bed all day?"

He chuckles. "We have an important appointment this morning."

I kiss him some more. "Where."

"At my investment firm."

I open my eyes. "Why?"

"You have accounts you need to make decisions on."

"What are you talking about? I don't have any accounts."

Something shifts in his eyes. "We need to discuss some things, kotik."

My stomach twists. "Do I need to be worried?"

"No. It's good stuff."

I release a breath. Since Dmitri got home over a week ago, we've spent all our free time wrapped up in each other between working on our projects. Even most of our work we've done side by side. But we've been at Chase and Vivian's. I thought it was strange, but Dmitri said we needed to spend time with them.

He and Chase seemed to have come to an understanding. They talked in Chase's office when he got back. Vivian and I cooked dinner and then the four of us ate. It was actually fun. We've spent some time with Chase and Vivian since, but most of our time, we're on my side of the penthouse, unable to keep our hands off each other.

I don't care where we are, as long as I'm with Dmitri, but I miss his place. I asked when we are going to go back, and he said today.

I sit up. We've avoided talking about his trip to New York. He gave me my laptop when he got home but, other than that, we didn't discuss it. It's like we're both avoiding it. "Okay, talk."

He sits against the headboard and pulls me into his arms. "The money Mitch stole from you is in an account at my firm. I had them transfer it so he had no more access. You need to decide what you want to do with the investments inside the account. You can keep it with my advisor or move it to someone else."

"How...why...how did you get Mitch to agree to that?"

He tucks a lock of my hair behind my ear. "I spoke with the CEO of the firm and told him what happened. I demanded they fire him and transfer the account to you."

My mouth goes dry. *Mitch got fired.*

I should feel bad for him. He worked long hours and spent years building his career and clientele with that firm.

He stole my money. I shouldn't feel an ounce of pity for him.

"Are you going to say anything?" Dmitri asks.

"Sorry...umm...how much did he steal from me? I know I sound foolish, but I honestly don't know."

"The account has over five hundred thousand dollars in it."

My mouth hangs open. I try to figure out in my head how that is possible. "I don't think that is possible."

"He invested it. He actually did a good job. My advisor says the investments are solid."

"Five hundred... I'm sorry, but you said half a million dollars."

Dmitri's lips twitch. "Yes."

"What do I do with it?"

"Whatever you want. It's your money."

I tilt my head. "You aren't going to tell me what to do with it?"

He shakes his head. "No. It's yours."

"But..."

He cups my cheeks. "This is your money, kotik. You don't have to make any major decisions today, but you need to sign paperwork for the accounts. Talk to my advisor. Talk to your brother. He's done well. Interview whomever you want."

I release a big breath.

Dmitri furrows his eyebrows. "Why do you seem stressed? You should be happy about this."

"I am. I'm very grateful to you. Thank you. But I've never managed money. I didn't even start investing until I met Mitch. Well, he told me he was investing it. Chase tried to get me to put money away for years, but I wasn't making a lot. It didn't seem important at the time."

Dmitri smiles. "You're smart. You'll figure out what to do with it. We should get moving, though, or we'll be late."

I sink my knees next to his hips. "I thought you were going to warm me up?"

He slides his hands over my ass. "Let's stay at my place tonight."

"Yes. I'm ready to go back."

His eyes brighten. "You are?"

"Yes."

"Good. That makes me happy."

I lean into his lips. "You like me at your place?"

"So much, kotik." He kisses me, consuming all my breath, lighting up every ounce of blood pumping through my veins.

He groans and squeezes my ass. "We have to get ready."

I sigh. "We should have a no-morning-meeting rule."

He snorts. "Eventually, I need to get back on my workout schedule."

"Then we'll have to wake up earlier."

He chuckles. "Deal. Okay, time to shower."

We get ready then leave. Dmitri's investment firm is located a few blocks from Chase and Vivian's, so we walk. It's a crisp fall day, and the wind blows hard. Dmitri wraps his arm around me and shields me from most of it.

When we get to the office, there are quite a few forms I need to sign. The woman named Nina, who is Dmitri's investment advisor, says, "Signatures are needed in all the places where there are stickies."

I pick up the pen but hesitate. I wince. "Sorry. My parents had this thing about us signing forms without reading them."

And I did it with Mitch.

"Take your time, Anna. Read every word if you want," Dmitri says.

"Yes. There is no rush," Nina adds. "Ask me any questions you want."

I read it all and ask questions along the way. It's exhausting, but she answers all my questions, and I sign everything.

"Do you want to go through the investments now?" she asks.

I glance at Dmitri.

"What is it, Anna?"

I turn to Nina. "Is there a way to get an overview of the account? Like a cliff notes version? It's not that I don't care, and I think I should learn about this, but I didn't even know about this until I woke up today. It's overwhelming for me."

She smiles. "Sure. The accounts are positioned well. I wouldn't recommend you change anything right now unless you want to change your risk."

"Am I in risky things?"

"I'd say you're middle of the road."

I can handle the middle. Not too high and not too low.

"Okay. So I'm good with my risk right now. But I can change it later, correct?"

"Sure. Any time."

"All right. Is there a book or something I can read to learn about this?"

"I think I have something better for you." She opens a folder and pulls out a flyer. "This is our women's investment class. If you want, you can join. It's starting in a few weeks."

I read over the flyer. "If I decide to come to this, can I bring my friend with me?"

"Sure. It's open to the public."

"Okay. I think I'll drag my friend, Harper, with me. Maybe I'll see if Vivian and her friends want to come, too."

Nina smiles. "Tell your friends we have drinks and food."

"Alcoholic ones?"

"Yep."

"That makes it easier to sell."

She laughs and hands me the folder. "This is all your account information, and my card is in there. Call me with any questions."

I hold the fancy folder embossed with their firm name in metallic foil. I point to it. "Is this to make me feel like a legit investor?"

She raises her eyebrows. "Does it?"

"Kind of."

"I'll tell the marketing team."

"Thank you. I'll let you know about the class."

Dmitri and I leave, and we stop in a cafe for a late breakfast.

"I like Nina. She's nice."

"She's excellent at what she does."

"I'm surprised you have a female advisor."

"It's proven women manage money better than men."

I tilt my head. "Is that true?"

"Statistics show it."

"Hmmm." I pull out the statement and put it in front of him. "Do you know how to read this?"

"Yes."

"Will you explain it to me?"

"Of course." We spend the next few hours eating and reviewing my investments. Dmitri patiently answers all my questions and keeps telling me to take my time. When we leave the restaurant, I feel empowered, as if I'm capable of handling my account.

We decide to walk to his place. "Why aren't you telling me what to do with my money?"

He puts my hand to his lips. "It's not my money. And you are capable of making decisions about it."

It's strange to have someone like Dmitri, who understands money and is super successful, not tell me what to do. It's totally different from Mitch and my relationship. Part of me wants him to tell me what to do with it. Another part respects him more because he believes I'm smart enough to make decisions.

I stop and he turns to me. "Kotik. Why are we stopping?"

I pull his lips to mine. "Thank you. For everything."

We kiss until someone bumps into us then continue the journey to his penthouse.

When we get inside, he says, "I have something I want to show you."

"What is it?"

His eyes twinkle. "You'll see."

He leads me down the hallway. I've spent a lot of hours in his penthouse, but I've never seen all of it. This hallway I've never even been in.

When we get to a door, he says, "Open it."

I'm not sure what is on the other side, but I turn the knob and freeze.

The entire space has been converted to a design area. Shelves line the walls with samples of materials. My new and old samples are mixed together. A large table sits in the middle of the room with bright lighting above it and four large monitors. An oversized rug fills the space in front of the fireplace with plenty of room for me to stretch out on the floor if needed, along with couches and chairs. Anything I could ever need to work, complete with a stunning view of Lake Michigan, and a full bathroom is in this room.

I look at Dmitri.

He has a nervous expression on his face. "What do you think, kotik?"

"This is for me?"

"Yes. Unless you don't want it."

Tears fill my eyes. "How could I not want it? This is..." I glance around the room again. "How did...it doesn't even look like the rest of the penthouse."

"It's why we stayed at Chase and Vivian's so long. I called your old boss. She created this and made some phone calls to rush the shelving and furniture. My brothers made sure it was all implemented and tore out the walk-in closet to make it bigger. If there is anything you don't like, you can change it." He steps closer and puts his hands through my hair, tilting my head up. "You can come and go as you please. But if you wish, I want you to move in."

My insides quiver. "You do?"

"Yes. What do you think?"

I put my hand over my stomach and the other one on my mouth. "I... I..."

His face falls. "I'm sorry. If it's too fast—"

"No! That's not what I'm trying to say. This is the nicest thing anyone has ever done for me. And I can't think of anywhere I'd rather live than where you are."

His lips turn up. "No?"

"No. I love you. I... I didn't think I would be able to love anyone again. But everything about you shows me it's because I didn't know what love was. And I thought I loved him, but I couldn't have. Because he didn't love me. And you show me, every day, what it's like to be loved and..." I'm too choked up to continue.

He pulls me closer and kisses my tears. "I love you, too, kotik."

"I know you do. And you told me once I wouldn't be able to fall in love with you if I knew all your sides."

His face hardens.

"It's not true. No matter how dark that side of you is, I love you. And I will continue to love you."

He closes his eyes. "Anna—"

"No. You don't have to tell me right now, but someday, you will. I will know every side of you. And I will still be here. Because your love for me isn't selfish or unkind. And my love for you isn't, either."

He opens his eyes, but I see his doubt in my promise.

"You gave me your trust." I kiss him. "Trust in my love for you. All of you."

22

Dmitri

ANNA'S A FLOWER BLOOMING INTO FULL BRILLIANCE. EVERY DAY, I watch her grow more confident in her abilities with work but also herself. The talent she has is incredible, and she still doesn't realize how special she is. Any opportunity to tell her, I do, but she stays humble.

She wants to learn Russian, so I'm teaching her a little bit each day. Sometimes she wakes me up whispering Russian in my ear.

She's spending a lot of time in her office working on our roof design and the new project for Sacha. We haven't gone out in a week. The grand opening for a restaurant my brothers and I invested in is tonight, so I want to take Anna.

I knock on her office door.

She's at the table and spins toward me. Her face lights up whenever she sees me, and it's an expression I hope she never loses. In Russian, she says, "Hello, my sexy man."

I chuckle and kiss her. "What are you working on?"

She beams. "I'm glad you're here. I want to show you something." She turns to her monitors, types something on her keyboard, and a 3D design of the rooftop relaxation area pops up.

"Wow! That looks incredible. Is that a firepit?"

"Yes. We have to bring gas up for the grills, so it's not much more to run the line over here." She points to the edge of the roof, where glass will be installed. "And these loungers are concrete so they don't get destroyed. But I think we should install a closet room against this back wall to store pillows and padded cushions."

"I love it. Great idea."

She points over my shoulder. "What's that?"

"I'm stealing you away from your work and taking you out tonight." I hold the plastic bag in front of her. "This is for you."

She pulls up the plastic and touches the gold dress. "Wow. You have good taste, Mr. Ivanov."

"Of course I do. And my good taste can't wait to see your ass in this dress," I cockily state.

She turns slightly, pumping her ass cheek in the air, and points to it. With an innocent expression, she says, "This ass?"

I slap it and pull her into me. "Don't tease me with your ass. You know I take it seriously."

She laughs.

"Your stilettos are on the kitchen table."

"New shoes, too? You're spoiling me."

I lean into the curve of her neck and kiss it. "Mmm...is it if I get benefits?"

She smiles. "When do we leave?"

"We have a few hours. Take your time."

She strokes her hand above my ear and tilts her head. "Why don't you ever tell me I have five minutes and to hurry up?"

I kiss her until she's breathless and I'm hard. "Why would I want you stressed, kotik? Hmm? I want you relaxed and happy. And all night, I'm going to stare at you, thinking about how later I'm going to be wrapped up in your perfection."

She pecks me on the lips. "Then I better start getting ready. I shaved today, but I think I'll shave again." She winks and pats my cheek.

Naughty girl.

God, she's sexy as hell.

She spins and leaves the room.

I follow her out of the room and work on a few things then go into the bathroom. Anna's at the vanity, drying her hair. I squeeze her ass, and she jumps.

"Just practicing," I tease.

"Ha, ha."

I shower and put on my clothes. When Anna finishes her hair and makeup, she unzips her dress and steps into it.

"Can you zip me?"

I step forward, zip her up, and her stomach growls. "Did you eat today?"

"Mmm... I forgot about lunch."

I sternly say, "You need to eat, kotik."

"It wasn't intentional. I got engrossed with work."

I grab the shoes off the bed and pull her into the family room to the couch. "Sit. I'll get you some food."

"We're going out for dinner."

"Yep. And you need something in your stomach."

"I'm not going to waste away."

"We've talked about this," I say and go into the kitchen.

"Dmitri, you're a bit overzealous right now, don't you think?"

I grab some cashews out of the cabinet and a bottle of water. Then I sit next to her. "Nope. Have some nuts."

"Your—" Her stomach growls again.

I cross my arms and raise my eyebrows.

She picks up a cashew. "Don't be arrogant now." She pops it in her mouth.

"You should set your alarm for lunch so you don't miss it."

"It's one meal. I'm not going to die. I haven't even been tracking what I eat or weighing myself."

"Good. You don't need to."

She rolls her eyes and eats some more nuts.

I hand her water, she drinks it then says, "I think you should make yourself useful and put on my shoes."

"Put on your shoes?"

Her lips twitch. "Yeah. I'll eat. You put on my shoes. It'll give you something to focus on besides what's going in my mouth."

"I love what goes in your mouth. Especially when you wake up," I tease her, referring to how she woke me up with a blowjob this morning.

She teasingly moves her foot up my thigh and close to my groin.

I move my hand up her smooth inner leg.

She inhales deeply and squirms.

"What's wrong, kotik?"

She seductively licks the cashew then pops it in her mouth. "Nothing."

Little vixen.

I hold her leg in the air and brush my lips on the inside of her calf while dragging my fingers down her leg.

Her chest rises and falls faster.

"I think I want my appetizer now." I graze my finger over her panties.

She holds out her hand. "Do you want a nut?"

I grunt. "Is that what you'd prefer me to eat?" I kiss the inside of her thigh.

"No," she whispers.

"That's good, kotik. I think I need something a bit more substantial." I bunch the bottom of her dress in my fists, and she lifts her hips. I push it up to her stomach.

I groan inside when I see she's wearing a thong. Her ass was made for one. It's going to drive me even crazier all night.

To taunt me, she holds her hand out again. "Sure you don't want to try a nut?"

I rip her underwear off her. The delicate material splits from her ass, and she gasps. "Put another thong on before we leave," I mumble while diving toward her pussy.

"Dmitri!" she cries out and grips my head with both hands.

I bury my face in her heat and massage her ass cheeks. I roll my tongue around her sweet sex, flicking it on her clit, sucking every delicious piece of her.

She squeezes her thighs around my neck, writhing and moaning, her whimpers getting louder until she's begging me to let her soar.

If we didn't have to be at this event, I would feast on her all night. Her pleasure is my drug. Every tremble of her body stokes my adrenaline until she's digging her fingers into my head so hard, I think I might bleed.

"Oh fuck!" she screams and convulses harder when I don't remove my mouth, sucking her clit and flicking it at the same time, faster than before.

When she can't come anymore, I release her.

She pants in her aftermath, and I kiss her mound and stomach. "We need to go. I'll grab you some new panties."

I go into the closet, select a thong, then go back to the couch and slide them up her legs. She grins and wiggles her foot.

"Demanding little kotik, aren't you?" I tease and slide her shoes on her feet. I help her off the couch, and she straightens her dress out.

She hands me the bottle of water. Her beautiful face is still flushed.

I drink half of it then tug her into me. I palm her ass. "This dress is sinful on you."

She unfastens a button on my shirt then traces over part of my chest tattoo. "I think clothes are overrated." She presses her lips to mine. "Maybe we should stay at home?"

I groan. "We have to go. Besides, if I don't take you out, you're going to become a hermit." I spin her and lead her to the elevator. A new coat is in the closet for her, and I pull it out.

"Where did this come from?"

"I bought it for you today."

She pecks me on the lips. "You're spoiling me."

"Not even close. Turn." I hold the jacket open, and she slides her arms into it. We leave and get into the car.

"So, where are we going?"

"My brothers and I invested in a restaurant. It's the grand opening."

Her eyes light up. "Fun! Do you own a lot of restaurants?"

"Not a lot. A handful. The Russian restaurant you've been to a few times, we have a stake in. But we're investors only. We don't deal in the operations."

"So you develop real estate, own restaurants and a boxing gym. Anything else?"

"Yes. Lots of things."

She tilts her head. "How do you know what to buy into?"

"It depends on the investment."

She taps her fingers on her thigh.

I put my hand over it. "What are you thinking right now?"

She turns in the seat. "Harper said she'd go to the investment classes with me. Vivian and her friends don't want to go. Piper made them spend their twenties learning about investments. She dragged them to too many classes to count, Vivian said."

"Piper. Is that Noah Parker's wife?"

"Yes."

"I met her at an event for Vivian's foundation. She's sharp."

"Yes. Piper, Noah, and Steven are all number gurus. But you are, too, aren't you?"

I shake my head. "No. I wouldn't say I'm a guru. They have special skills I don't."

"But you've created what you have, right? Or were your parents rich?"

I snort. "My parents were anything but rich in America. They lost everything when we fled Russia. The language barrier was too much of a problem for them to thrive here. And they had four growing boys to feed. It's why we try to help our community and other immigrants when we can."

She bites her lip, thinking. She slowly says, "Would you consider yourself poor when you grew up?"

"Yes."

"But now you aren't."

"No."

"So, how did your family pull itself out of poverty?"

My chest tightens. I growl, "All of our businesses are legal."

She scrunches her face. "I didn't assume they weren't."

What am I doing?

She never insinuated that.

She can't ever know.

I'm losing it.

"Sorry. We saved and invested in businesses."

She looks at her lap and fidgets with her fingers. It's dark, but I can see her hurt expression.

I put my hands over hers. "Anna, I'm sorry. I didn't mean to snap."

She closes her eyes but then says, "Why won't you trust me?"

"I do trust you, kotik."

She shakes her head then locks eyes with me. "You don't. There are only two times I've ever heard you speak to me like that."

"I'm sorry—"

She puts her fingers over my lips. "You accused me of assuming you were in the Russian mob. Now you just said I didn't think your businesses were legal. I don't know what the situation is, but there's a reason you got triggered."

My pulse beats hard in my neck, and I wonder if she can see it.

"I'm not sure what else happened in New York, but I do have assumptions. I've not asked you. Mitch hasn't contacted me in any way. I doubt it's only because he lost his job. And I haven't been asked to press charges for him stealing my money. So something happened. I'm naive about a lot of things, but I'm not so ignorant I don't realize this."

The air is thick in my lungs. I may break out in a sweat. Blood pounds loudly between my ears.

I don't want to lose her. No one has ever meant so much to me. I also don't want to hurt her or lose her respect.

"You are right. More happened in New York."

"Is he alive?" she asks in a deadpan voice.

"Yes. I promised you I would not kill him. I kept my word. And I have eyes on him."

Surprise registers on her face. "You're watching him?"

"For the time being, yes. To make sure we got the message across forever that you are not his."

She takes a deep breath and stays silent.

"Say something, Anna."

"Do you want to tell me what you did?"

"No. I don't want to go into details other than he didn't get anything from us you didn't receive from him."

She inhales sharply and puts her hand on her rib cage. "'Us' meaning you and Boris?"

"Yes."

She continues gripping her rib cage and turns to the window. The car stops at a light, and traffic passes in front of us.

My stomach twists. I quietly say, "You did not ask me what happened because you do not want to admit the man I am."

She jerks her head and glares. "No. I didn't ask you because I thought if I needed to know, you would tell me. I already know the man you are and what you are capable of."

"You don't, kotik. No matter what you think you know, you don't know all parts of me."

"Then why don't you tell me?"

"I've already told you why I can't."

"No. You said I would never be able to love you. I already do. So your fear is not valid anymore. And you expose every layer of me so I have no secrets from you. Every insecurity and flaw in me, you are privy to. And I trust you with all of it. You require I do this, or there is no us. You didn't even give me a day into our relationship to give you my full trust. And I did. I chose you. Yet, you don't believe in my love for you enough to handle whatever it is you're hiding."

I close my eyes and try to figure out how to make this right. She's right about everything, except one thing. She loves the man she knows, not the one raging at times inside me. And that man isn't worthy of her love.

If I weren't selfish, I would never have attempted to make her mine. But there isn't a part of her I can't imagine not having in my life. And her love feels so good, I can't give it up.

The car stops, and the driver opens the door. I step out and reach for her. She takes my hand, and I tug her into me. I palm her ass and head. I lock my eyes onto her blue ones. "You are my everything."

"I know. And you are mine. All of you. Why can't you trust me?"

"I do, kotik." I kiss her. "Let's go eat. We will talk more about this later."

It's a lie, and I cringe inside. I don't plan on ever talking to her about who I am or how the Ivanov brothers got where we currently are. And I don't want her to ever know what any of us have already proven.

Anna

MOST OF THE TIME, I DON'T DWELL ON THE SECRET LINGERING between Dmitri and me. Sometimes, it stirs. The same voice in my head telling me Mitch was cheating on me and I should leave him says Dmitri needs to tell me his secret.

I couldn't turn the voice off when it was about Mitch. I can't turn it off now. And I don't believe anything Dmitri can tell me could change my love for him.

Mitch's secrets hurt me. Dmitri's do, too, but in a different way. If I look back, I was constantly trying to get Mitch to love and approve of me. I don't have to try with Dmitri. I know he adores me and would do anything to protect me.

The hurt comes from the hatred for himself that fills his eyes whenever the topic comes up. And the inability for him to believe in my love for him.

I know he's a dangerous man. I don't think he's the type who pays others to take care of issues. If this is true, then he's a violent man. And while I grew up in a bubble, Mitch taught me about the evil residing in a violent man.

So I should run from Dmitri. But I don't believe he would ever harm me. And while Mitch was violent without cause, my gut tells me Dmitri wouldn't hurt anyone unless there was some reason justifying it.

And that's another way I've changed. I never thought assault could be justified. I assumed it was always wrong. But something changed in me when I got away from Mitch. I would never have been strong enough to overpower him. His threats to find me in Chicago were always in the back of my mind. So I find peace in whatever Dmitri and Boris did to him. A part of me hopes they inflicted more pain than what he did to me. And if these are my thoughts and wishes, how is Dmitri any worse of a person than I am?

He says we will talk later, but I don't have confidence we will. There are too many people around, so I drop it for now.

Dmitri escorts me through the restaurant to the back. His brothers are already seated with women. I've never met any of them before, and I'm not sure if they are girlfriends or casual dates.

Maksim, Boris, and Sergey rise when we approach them. They all hug me and kiss my cheek, telling me I look nice. Dmitri does the same to the women they are with, and we are all introduced.

Maksim brought a woman named Jade. She's a beautiful Asian woman with flawless skin and black hair. It hits her chin in an edgy bob. She's half the size of Maksim but has a cold air about her, as if she'd slice you to pieces with her stare alone should you mess with her.

Boris's date is a red-haired woman named Nora. Her hair is long and curly. She blushes a lot and nervously glances at Boris often, as if looking for his permission or she's unsure of him. I can't figure out which.

Sergey's date is a beautiful black woman named Eloise. She's tall and so stunning, I wonder if she's a runway model. Her French accent is thick and she rolls her dark eyes from time to time, as if annoyed at his attention.

Dmitri pulls out my chair. I sit next to Nora, and Dmitri sits next to Maksim. Dmitri's arm is around me, but he's pulled into a conversation with Maksim.

I turn to Nora. "Are you from here?"

Nora nods. "Yes. I've lived here my entire life. You?"

"I just moved from New York City."

Her face lights up. "I love it there. What made you move?"

It's a question I get asked often, and I am learning to answer it better. The first few times someone asked me, I stuttered, trying to figure out how to answer it. But now I ignore the increase in my pulse. "My brother and his wife live here. They are having a baby, and I thought it would be nice to be near them."

She smiles. "That's nice. My sisters and brothers all have kids. It's fun being an aunt."

"They are here in Chicago?"

"Oh, yeah. The O'Malleys would never leave Chicago. That would be a sin, according to my grandfather."

"Ahh, you're Irish. That explains your beautiful red hair."

She touches it. "Yes. It's hard to escape in my family."

Boris slides his hand around her and drags his finger down her bare arm then twists a lock of her hair around his finger.

She flushes and inhales sharply.

He leans in near her face, giving her an intense set of fuck-me eyes. I know those eyes because Dmitri looks at me with the same expression. Boris says, "Anna is Chicago's newest, up-and-coming interior designer."

She turns redder then tears her eyes away from Boris. "You're an interior designer?"

"Yes."

"Do you design restaurants?"

"I worked on several over the years before I started my business, but I've not designed one on my own before."

"Could you?"

"Yes, I suppose."

Boris says, "You two should meet up and discuss this. Nora's been struggling to find someone good, haven't you?"

"Yes. There have been some issues."

Boris leans closer to Nora's ear and strokes her neck from her ear to her collarbone. She squirms in her seat. "But all of them are going to go away. Sometimes a clean slate is best, don't you think?"

Worry fills her eyes. She nods.

He strokes her cheek.

Why don't you throw her on the table and screw her right here, Boris?

His attention to her makes me slightly uncomfortable. It's like experiencing foreplay, except I'm not the recipient.

I clear my throat. "Well, I'd love to meet up and talk with you if you want."

She turns to me. "I would. Very much. Please."

"Okay." I pull out my phone, and we exchange information.

A waitress comes over and puts bread on the table. Maksim orders wine and champagne for the table.

Dmitri butters a piece of bread then holds it to my mouth. His lips twitch. "Something for you besides nuts, kotik."

I try to stop my smile but can't. I take a bite, and he pops the left-over part in his mouth.

He leans into my ear. "I prefer your nuts."

I elbow him, and he kisses my head. He opens the menu, and we read it together.

"What's good here?" I ask.

"Everything, hopefully. Do you like escargot?"

"Yes."

"Should we get it as a starter?"

"I thought you already had your appetizer?" I tease.

He gives me the same eyes Boris just gave Nora, and my flutters take off. "I'm extra hungry tonight, kotik."

"I think—"

"Imagine finding all the Ivanov's here tonight," a man behind me says. It's not a pleasant tone. It's more of a sneer.

Dmitri's body stiffens. His face hardens, and his brothers and he all exchange glances.

"Lorenzo. Didn't expect to see you here, either, " Maksim replies in a deadpan voice.

Lorenzo Rossi, part of the Italian mafia?

"Time's ticking. I'm getting impatient," Lorenzo says.

Dmitri leaps off his seat and gets in Lorenzo's face. He bites out, "Don't threaten us."

The brothers all jump up and crowd around him.

"Or what?" Lorenzo replies, and three men behind him step forward.

My heart pounds hard.

Maksim steps between Dmitri and Lorenzo. In a firm voice, he states, "We're having a night out. If you have something to discuss, we'll do it at a different time. Not now."

Lorenzo scoffs. "Tomorrow. And I expect to move forward."

"You don't make demands from us," Dmitri growls.

Lorenzo lowers his voice. "I own this town. You know it. I know it. Everyone knows it. The price just went down another ten percent."

Dmitri clenches his fists, and Maksim pushes Dmitri back. He points at Lorenzo. "We're done with this conversation."

Lorenzo laughs, and he and his posse begin to walk away. When he gets to the front of the table, he freezes and stares at Nora. "Aren't you an O'Malley?"

She swallows hard, and her face turns crimson.

I grab her shaking hand. I'm not sure why, but something about Lorenzo even knowing who she is worries me.

"What's it to you?" Boris asks.

Lorenzo's grin widens. "Oh, how the Irish have fallen."

Boris and Sergey almost leap over the table, and Maksim and Dmitri grab both of them.

There's no screaming. No threats. No scene besides Maksim and Dmitri holding back their brothers while the four Ivanov's scowl at Lorenzo.

He sits at a table with his men several rows over. Women are already seated, and the waitress begins filling their wine glasses.

"Dinner's over," Maksim orders, and each brother puts his arm around their date, and we all leave.

When we get in the car, Dmitri pulls me onto his lap. "I'm sorry about dinner, kotik."

"Is he coming after you?" I ask.

"No. Don't worry about it."

"Dmitri!"

His eyes widen. I've never yelled at him before.

"You can't act like I wasn't even in the room. I'm not a child. Do not treat me like one."

He closes his eyes and puts his forehead on mine. "I'm sorry. I don't want you anywhere near this."

"What does 'this' mean?"

He opens his eyes. "Him. I don't want him or any of his men near you."

"Is he coming after you?" I repeat, this time sterner. I already know the answer, and I'm not sure why I'm even bothering to ask it.

"No."

"Liar. Why are you lying to me? Just be honest," I cry out.

"You don't need to worry. He won't survive if he tries." He clenches his jaw and looks out the window.

I softly ask, "What does that mean?"

"Nothing."

"God dammit! I'm so tired of you lying to me."

"I'm not—"

I slap him. It happens so fast, I don't even know I'm doing it. My hand shakes from shock and the sting. "Oh God. I'm sorry. Dmitri." I pull his face to mine. I've never slapped anyone before. And shame fills me for hurting him.

His eyes darken. "Don't push me on this, kotik. We have a good thing going. If you push, you're going to destroy everything we have. It'll take the perfection of us and tear it to pieces until there is nothing left but painful memories."

"Why do you say that? Has this happened to you before with other women?" Jealousy skyrockets through me as I ask.

"No. I've never loved any woman the way I love you. I've not allowed anyone to get close but you."

"Then how do you know?"

"I do. You need to trust me."

The car stops, and Dmitri steps out before the driver even gets out.

I need to trust him. When does he trust me?

He reaches for my hand, and I take it without thinking. He leads me into the penthouse. As soon as we step off the elevators, he slides my coat off my shoulders.

We get into the main room, and I spin into him. I put my hands on his cheek. "I'm so sorry I slapped you."

"It's okay."

My insides quiver. "No. It's not. And this thing between us, it's not okay, either."

"Kotik—"

"I can't do this with you."

His head jerks back, eyes widen, and he sharply inhales. The color drains from his face then fills with hurt.

Tears drip down my cheeks. "I love you."

"Then why are you doing this?"

"You know why."

"No. I don't. We're happy together."

"Yes, we are. So happy," I admit.

He clenches his jaw. "Then why would you break us apart?"

My voice shakes. "You gave me an ultimatum. You told me you wanted my permission to take care of me how you saw fit. And I had to trust you. No matter what, you would never do anything to hurt me."

"Yes. And I wouldn't."

"I've given you what you needed. It was a vow. An oath that I took seriously. And I have trusted you to do whatever you saw fit."

"You have."

I take his hand and put it over my heart. "You promised me you would give me your trust. You said I got to decide how to take care of you. And you wouldn't question anything. You would know everything I did came from in here."

"That's true. It still is."

"No. It's not." Tears fall faster. "You said if you can't be the man you know how to be, then we're living in a lie. And neither of us deserves that."

"Anna—"

"No, Dmitri. You want all of me. But you don't give me all of you. You think I only deserve to see the good part, but you see every ugly thing about me. And it may not be as dark as whatever it is you're hiding, but it's still me. I trust you with it all. You know my truth. I don't know yours, and not because I don't want to. Because you haven't given me your trust. So we're living in a lie. And I've spent too much of my life doing that. I won't do it anymore."

I've never seen the expression on Dmitri's face before. I'm not sure how to take it.

I kiss his cheek. "I love you. I'm not sure how to stop. But I can't live in a lie with someone who expects me to put all my faith in them, yet they won't put their faith in me."

I leave the room, unable to look at him anymore, my heart shattering into pieces, the pain worse than anything I've ever felt.

He's my heart. But without the truth of who he is, we'll never be real.

Dmitri

"Anna!"

She can't do this.

"Anna!" I call after her while following her to the bedroom, but she ignores me and goes into the closet.

I need to tell her. I can't lose her.

I can't tell her. She'll never be able to look me in the face again.

It's too dangerous for her to know.

I step into the closet, and she's crouched over her suitcase. A few random items are in it, and she's trying to silence her tears. Her hand is over her face, and her body is shaking.

I slide on the floor and pull her into my lap. "Don't go. Please. I love you."

She sobs into my chest. "It's not about love."

I hold her head to my chest and kiss her forehead. "We have nothing without love. It's everything, kotik."

She looks up. The anguish in her eyes almost kills me. "We can't have love without trust. You insisted on it."

More tears fall, and she turns away.

I tighten my arms around her, conflicted about everything I thought I needed to do, or keep from her, for us to survive the truth.

"You're hurting me by not telling me. You promised you'd never hurt me," she mumbles into my chest.

Pains shoot through my heart. I meant all the things I've said to her. When she repeats them back to me and tells me I've not held up my end of our vow to each other, I despise myself even more.

I'm a hypocrite. There are no ugly parts to Anna, but she believes there are. I don't see anything but beauty in her. But she's unveiled every aspect of her soul to me, even pieces that make her feel shameful. She's put herself in the most vulnerable position possible because I required it, but I haven't done the same.

I wanted to give her the best parts of me and hide everything else. I've been ignorant. Maybe it's why I've avoided getting close to any other women over the years. What I thought I could do with Anna isn't possible, and deep down, I know it.

But once you're involved in what weaves through my past, you can't get out. Even when you think you're out, you're still in, watching your back and waiting for the other shoe to fall.

After what happened at the restaurant tonight, there is no more denying it. There's about to be a war. And Anna witnessed the beginning.

It's ignorant for me to believe I can tell her everything is fine and not to worry about anything. She's smart. But I hate that she got a glimpse of Lorenzo Rossi.

"I have to go. I can't stay here," she whispers and tries to get off my lap.

I hold her so she can't get off me.

"Let me go."

"I don't want to ever let you go, kotik."

She shuts her eyes, and more tears fall. "Dmitri, don't make this harder for me."

"I'll tell you."

She freezes and pins her blue eyes on me. "Everything?"

My jaw twitches and I gaze up at the ceiling.

She pulls my head down.

I shake my head. "I won't tell you the little details. But you won't need to know them. The broad truth is enough for you to understand." I take my thumbs and wipe the tears off her cheeks.

Where do I even start?

Minutes pass, I focus on her suitcase.

She can't leave. I need to figure this out.

As if she can understand my anxiety, she rises and holds her hand out. "Let's get out of the closet."

I take her hand. We lie on the bed.

She cuddles into my chest.

"I've never spoken of this. I don't know where to start."

She cups my cheeks and kisses me. "Tell me. I promise I'll still love you."

I don't see how you will be able to, kotik.

Don't be a coward. There's no getting out of it. Just tell her.

I stroke her hair. "When my parents fled Russia, they came to the US but didn't speak any English. Maksim was ten. I was eight. Boris was three. Sergey wasn't even born yet. My mother and father were always working three or four jobs. Anything they could find to support us they took. The Russian community was full of people in the same position, so everyone helped everyone out."

"And that's why you try to hire Russians and other immigrants?" Anna asks.

"Yes. But there's another reason."

"What?"

My pulse beats in my neck. "It is also to try and keep them away."

"Who's them?"

"Not everyone in the community is there to help. Some are there to profit off those who are hurting. And they still are."

She stays quiet.

My stomach flips. I inhale her scent, but it doesn't calm me how it usually does. "My parents struggled to give us everything we needed. My father was the equivalent of an engineer in Russia, and my mother was a nurse, but since they couldn't speak English, and they weren't educated here, it's like they had no specialized skills. The jobs they took were often under the table and below minimum wage. It didn't go very far with four boys.

And the vultures were always there, waiting to prey on my father's hardship."

Anna traces the no past, no future tattoo on my chest. She softly asks, "Did your father get involved with bad people?"

My father's face, the last time I ever saw him, pops in my head. I blink hard. "No. He and my mother often fought about this. She thought the jobs they offered them were harmless. But my father knew. He warned her about the danger of taking any job from them. He forbade her from associating with them and made it clear to my brothers and me who to stay away from. But he got sick, and everything changed."

Anna strokes my cheek, and my jaw twitches under her fingers.

Stop now. She doesn't need to know.

She'll leave me.

She's going to leave me regardless after this.

I tighten my arm around her and palm her ass. It's a comfort, as if holding her will ease the blow of my truth. But it won't.

"What happened, Dmitri?"

"We didn't have insurance and could barely put food on the table. I was fourteen. Maksim was sixteen. We tried to find jobs to help, but my mother insisted we stay in school. My father made us promise to get our education."

I close my eyes. The flashback of my father reduced to skin and bones, barely able to sit in the chair, lecturing my brothers and me about staying in school is as clear as when it happened thirty years ago.

"When my father died, the community helped us as much as they could. But they were struggling, too. Four boys were too much for my mother to support on her own. Maksim quit school to work. My mother reminded him we promised my father to stay in school. They had a horrible argument, but he wouldn't return, insisting he needed to step into my father's role. Several weeks later, my mother came home. She slapped cash on the table and informed us she got hired full time to be a secretary for a good friend of my father's. He was a Russian man with several businesses. My mother insisted Maksim was to return to school."

"Did he?"

"Yes. When he graduated, my mother had the money for him to go to community college. He wanted to get a full-time job to help out. She stood her ground that she was making enough, and he needed to continue with his schooling. So he found part-time work and went to classes. I followed in his footsteps, and for several years, everything seemed okay."

Anna slides her hand in my shirt. "Your heart is racing. Do you want to take a break?"

My mouth is dry, and I swallow the lump in my throat. "If I stop, I won't finish."

Tell me to stop.

She nods. "Okay. Keep going, then."

The breath I exhale tastes stale. "Maksim finished college. I was in my last year when Boris found out."

"What did he discover?"

"Who my mother really worked for."

"Who was it?"

I focus on the ceiling, hating this part of my family history. "Zamir Petrov, the Russian mob boss."

Anna slides up and pins me with her gaze. I'm not sure what I expected, but her voice isn't scared or angry. It's calm. "Are you and your brothers part of the mafia?"

"No." I exhale. "Yes. It's complicated."

A line forms between her eyes. "How?"

"The food in our bellies and clothes on our backs was from his money. The degree Maksim earned, and the one I almost obtained, he paid for. Boris interrupted a meeting with him and my mother. Zamir explained to Boris how he owned us. My mother claimed it wasn't true and not part of their deal. She insisted only she was indebted to him. But we all were. And he was ready for us to pay off our growing debt. Four boys were more valuable to him than one mother could ever be."

My stomach flips so fast, I feel dizzy and have to look away from Anna. I sit up and try to get more air into my lungs.

She doesn't let me go. She moves closer and puts her arm around my back and head on my shoulder.

I don't deserve her affection. I shouldn't be telling her any of this.

"Whatever you tell me, I will still love you."

She won't. It's not possible.

"I'm a bad man, my kotik. No matter how much good I do going forward, it will never erase the demon of my past, or even allow him to escape me. And I will always be a man who can call upon the evil within me at any time and utilize it how I see fit."

She sternly says, "Dmitri, tell me what happened."

I get up and walk to the window. Her touch is too much for me. It shouldn't mix with my truth. I cross my arms, fixating on one of the buildings and the windows lit up against the night sky.

"Zamir took my mother. He instructed my brothers, even Sergey, who was only twelve, to meet him in a warehouse to get her back. If we didn't come, he said he would put her in his whorehouse before killing her."

My insides shake with rage so intense, I have to swallow back bile. It's the same as back then. Helplessness mixes with the rage, creating a concoction so potent, I reach out for the window to steady myself.

Anna steps behind me and circles her arms around my waist.

"Don't touch me right now. You are the good in my life. I can't have you mixed up in this," I mumble, barely able to breathe.

She holds on to me tighter and presses her cheek against my spine. "I love you. I am part of you, including anything you don't like."

"You will never be part of this, and I don't want you to be. Only good resides in you."

"You think too highly of me. We all have parts we hate."

"Not like this, Anna."

"Maybe not, but there is nothing you can say that will make me not love you. And I will find a way to love even this part of you that you despise."

She doesn't know what she's saying.

Minutes pass. I don't move, and neither does she.

"Dmitri, tell me the rest."

The twitching in my jaw intensifies. "When we got to the warehouse, his thugs took us to a back room. Plastic covered the walls and floor. Six metal chairs lined up perfectly straight with six warm bodies in them; five men and one woman, tied to the seats, with gags in their mouths. The woman was my mother." I swallow more bile, remembering my mother's fear and tear-filled eyes. "Zamir's thugs held knives to our throats while he explained how we would get our mother back."

Anna squeezes me harder then takes a deep breath. Her chest presses against my back as air fills her lungs.

I don't want to look at her.

Don't be a coward.

I spin into her. "This is violent. I don't want you to know about it."

She cups my cheeks. "Yes. It is. And you must continue. What happened?"

I place my hands over hers and remove them from my cheeks, holding them to my chest. "We had a choice. Leave or earn our mother back. We chose our mother. And that night, we were all given a man to torture and spilt to shreds with a knife. One of Zamir's thugs would do something to the man assigned to him who sat helpless in the chair. We would each have to replicate that torture on the man Zamir declared as ours. Our mother watched for hours as each of her sons slowly stole the last breath of air and drop of blood from a stranger."

Anna's eyes glisten. The color in her cheeks disappears. I'm sure I've now lost her. If I haven't, the rest will be the final blow. But I'm too far in. The rest of the truth now has to come out.

"That night wasn't the end of it. They kept our mother. We had ten jobs each to do. Each incident, our mother was tied to the chair and gagged. After the fourth evening, my mother stopped crying when she saw what we did. When we finally got her back, Zamir made it clear he owned us. We were still in debt to him.

The men we killed were only to pay for my mother. For years, we tortured and killed men for him."

Anna swallows hard. "So, you are in the Russian mafia?"

"It's not black-and-white, Anna."

She furrows her brows. "Explain it to me."

I release her wrists and pace the room. "Boris got into betting. He has a knack and somehow almost always wins. We didn't know about it. He was only twenty-two, and he won over fifteen million dollars one night in Vegas. When he came back, he used it to his advantage."

"How?"

"He went to Zamir. Our freedom for ten million dollars. And anyone with the Ivanov name was never to be touched again."

"Zamir agreed?"

I shake my head and turn to her. "Not entirely. Boris will never be free. He is a master at what Zamir's thug taught us to do. He has control others don't, including me. Zamir saw it. Once a year, Zamir calls on him. He owns him on those nights. Until Boris or Zamir dies, the agreement will not cease. And it will always tie our family to the mob. No matter how many people we help, or how legitimate our businesses are, we are still part of it. We cannot escape it. And Zamir is always looking for a way to pull us all back in."

Anna bites on her lip, and her head bobs in tiny movements. Minutes feel like hours. Silence and the air are thick, suffocating my every breath and thought, except for the fear I'll never see my kotik again after this night.

"Why didn't Boris offer him the other five million for his freedom?"

My gut pitches. "In some ways, Boris and Zamir are the same. He understands how Zamir thinks, and even at twenty-two, he knew Zamir would never allow him out. He kept the money so our family could have a future and never have to rely on anyone else again. He gave the five million to Maksim, and we bought properties with it. For years, we didn't use a dime and lived on scraps, reinvesting everything and only hiring Russians so we could prevent others from having to rely on Zamir."

Anna tilts her head. "Where is your mother now?"

I close my eyes. "She passed shortly after we got her back. She couldn't handle the guilt of what she did and..." I squeeze my eyelids tighter.

Anna's hands are on my cheeks, but I can't finish. She whispers, "Did she kill herself?"

I nod.

Anna wraps her body around mine, and the perfection of her almost destroys me. I don't dare open my eyes for fear I will break down.

She pulls my head down and kisses me. I don't expect it. I shouldn't allow it and should stop her from ever touching me again. Now that the truth has been spoken, she should run. I was foolish to assume I could keep every part of me separate and not taint her.

No past, no future. I know better.

"Anna—"

She shuts me up by sliding her tongue in my mouth, hot, possessive, as if we're in a famine, and I'm the only piece of meat around. Her hand glides over my head, holding it firmly to her, and she unfastens the buttons of my shirt, pushing it off me.

"An—"

"I still love and need you." She goes back to kissing me, encasing me into the world I want with her.

My body responds, thirsty for every part of her and me, the beautiful mix of us that doesn't exist outside of our proximity.

And I want the life I've been living with her. I'm not sure how to move forward with her, now that she knows who I am, but I can't stop my body from responding to hers.

Our clothes get shed. We end up next to the window, and I pick her up, holding her against the glass, entering her in one thrust.

"Yes," she whimpers against my lips, her breath merging with mine, her body already quivering.

"I don't want to lose you," I admit, choking back emotions.

She kisses me harder. "You aren't." Her fingers dig into my shoulder and the back of my head.

"This isn't a world for you."

"Shh. You're my world." Her tongue is fire, blazing against mine, scorching everything in its path, leaving no room for me to resist her.

I get lost in her, barely noticing the lights blinking on buildings. Her whimpers and cries soothe my nerves. She gives all of herself to me, like always, wrapping her perfection around me, as if I didn't just reveal every dark part of my soul.

"I'm yours," she whispers in my ear, her body trembling around my flesh. "You're mine."

"I love you, kotik. I'm selfish for it," I murmur in her ear.

"No. You're selfish if you discard me."

Her statement affects me. I choke up again at the suggestion she would ever believe I could ever toss her aside.

"I...oh...oh...God!" she cries out, her body arching off the glass and pressing into me. "Dmitri!"

I release all of me into her. Violent as the man I am, growling her name and creating no air between the glass, her, and me.

I'm only whole with her. Without my kotik, I'm broken, and I never knew how much until she entered my life.

In our aftermath, the fog on the glass dwindles, and streaks of moisture drip down it, outlining the edge of her body. But I don't move.

She doesn't loosen her hold on me. In a firm, don't-argue-with-me voice, she claims, "The truth is out. There are no more secrets between us. Going forward, we won't have them, either. And I will decide how to take care of you now."

Everything I assumed was wrong. I thought I was the one who needed to take care of her. But her words cut into my soul, and I can't deny it. Every part of me needs her to do whatever she sees fit. She, and she alone, is the only person on earth who understands how to find any salvation within me.

Anna

TRUTH IS A FUNNY THING. IT CAN DESTROY YOU OR MAKE YOU stronger. In Dmitri's and my case, it only binds us closer together, creating a bond so thick, no one could ever unravel it.

Our love is untouchable. I don't say it to be arrogant. It's my truth. It's weaved so tight in my heart, there's no room for error.

I don't disregard his past or the beast that lies within him. I know at any point, he could shred someone to pieces and go on with his day, as if nothing occurred.

Before I met him, I would have run and assumed I was safer away from a man who could do what he can. But it is his demon who would die to protect me. It's the man who stopped Mitch from harassing me and eliminated my anxiety that he would find and hurt, if not kill, me.

My acceptance is selfish. I want Dmitri's protection. At this point, if I left him, he would still give it to me. He would let me go and allow me to live how I wanted, but he would always have someone watching me, making sure I am okay. He told me this when he tried to understand why I refused to leave him.

But I can't exist anymore without his love. And those two things allow me to let the truth be what it is and not run from it. Instead, I embrace it.

I tell no one our secret. My family wouldn't understand. Harper or any of my other friends would never stop urging me to run. Part of me does wonder if Chase has any idea about Dmitri's ties. But since I made it clear that I would choose Dmitri over Chase, my brother hasn't said anything. He treats him like anyone else I would date. Well, excluding the last few years with how he acted around Mitch.

Dmitri keeps teaching me Russian, and I pick up more bits and pieces of conversations he has. I don't ask about things. Once he told me the truth, a calm swept over me. If he needed me to worry about an issue or be aware, he would tell me.

Viktor goes everywhere I go. I should be annoyed, but I've gotten quite used to him. He stays in the shadows most of the time, but I always know he is there. It's also become a daily challenge to see how many times I can get him to talk or smile. As much as he tries to maintain his stoic demeanor, I think I'm growing on him and wearing him down. I caught his lips twitching three times yesterday.

"Try this. I added coconut flakes today." Dmitri leans over me and sets two bowls of yogurt, fruit, nuts, and seeds in front of me. He just got back from his workout with his brothers. I'm still in my robe.

I tip my head back for a kiss, and he dips down to meet me. I glide my fingers over his head and deepen our kiss. "What's your schedule today?"

He sits next to me. "My brothers and I are going through which of our guys to send over to work on Vivian's foundation project."

I snap my fingers. "I forgot to show you the design. Vivian and Charlotte were excited about it. They both said if you were okay with the labor costs, it would be great."

"I'm sure there won't be any problems."

I take a bite of my breakfast. After I swallow, I dip my spoon in for another taste. "This coconut is a good addition."

Dmitri puts some in his mouth, and we eat in silence for a few minutes. "Do you want to come to the meeting and show my brothers the design?"

"I can't. I have my first meeting without Maksim today," I chirp.

His eyes narrow. "Who with?"

I snicker. "No one who's going to try to take advantage of me. Besides, I think Maksim has converted me." I chant, and put my fist in the air, "No discounts. No discounts."

Dmitri laughs. "Good, kotik. Glad you finally see your worth."

I've signed three contracts in the last week alone with Maksim's assistance. And Dmitri said they have a few more projects coming up he and his brothers want me to work on.

"So who is this mystery meeting with? Do I know him?" Dmitri asks.

"It's a her."

He winks. "Sorry. Do I know her?"

"Yep. I'm meeting Nora."

His body stiffens next to mine. "Nora O'Malley?"

I put my spoon down. "Is there something about Nora I should worry about?"

His jaw clenches. He taps his fingers on the table and gazes out the window.

"Dmitri?"

"Nora's a great girl. We've known her and her family forever. Her brother is the boxer who Boris fought."

"Oh. What's wrong, then?"

"Nothing with her. But there are things..." He takes a deep breath.

I place my hand on his cheek and pin my eyes on his. "We don't keep secrets from each other. There is something I need to know, so tell me."

He takes my hand and kisses the back of it. "You're right. Her family has ties to the Irish mob. It's several generations away, but they are still tied. Issues are going on with her restaurant. There were things intentionally done to hurt her business. Boris got involved and shouldn't have."

"I'm going to need a little bit more clarity on what you're telling me."

The green in Dmitri's eyes darkens. "It was a loud and clear attack from Lorenzo Rossi. Boris should have let her family handle it."

My stomach flips. "Ah. I see. And is Rossi coming after us harder now?"

Dmitri's voice drops. "He does not know it was Boris."

Chills dig in my bones. "Will he?"

"Boris always covers his tracks."

I take a deep breath and smile to try and cut the tension. "Okay. So are you telling me you don't want me to work on Nora's project? Boris is the one who originally suggested we meet."

He hesitates but then says, "I'm sure it is okay. You would do an amazing job, and we only want the best for Nora and her family. But I want to speak with Boris first, if you don't mind?"

"I'm sure if I said no, you still would, but thanks for asking," I tease.

His lips twitch. He leans to mine and pecks me on the lips. "I don't deserve you, kotik."

"You know I don't like it when you say that," I reprimand.

"I'm a man who knows the importance of the woman he is with. It's not something I am going to forget." He kisses me again.

I groan. "You're impossible."

"Yeah, but you love me."

"That's right. I do. Don't forget it." I glance at my watch. "I need to shower. I sadly see you already did at the gym."

His eyes twinkle. "If I didn't need to speak to my brother, I would take another."

I rise and put my arms around his shoulders then give him a final kiss.

He squeezes my ass then pats it. "We will discuss things after my call with Boris."

"Okay. Keep in mind I like Nora and already have ideas floating in my head. It would be super fun to design her restaurant."

He chuckles. "Noted."

I shower and get ready.

When I come out, Dmitri eyes me up and whistles. "It's a good thing you're only going to meet with a woman. I might be worried all day."

"Ha, ha. You know I only have eyes for you, lover boy. Do I get the clear to go?"

"Yes. Viktor will go with you."

I smirk. "Like everywhere else I go?"

"Point taken. Is it bothering you?"

I shake my head. "Not really. Viktor's grown to adore me. He hasn't admitted it yet, but one of these days he's going to."

Amusement crosses Dmitri's face. "I'm also sending Peter."

My pulse increases. "Why do I need two bodyguards?"

"It's only precautionary. I would send Boris, but he needs to be in our meeting today."

"No offense, but I'm ready to wear my big girl panties and be Ivanov-free to close this project."

Pride sweeps his expression. "I'm sure you will, kotik. Tell you what. Why don't we go celebrate your win tonight?"

"She hasn't hired me yet."

He pulls me into his arms. "Pretty sure you'll have a signed contract in your hands. Should I plan something?"

"Sure."

He kisses me. "Viktor is waiting by the elevator."

I steal his lips one last time then leave. Viktor escorts me to the car. He sits in the back with me, since Peter is in the passenger seat. It takes ten minutes to arrive at Nora's.

Her restaurant is a stereotypical Irish pub with thick wood, mirrored Guinness signs, and four-leaf clovers. Tape covers ripped spots on the green vinyl booths. It's faded and worn in many places. A mix of stale beer, fried food, cabbage, and potatoes floods my nostrils.

Nora is on the phone when I come in. "We can't keep doing this." She twists the old-fashioned cord around her finger. "My brother —" She nods her head and sighs. "I'm working tonight." There's a long pause. "You know I do."

I clear my throat, feeling like an eavesdropper.

Nora turns, flustered. "Oh, sorry, Anna." She holds up her finger. "I need to go. Anna is here."

Is she talking to Boris?

Her face flushes, and she turns and murmurs, "I have to go." She hangs up, takes a deep breath, and turns with a smile. "Anna, how are you?"

"I'm doing well. I love the authenticity of this place."

Her smile widens. "I'd like to keep it but not be lost in the past, if that makes sense?"

"Sure."

"Why don't we—" She glances toward the door, and her face falls.

I turn. Viktor and Peter are standing at the entrance.

"Sorry. Dmitri has me on bodyguard lockdown right now," I joke.

"It's okay. I understand." She points to a booth. "Do you want to sit? Can I get you a drink or food?"

"I'm good." I slide into the booth and take my laptop out then glance around. Part of the restaurant has clear plastic sealing it off, and everything behind it is black. "Did you have a fire?"

Her eyes glisten. She twists a lock of her curly, red hair around her finger. "There was an issue..."

My stomach flutters. *This is what Dmitri was talking about.* "I see. Well, why don't you tell me what you're trying to do?"

"I want to redesign everything. Bring it up to date. I inherited this pub from my grandmother. She passed a year ago, and I was her favorite, so..." Sadness fills her eyes.

"I'm sorry about your loss."

"Thanks. Anyway, I need to update the entire place. The fire is shortening my timeline. I hoped to wait another year, but I don't want to keep staring at that mess." She points to the burned area. "I don't want to lose the old-school Irish feel, but I'd also like to bring it into the current year. We're a neighborhood pub. Generations of families have supported this place, and my grandmother inherited it from her mother. I don't want to dishonor the memory or what they built, or make it so different the people who love this bar still don't feel at home here."

"I understand. Maybe a facelift with some new edge to it?" I suggest.

Her eyes light up. "Yes."

I rise and walk around the restaurant. I stop in front of the burned area. "What was this?"

"The game room. Dartboards and pool tables, mostly."

"I'm assuming you want it to continue to be one?"

"Yes. The patrons are dying without it."

"I bet." I step closer to the plastic. "It's a large area."

"I have the dimensions of the entire floor plan. My brother and Boris measured it out for me before the fire occurred."

"I have some ideas. They were floating in my head before we met, and I put a few things together. Can I show you to get an idea if you like anything?"

Her face brightens. "Yes. Please."

I know Maksim and Dmitri have told me never to give ideas before getting the job, but I don't think Nora is out to screw me over. They've been right about the other men I've signed contracts with, but I'm going to go with my gut on Nora.

We spend an hour looking over design ideas I put together and discussing how we would work together and my involvement with her contractors.

"My family will do the work. Mostly my brothers. They are pissed I'm letting the burned area sit right now, but until I know what I want done to it, I don't want to touch it."

"That's smart."

"So, how do I work with you?"

I pull my folder out of my bag. "This is my contract. All the rates we discussed are on it. I can leave this with you and answer any questions you have."

She pulls a pen out from behind her ear. "I'll sign it now. I want to get started right away. Boris wouldn't have recommended you if I couldn't trust you." She skims through the contract, signs, then sets it in front of me.

"Can I borrow your pen?"

She holds it out.

I sign. "I can email you a copy when I get back."

A grin forms on her face. "Perfect. So we can get started right away?"

"Yes. I'm excited to work on this."

"Great. Thank you."

We schedule the next time to meet, and I leave with Viktor and Peter. When we get in the car, I call Harper.

"Hey, girl! Are you on your way?"

"Yes. I just got done. Do I need to bring anything?"

"Nope. Just your fabulous booty."

"Okay. I'll be there in five."

I tell the driver where to go, and when we get to the building, Viktor comes in with me. At the door of the suite, I turn. "You can't come past here."

He raises his eyebrows. "Why?"

"It's girly stuff," I tell him.

He crosses his arms.

"I'm serious. You have to stay out here. If you come in, Dmitri would kill you."

He furrows his brows.

I knock on the door.

Harper opens it. "Hi!!" She hugs me then glances up at Viktor. "Hey, Viktor. I'm glad you're here. There's this woman I met, and she's totally into the bad boys. I think you should meet her. Are you taken?"

Viktor's face only grows more rigid.

"Is that a yes? No? Come on, help me out here."

He stays silent and continues to give Harper the stare down.

"Tell you what. We're going to do what we need to with Anna, and when we finish, I'll bring you a picture of this woman. Oh, and she's freshly divorced and really in need of a good time, if you get my drift." She pulls me through the door and shuts then locks it. She wiggles her eyebrows. "I picked up a few more pieces for you. Something to show off your ass more."

I laugh. "Well, Dmitri does appreciate my ass."

26

Dmitri

"IF WE DON'T END THIS NOW, WE'RE ASKING FOR MORE TROUBLE," Boris insists, pacing the room. "He torched Nora's pub. She could have died."

He's not typically agitated like this.

It's Nora.

No. That's not the only reason.

I glance at Maksim, who's assessing Boris as well.

"Zamir contacted you, didn't he?" I blurt out, and the room goes silent. Boris stops pacing, crosses his arms, and his face hardens further. He doesn't have to confirm. His expression tells me I'm right.

My gut flips. For three-hundred-and-sixty-four days a year, Boris makes his own decisions. But the one day a year he isn't free keeps him a prisoner to Zamir. It ties him and us to the

Russian mafia. And it reminds us all where we learned everything we know about dealing with people like Lorenzo.

But it also reminds us our mother killed herself due to what Zamir made her watch. No mother should have to watch her son torture and kill another man. My mother watched all four sons and ten times over. And Sergey wasn't even a teenager. So our mother's death is on Zamir's head.

"That's the real problem we should be discussing," Maksim seethes.

Lorenzo is screwing us. Hatred for him grows each day. But Zamir stirs something in each of us we will never release.

"It's not your problem," Boris states, as he does every year.

"You know it is," I reply.

"It's one day a year. Everything else works around it. Zamir is not our issue right now. Lorenzo is. And I'm ready to unleash what he has coming to him," Boris says.

Sergey rises. "I'm with Boris. Enough is enough. His threats are getting worse. There's only so much time we can sit back before he comes to attack. Better to be on offense than defense."

Maksim shakes his head. "We all know access to him isn't easy."

"I'll handle it," Boris says.

"You have enough on your plate with Zamir right now, don't you think?" I point out.

Boris scowls. "Since when am I not able to handle more than one thing at once?"

"You're agitated. You only get like this when Zamir calls."

"He torched Nora's pub," he growls.

"This isn't the time to get into a pissing match," Maksim barks.

"Why are you messing with Nora anyway? You can get ass anywhere. Killian will rip your head off if he finds out you're screwing her," Sergey adds.

Boris spins, grabs Sergey's shirt, and shoves him against the wall.

Sergey's eyes widen. "What the fuck! Get off me."

Maksim and I pull Boris back as he yells, "Nora isn't a piece of ass!"

"Jesus. What's gotten into you?" I holler.

Boris scowls. "So, I'll call Anna your piece of ass."

I grab his shirt. "You better watch your mouth."

Sergey pushes me away from him, and Maksim forces Boris to the wall. "Cool it! All of you! And Sergey is right about Killian. You're playing with fire with Nora. We don't need a war with her family next."

"You can all mind your own business. I know what I'm doing. And you better get your head straight, Maksim," Boris says through clenched teeth.

"About what?"

Boris shakes out of Maksim's grasp. "Lorenzo is not going to wait. He's going to attack us. It'll be dirty, just like his father. Everyone will be in danger. Us. Our workers. Our women. Stop being stupid and give me the go-ahead to take care of this."

He's right. Anna is in danger while Lorenzo is alive.

"This isn't just anyone. It's the mob boss. We have to strike at the right time. It can never be linked back to us," Maksim reminds him.

Boris points in Maksim's face. "Figure out a time—this week. If you don't, I will. I'm not letting that little weasel shove us around anymore. We're losing millions because of him. And I'll be damned if I let him continue to threaten us."

"You need to take a breather," I state.

"You want him coming after Anna?" Boris fires out.

My stomach twists. "No. You're right. He needs to be taken down. But Maksim is correct, too. And you're dealing with Zamir right now. What night are you meeting him?"

Boris scowls. "You know how it works. He reminds me. Then he calls, and I have to drop everything and go."

"So, you see why you cannot move on Lorenzo until we are past the other situation?"

Boris sniffs and stares at the ceiling, clenching his teeth.

Maksim puts both hands on his cheeks and makes him look at him. "We all want the same thing. One thing at a time, little brother."

"I want him tracked. At the very least, it's time to follow his every move."

Maksim nods. "Okay. I will implement it immediately. He won't shit without us knowing."

Boris steps back. "I've gotta go. I'll be late for my session with Aleksei." He gets to the door, and I stop him.

"You tell us when Zamir calls."

He closes his eyes briefly and nods.

I pat his back, and he steps out. I nod for Sergey to go with him.

When they both are gone, Maksim says, "Zamir needs to be dealt with."

"We've gone around and around about this. Zamir is not stupid like Lorenzo. He doesn't make mistakes."

Maksim rubs his face. "Why didn't I see it?"

"Don't," I sharply demand. Every year, Maksim goes on a guilt spree about how he should have known about our mother's involvement with Zamir. He blames himself for everything we've been through and my mother's death.

He crosses his arms and stares out into the city. "We need a plan B for the lots. Taking care of Lorenzo doesn't guarantee we'll end up with the land."

"We overpaid for all seven if we can't develop it. The cost of the chemical cleanup alone makes it undesirable if we can't build what we planned."

Maksim sighs, and it comes out as a growl. "We need to sell the East Bay project out quickly. Now that we know the design and have the first units done to show and the roof concept, we need to get contracts. There's too much cash tied up on those seven lots."

My stomach clenches. Money tied up means we can't use it to expand. It creates a possible layoff situation in a few months for our workers. "Boris can't handle Lorenzo right now. Not with Zamir in the picture. One of us will need to do it."

Maksim turns. "We track him first. You know this. We do not skip steps. War with the Rossi family is not something we can afford. His death needs to trace to another crime family."

"The only beef I know he has right now is with the O'Malleys."

"That isn't happening."

I put my hands in the air. "I'm not suggesting that."

Silence ensues. We lock eyes, both trying to figure out who to pin his death on. Then it hits me.

"Zamir. He's the fall guy. Let the Rossi family fight it out with the Petrovs."

Maksim shakes his head. "It could backfire, and Zamir could gain more control. It puts our people in more danger."

"What if it's the way to destroy Zamir?"

"We can't risk it. You know what happens if Zamir gains more power."

"If we—"

The buzzer rings. Maksim goes to the intercom. "Yes?"

"We have a package for you. It requires your signature. Do you want me to send the man up, or would you like to come down?"

"Send him up," Maksim orders. He turns. "Every move we make has consequences. Both our problems need to go away, but we cannot afford to be careless."

"I agree. But the longer this goes on, the more danger this puts everyone in, including Anna. Lorenzo is a loose cannon. He's cocky. It makes me nervous."

"His arrogance will be his downfall. When the—" the elevator dings, and Maksim goes to sign for the package.

"What is this?" Maksim asks.

"I'm just the delivery guy," a younger man's voice claims.

"Thanks."

Maksim comes back into the room and sets a box on the table. It's not an ordinary box. It's white and expensive looking. There's a fancy, red bow around it.

"Secret admirer?" I tease.

"No idea who would send me a gift."

"Are you seeing Jade again?"

Maksim shrugs. "You know how she is. Doubt she sent me something."

Maksim furrows his brows and tugs at the ribbon. It falls, and he takes his knife out of his pocket, flips it open, and slices through the tape. He opens the flaps and pulls out bubble wrap then sharply raises his hands in the air. "What the fuck!"

The hairs on my arms stand up. I step forward and glance in the box. "Fuck sake! Whose arm is that?" A man's hand and arm, up to his elbow, is in the box, frozen from death, and the stench flares in my nostrils.

Maksim reaches into the box and pulls out an envelope. He opens it. He growls, "Mother..."

"What does it say?"

"Sign while you still are capable." His eyes turn to slits.

"We can't wait. He's escalating," I bark.

Maksim picks up his phone. "Tolik. I need everything you have on the Rossi family and then I need you to dig some more. And put Obrecht on Lorenzo, starting now."

Obrecht moves between New York, Chicago, Atlanta, and Los Angeles. He goes where our family needs him, tracking down the most dangerous men who threaten any Ivanov. His data will enable us to decide when Lorenzo meets his fate, and who else around him needs to experience our wrath.

"Move him out of Atlanta. Transfer Kaapo there. He can handle that matter. This snake is more pressing," Maksim demands and hangs up.

"I'm putting Anna on lockdown."

Maksim nods. "It's best. We can't put anything past him. He doesn't abide by code."

Code involves keeping women and children out of your battles. Mafia men tend to adhere to it with other mob families so everyone keeps their families safe. It's an unspoken agreement and rarely broken. Full-out war occurs whenever there is an incident. But Lorenzo doesn't seem to play by the same rules his father honors. I won't risk Anna's safety to find out what he has up his sleeve.

"Do you want me to get rid of this, or do you want to take care of it?"

Maksim glances at the arm. "I will. Go do what you need to do with Anna."

I start to go then stop. "Boris is right. This needs to happen this week. Next week may be too late."

"We wait for Obrecht to do his job. And the time has come for us to move on Zamir as well. We will put Obrecht on Zamir and finish this once and for all. No one will continue to threaten our family. And when that bastard breathes his last breath, he will stare into all of our eyes and understand what he has created."

"I welcome the moment, brother." I pat him on the back and leave.

When I get into my car, I try to call Anna, but it goes to voicemail.

I am supposed to take her out to celebrate tonight.

God, I hate disappointing her.

I tap my fingers on my thigh, trying to figure out what I can do to still celebrate her success. She hasn't told me if she got the contract or not, but I'm sure she did.

I pick up my phone and push the button for Vivian.

"Hey, Dmitri."

"How are you?"

"Not sick anymore. Just super pregnant."

I smile. "How long do you have left?"

"About a month."

"Almost there."

"Yep. So what's up?"

"I want to throw a party for Anna tonight. She's closed several jobs, and I want to surprise her. I know it's last minute, but do you think you could help me pull it off and invite her friends?"

"Sure. At your place?"

"Yes. Does eight sound good?"

"Perfect."

"Thanks." I hang up and call the chef at the new restaurant we didn't eat at because of Lorenzo. He tells me he can cater the party. I talk to Viktor next.

"Is Anna with you?"

"She's with Harper. I'm outside the suite. She didn't want me to come in."

I debate whether to make Anna come home now or let her finish whatever she's doing with Harper. "She's safe right now?"

"Yes. You know I won't let anything happen to her."

"Okay. As soon as she finishes, bring her directly home. We're on lockdown, starting now."

27

Anna

IT'S ALMOST SEVEN BY THE TIME I FINISH WITH HARPER AND CINDY. When I get home and step off the elevator, Dmitri's face lights up. "Wow. Why do you look like you've been in a photoshoot?" He dips down and kisses me.

"There's a new makeup artist Harper's obsessed with. Cindy needed a few normal people for her to work on," I lie.

"You look great. Can we sit for a minute?"

"Sure. Is everything okay?"

He takes my hand and leads me to the couch. "I don't want you to stress out, but Lorenzo is increasing his threats. We need to take some more precautions."

My stomach flips. "Okay. Can you tell me what happened?"

"I'd prefer not to. It isn't pertinent you know."

I take a deep breath, but he misinterprets it.

He furrows his brows. "Honestly. It—"

I put my fingers over his lips. "I trust you. If I needed to know the details, you would tell me." I lean into him and kiss him. "So, what are the new safety measures?"

"It's best if you stay home most of the time and have limited time outside the penthouse. Chase and Vivian's place is okay, or any of my brother's places, but only with Viktor."

I stay quiet.

"It won't be forever."

My chest tightens. "I see. And what about you?"

He tucks a lock of my hair behind my ear then pushes his fingers through it. "I will be okay, kotik."

I don't like the thought of him exposed to danger, but it is what it is. I can't change it. "I guess we're staying in tonight?"

"Yes. But I have a surprise for you."

"You do? What?"

"We're having a party to celebrate your success."

"Oh! I forgot to tell you, I got the job!"

He grins. "Doesn't surprise me. Congratulations." He kisses me.

I move on top of him, straddling his body. "Are we really having a party tonight?"

"Yep. All your friends and my brothers will be here to celebrate you."

I stroke his cheek. "No one has ever thrown me a party before."

He palms my ass. "That's a shame. But I'm sorry I couldn't take you out tonight."

"It's okay. It isn't your fault. I'm happy with a party. How long do we have before company comes?"

"The caterer will be here in ten minutes. Everyone else in about an hour."

"An hour? I have to get ready."

He drags his fingers over my ass cheek. "You look pretty good to me already, kotik."

I glance at my dress pants and sweater. "I'm going to go change and freshen up. If this is my party, I'm putting on a dress."

He wiggles his eyebrows. "What about the purple one you haven't worn yet?"

I try to stop my smile. "Have you been snooping in my closet?"

"Yep. I might have put something else in there for you, too."

"What?"

"Go look."

I slowly get off him, wondering what it could be. He follows me into my closet. I stop and gape when I get inside.

A brilliant, round, purple topaz surrounded by diamonds sits on a platinum chain. Diamond stud earrings—I'm assuming several carats—are next to it.

Dmitri stands behind me, puts his hands on my shoulders, and his cheek next to mine. "What do you think, kotik?"

I spin. "Are those for me?"

Dmitri chuckles. "You don't think I'd buy another woman jewelry, do you?"

I blink hard. "I love them. Thank you!" No one has ever gotten me jewelry before. All the years I was with Mitch and not once did he even buy me a piece of costume jewelry. He claimed it was a waste of money.

These two pieces are real. They probably cost a fortune. But it isn't even about the price. Dmitri could have gotten me a cheap ring from the drugstore, and I would find it valuable.

He puts his arms around me. "I'm so proud of you. You're talented and have done amazing with your business in a short time."

"I wouldn't have gotten those deals if Maksim hadn't been there."

"Shh. Don't. He made sure you didn't get taken advantage of. If you weren't talented, you wouldn't have signed contracts. And today you closed one all on your own. So tonight is about you and your success."

I wipe my eye. "You're going to make me cry and ruin my makeup."

The buzzer makes me jump.

He pecks me on the lips. "Get ready. Put your dress on. That's going to be the caterer. I'll take care of everything, and you take your time doing whatever you want." He leans closer to my ear. "But I can't wait to see your sexy little body in that dress, kotik."

"I guess I'll shave again, even though I already did this morning," I tease.

He groans. "Now I'm going to be thinking of your smooth legs all night."

"Only my legs?" I tease and bat my eyes.

He circles his hand to the front of my body and strokes my sex through my pants. "It's a given I always have multiple body parts of yours on my mind.

I push his chest, laughing. "Go!"

He pinches my ass, pats it, then leaves.

I spend the next hour getting ready and style my hair up so my new jewelry shows off. I put on the earrings and slide into my stilettos.

Dmitri comes out of his closet in black pants and a purple dress shirt.

"You look nice in purple. Can you zip me up and clasp this for me?" I hold out the necklace then turn.

He steps forward, zips me, kisses my shoulder, then secures the necklace. "You look stunning, my kotik."

I spin and circle my arms around him. "Thank you for my gifts. And for tonight."

"We'll just have to make the best of lockdown, okay?"

I stroke the back of his head. "I have a lot of design work to do. I'll utilize this time to create. And I can think of lots of things we can do by ourselves..."

He grins. "We'll start exploring those options after our guests leave tonight."

"Deal."

He gives me a panty-melting kiss, and the buzzer goes off. "I think our guests are here."

Over the next hour, people arrive. I give tours to everyone, except Dmitri's brothers. Nora shows up with Boris.

I hug her. "I'm so glad you're here. I thought you had to work tonight?"

Her face falls.

Boris tugs her close to him. His face hardens, and he speaks directly to Dmitri. "The city came in and found some loophole to shut the pub down due to outdated electrical wiring."

Dmitri's body stiffens. He stays silent. The brothers continue to stare at each other.

Nora blinks hard. Her smile appears forced. "Hopefully, you'll have time to start the redesign soon so I can get these issues fixed and reopen?"

"Yes. Of course. Tomorrow, I'll work on it."

She nods and scrunches her forehead. "Thank you."

"Of course. Actually, I have something in my design studio I'd like to show you. Do you want to come with me?"

"Sure."

Boris releases his arm from around her, and he and Dmitri speak in Russian. Boris sounds more aggressive than Dmitri. I recognize the phrase, "this week," but that's it.

I lead Nora into my studio. Chase and Jamison are in the room. I introduce them to Nora.

"This is impressive, Anna," Jamison says.

I can't help but beam. "Thank you. I love it. I still can't believe Dmitri surprised me with it."

"I'm glad to see you've got a good space to work in," my brother quietly says.

I'm not sure what he's thinking. It's the first time I've had anyone besides Harper over. Not because I didn't feel I could, I just hadn't had time.

I pull out a few samples of flooring and open my wallpaper book. I skim through it and show Nora what we discussed earlier at her restaurant.

"I love it. I think it's perfect!"

"Okay. This will help me create the rest of the design."

Steven and Harper walk in, and more guests follow. Soon, everyone is in my studio.

My stomach growls. "Well, you can all stay here, but I'm going to eat. I'm starving."

When I get to the main room, Dmitri and his brothers are all huddled together, speaking Russian. They all seem upset.

The others enter the room. Dmitri pats Boris on the back and comes to the food table. "Kotik, did you eat yet?"

"No, but I'm about to. It smells awesome."

He hands me a plate.

"Is everything okay?" I quietly ask.

He puts his arm around my waist and kisses the top of my head. "Yes."

"Dmitri, you did a great job on Anna's studio," Chase says.

"I can't take all the credit. My brothers made sure everything got implemented."

His brothers come over and Dmitri introduces them to Chase.

"Your sister is really talented," Maksim says.

"I've heard you've been assisting her in meetings. Thank you."

Maksim grins at me. "She's a quick learner. No one is going to be able to mess with her soon."

Dmitri pulls me closer and brags, "She didn't need you today."

Maksim's face brightens. "That's great."

"Well, I appreciate you making sure she doesn't get taken advantage of," Chase says.

I clear my throat. "I am right here."

My brother shakes his head in annoyance. "You've been undercharging, and I had to convince you to use a contract."

"It's a good one you had written up," Dmitri adds.

Boris's phone rings. His face hardens. "Excuse me."

The brothers all exchange a glance, and my stomach flips.

"You want another drink, Chase?" Sergey asks.

He nods. "Sure. I'll go to the bar with you."

Sergey glances at Dmitri and leaves with my brother.

Dmitri and Maksim quietly talk in Russian. I recognize, "it's him."

Are they talking about Lorenzo?

Boris finishes his call. He steers Nora over to us.

"Where do you have to go?" Nora asks.

He avoids everyone, except Maksim and Dmitri. "Maksim, take Nora home later."

"Sure. Call me later."

He nods.

"Boris—"

He cups her cheeks. "Maksim will take you home. I will talk to you tomorrow."

"Tomorrow? What—"

"Nora, do what I say. Please."

She bites on her lip. "Okay."

He leaves, and she watches him, her forehead scrunched in confusion.

Dmitri holds out a plate. "Have some food, Nora."

She puts her hand over her stomach. "He's back, isn't he?"

Dmitri's eyes widen in surprise.

She nods. "Yes. I know. Everything. When does it stop?"

I'm not sure if they are talking about Zamir or Lorenzo. But a chill digs into my bones.

"Soon. We're working on it."

What does that mean?

"He can't take much more."

"Boris knows what he's doing."

"He may be your brother, but I know him. This needs to end."

"We're fully aware."

She closes her eyes and turns to Maksim. "I'm sorry, but please take me home."

He nods. "Sure."

She addresses me, avoiding Dmitri. "Thank you for having me. Can we talk tomorrow about the design?"

I want to reach out and hug her. She looks so worried. But I'm not sure what to do. "Yes. I'll call you in the afternoon?"

"Please."

"Nora," Dmitri says.

Pain fills her expression. She blinks hard and stares at him. A tear falls down her cheek.

"We're going to end this," he repeats.

She wipes her face. "Killian promised that as well. We all know what happened to Sean."

Dmitri takes a deep breath. "We will end this."

She nods and leaves.

I lean into Dmitri's ear. "Who called Boris? Lorenzo or Zamir?"

His jaw twitches against my forehead. "Zamir."

So this is the one night a year.

How are they going to end this?

I shudder, and Dmitri only pulls me closer.

28

Dmitri

I'VE NOT SEEN BORIS SINCE HE LEFT MY PENTHOUSE TWO DAYS AGO. He usually needs a day of space after he does whatever Zamir makes him do.

"Why isn't Boris here?" I ask Sergey when he walks into the gym. It's seven, and Maksim and I both expected Boris to arrive.

"He texted he'd meet me here and not to pick him up."

"Have you seen him?" I ask.

Sergey shakes his head. "No. But you know he needs distance for a day."

"He normally—"

The door opens, and Boris steps through it. To anyone else, he'd appear normal. But the emptiness in his eyes worries me. It usually is gone by now.

Maksim is closest to him and embraces him first. "You alright, dear brother?"

He steps back, cracks his neck, and licks his lips. His face hardens. "It's over. Where are we at on Lorenzo?"

"Obrecht is on it. We will know more later today."

"I'm tired of waiting. Nora's bar is shut down because of him. He's gone too far. Tell Obrecht to give us the entry point, or I'll figure it out myself." Boris shoves past Maksim and goes into the locker room with his bag.

"Boris doesn't make threats. He follows through," Sergey reminds Maksim and me.

Boris comes back out and racks weights on the bar to bench press.

I work on the opposite side. "You filling this?"

"Yep."

Maksim starts, "Boris—"

"We aren't talking about it. Every year, you want to talk about it. I always tell you the same thing. I've not changed. There's nothing to say. It's over. Can we please focus on our current problem?" he barks.

Maksim's eyes turn to slits. "I'm worried about you. Out of all of us, you're the man who demonstrates patience the best. But I haven't seen it this week."

Boris slams a weight on the floor. He steps toward Maksim. "What do you not get? The Rossi's torched Nora's bar. She could have died. They put her out of business. And you know they were behind Sean's death."

"I know Nora means a lot to you, but—"

"I love her. She's carrying my baby," he growls.

Silence ensues, other than the blood pounding loudly between my ears.

Boris softens his voice. "I've always loved her. You all know that. No matter what Killian thinks, she has my baby in her belly. And this is no longer only an O'Malley war with the Rossi family. This is our war now, too."

Chills expand in my body like a spider web. The war the O'Malleys are in with the Rossi family is one already full of blood. But Boris is right. If she is carrying his baby, then this is now our battle as well. And even if she wasn't pregnant, he loves her. He's correct to say we already know it. As much as we have tried to steer him away, he's never been able to stay away from her. He can't stand back and not cross the line for her. It's not possible.

"How far along is she?" Maksim recovers first.

"Maybe six weeks."

Amid the tension, a grin grows so big, my cheeks hurt. I step forward and embrace Boris. "Congratulations. But I hope the baby gets Nora's stunning good looks and not your ugly mug."

"I'll second that," Sergey says and hugs him as well.

Maksim shakes his head. "An O'Malley-Ivanov. Good God." He chuckles and puts his arms around Boris.

Boris's face falls. "I want him dead, Maksim. And he needs to see my wrath."

"He will. For everyone's safety, Nora, Anna, us, and the O'Malleys, I need your head back in the game. No past, no future. We cannot make old mistakes. Patience is what I need from you."

Boris scowls.

"We're in this together. Do not jump the gun. We wait for Obrecht. He will not let us down. Then you can execute with perfection, which is what you do," I back Maksim up.

Sergey pats Boris's shoulders. "Listen to the old, wise ones."

I slap Sergey's head.

"Ouch."

"You better watch those old comments."

Boris lays down on the bench. "Fine. I will give it a few more days. But I will not wait forever."

I step behind him to spot. "Have you thought about the beating Killian is going to give you?"

Boris grunts and lifts the bar off the rack. "It's a good thing I fought him before he found out. I barely took him out that last fight."

We all get into our workout and shower when we're through. We agree to wait until Obrecht gives us information on Lorenzo. I'm walking out of the gym when Viktor calls.

"Morning."

"We've got a problem."

I freeze with my hand on the door. My stomach flips. "What's that?"

"We just got a package delivered."

I lock eyes with Maksim. "What kind of package?"

"Expensive white box. Pink, fancy ribbon. The delivery guy at the front desk demanded Anna sign for it."

"Anna?"

"Yes. Peter attempted to. Even said she was sleeping, but he insisted she had to sign."

My chest tightens. "You didn't let him or the box anywhere near her, did you?"

"No. But, Dmitri, he said he would be back."

"Tell security he's not to come anywhere near the building," I order.

"Peter is already talking with them."

"Does Anna know anything about this?"

"No."

"Good. Don't tell her. I don't want her to worry. I'm on my way home. Do not let her go anywhere."

"We won't."

I hang up. "That mother—"

"What is it?" Boris asks.

I tell my brothers about the conversation.

Boris tilts his head, scowling. "Do you still want me to be patient? He already came after Nora. Now he's coming after Anna."

Maksim growls, "We do this the right way. The dynamics have not changed since our conversation earlier. We wait for Obrecht. He will give us an update today."

My heart beats faster. "So help me God, if he or anyone comes near my Anna, I will slice him to pieces in the middle of the street."

"Have security pull the video footage. I want to see who this delivery person is," Sergey says. "I'll go with you."

"I need to talk to Killian. Nora can't be left alone."

"Boris, let me go with you," Maksim says.

"Are you going to step between us when he tries to beat me to a pulp?" Boris asks with an amused look on his face.

Maksim sighs. "No. I'm going to try and talk some sense into him before he tries to kill you."

"Good luck with that." Sergey snorts.

"Looks like you got the easy job today." I pat Sergey on the back. "Let's go. Good luck, Boris. I hope we see you again," I tease, but part of me wonders how Killian is going to react. There's no way Killian is going to take the news well. He and Boris may be good friends, but we're Russian. The O'Malleys are as Irish as they come and want Nora to marry a fellow Irishman. And Killian isn't going to like that one of his best friends was going behind his back with his sister.

We get in the car, and I call Anna.

In Russian, she answers, "Is this my sexy Russian?"

I smile and reply, "I'll show you what's sexy when I get home, kotik."

Sergey grunts and rolls his eyes.

I kick him. "Mind your own business."

"What?" Anna asks.

"Sorry. Sergey is in the car coming back with me."

"Oh. Is everything okay?"

"Yes," I lie, not wanting to worry her. "We've got a few work issues to sort out."

"Well, I thought I'd make you breakfast. Is he hungry?"

"Is the pope Catholic?"

"Point taken. I was planning on wearing nothing but my apron, but since Sergey is coming, I guess I need to put some clothes on."

I groan. "I'm dropping him off, then."

She laughs. "I'll see you soon. Love you."

"Love you, too, kotik." I hang up. "Anna's making breakfast."

Sergey fist-pumps the air. "Yes! I'm starving."

"I didn't want to say this in front of Boris, since he's so hot right now, but Obrecht better hurry up. He's coming directly at our women. Giovanni must have done a horrible job teaching him about code," I admit.

"It surprises me. His father is as old-school as they come. You'd think Lorenzo would step into those shoes, instead of trying to rock the boat. The rest of his father's guys can't be happy with that."

Silence ensues.

"What is it?" Sergey asks.

"Something you just said."

"What?"

"Why would he rock the boat?"

Sergey shakes his head. "I'm not sure."

My stomach pitches. "Who do you know that doesn't draw the line with women and children?"

The color in Sergey's face drains. "What are you getting at?"

"I'm not sure. But there's only one man I know in all the crime families who I'm aware doesn't keep the boundary."

Sergey shakes his head. "How would Lorenzo even begin to be mixed in with Zamir? The hatred the two families have stems back for generations."

"What if something changed it?"

"Like what?"

"I'm not sure. But what if Lorenzo is mixed up with Zamir?"

The car parks in front of my building.

"That's a pretty large what if," Sergey states.

"Yes."

Sergey leans forward. "Why would he be?"

"I'm not sure what Lorenzo gets out of it, but Zamir would love to have a reason to take us down. What I've been trying to figure out all these months is, why did Lorenzo suddenly get interested in that lot? We were all set to buy it then he swept in, and the mayor sold it to him for a tenth of what we were going to get it for. Why?"

Sergey runs his hand through his hair. "I assumed Lorenzo is in bed with the mayor."

"Yes, but how did he get interested in the property?"

Sergey's eyes widen and his voice lowers. "Zamir's always watching us. Every move we make. I try to forget he exists, minus the one night a year he calls on Boris, but he's never stopped trying to destroy us, has he?"

I shake my head. "No. And he never will."

Sergey shuts his eyes. "Do you remember when Mom couldn't look at me anymore?"

"Serg—"

"No, you don't have to deny it."

"She was filled with guilt. She loved you."

"I still hear her begging Zamir not to make her baby do it. Then I see her face, crying for me and telling me to stop. I smell Zamir's breath on my cheek and feel the blade of his knife on my throat."

I wish I had something to say to take it all away from him. Or I could somehow comfort him. But I have my own memories and don't know what to do with those, and I was ten years older than Sergey.

Sergey swallows hard. "If Lorenzo is involved with Zamir, we're dealing with a much larger problem."

Bile rises in my throat. You can take the entire O'Malley clan and the intricate network of Ivanovs we've developed over the years, but together they may not be powerful enough to go against Zamir. Add in power from the Rossi family, and we're in a position to be destroyed.

"Our entire strategy about how to go about this has been wrong," I tell Sergey.

"What do you mean?"

My Anna's safety is at risk. Boris's unborn child is in danger. Nora's life will be on the line.

"If Lorenzo is involved with Zamir, everything we hold dearest to us is in jeopardy. It's going to take the force of every alliance we have to survive. And there's no way of getting around it. We're going to need to figure out how to cap all their knees off, including Zamir."

Sergey's eyes darken. "An all-out war."

"There will be no way around it."

Anna

DMITRI COMES UP BEHIND ME AND PUTS HIS ARMS AROUND MY waist. "Smells good, kotik."

I spin and put my arms around his neck. "Are you hungry?"

He wiggles his eyebrows and smirks. "For lots of things."

"Get a room," Sergey groans.

I glance over at him and chirp, "Good morning."

He reaches over the island and snags a piece of bacon off the plate. "I'm coming here more often if you're going to feed me after workouts."

Dmitri pecks me on the lips. He hesitates then says, "We need to talk."

"What's wrong?"

"Let's sit and eat."

Something has happened. Goose bumps erupt on my skin.

"Is Boris okay?" Ever since the other night, I've been worried about him. Dmitri told me he hadn't surfaced yet from whatever Zamir made him do.

Sergey grabs the platters of bacon and toast and takes them to the table. "He's...well..."

"What?"

Sergey raises his eyebrows at Dmitri.

"Is he hurt?" I fret.

"No. Come sit." Dmitri pulls out the chair beside him.

I add eggs to three plates, and Dmitri carries two over. I take the third and follow him to the table. We add the rest of the food onto our dishes.

I turn to Dmitri. "Please tell me what is wrong."

He puts his arm around me. "Boris and Nora are having a baby."

My mouth drops open. I glance between Sergey and Dmitri. "Ummm... I want to be excited right now. Are we excited?"

"Once Boris survives Killian's wrath." Sergey shoves a forkful of eggs into his mouth.

"So, it's not good?"

Dmitri smiles. "We're happy about it."

Relief fills me. "Good. So is that what you wanted to talk about?"

Dmitri shakes his head. He lowers his voice. "I need to change your lockdown stipulations."

My chest tightens. "Why?"

"Lorenzo is increasing his threats."

I move my food around on my plate. "Okay. What does this mean?"

"It's best if you don't leave the penthouse until we have things under control."

Until they kill him is what he means.

I don't need to ask. I put my fork down. "I'm ummm..."

"I'm sorry, kotik. I know it isn't convenient for you to be confined to the house."

"I'm not worried about that. I can work. But..." My insides quiver. I blurt out, "I don't want anything to happen to you or your brothers."

"Don't worry, we'll be careful," Dmitri says, but he and Sergey exchange a glance.

It only makes my stomach flip. "What aren't you telling me?"

Dmitri strokes my cheek. "Nothing. Thank you for not fighting me on the lockdown changes."

"Of course. You wouldn't do it if you didn't think it was necessary."

"No, I wouldn't."

I force a smile. "Okay. I'll stay in. I was going to meet Harper at Vivian's today, but I'll have her come here instead."

Dmitri traces my jaw. "That's a good idea."

I pick up my phone and text Harper and ask her to come here instead.

She texts back, "Vivian said she's too tired to go anywhere today. Let's keep it at her place."

Great. What do I tell her?

I stare at the phone.

"What's wrong?" Dmitri asks.

"Harper said Vivian is too tired to go anywhere today and we should stick to her place. What do I tell her?"

I can't tell her the truth. What would I say? Hey, Harper, my man is, but isn't, involved with several crime families. And the son of the Italian mafia is making threats, so I can't leave the penthouse.

"Tell her you're behind on your projects and need the extra time," Dmitri states. "Hopefully, this will be over soon, and you won't be in these uncomfortable situations."

"What are you going to do to end it?" I ask.

"Anna, you don't want to know this information." Sergey takes a bite of toast. His eyes are hard.

"Sergey's right. This is not something you need to know, kotik," Dmitri says. "Information on anything about to happen could harm you."

Don't waver in your trust in him. He would tell you if you needed to know anything.

"Eat." Dmitri motions to my plate.

"Are you going to kill him?" I blurt out.

Sergey raises his eyebrows at Dmitri.

I wave my hand in front of Sergey's face. "I'm right in front of you. And I'm not stupid."

"No one said you were," Dmitri states. "But we will not answer questions about this. I will not put you in more danger."

My stomach twists. Not at the thought of Lorenzo dying but that something could happen to Dmitri or his brothers.

"Finish making your plans with Harper," Dmitri gently says.

I sigh and text Harper I'm behind on projects and can't make it to Vivian's but hope Harper can still come over.

Dmitri holds a forkful of eggs to my mouth. "Eat before it gets cold."

I eat the eggs but not much more. Harper replies she'll come to my place. We finish breakfast, and Dmitri takes me into our bedroom.

He cups my cheeks. "You hardly ate."

"I trust you, Dmitri, I do. And if you say I shouldn't know what you are planning, then I won't push. But I have this feeling something bad is going to happen."

He pulls me into him. "I don't want you worried, kotik. I'm sorry you have to stay in the penthouse right now. I know you deserve better."

I glance up. "There is nothing better than us together. As long as I'm with you, I have the best. But I don't want anything to go wrong. If something happens to you..."

"Shh. Nothing is happening to me." He kisses me. "What time is Harper coming over?"

"Noon. What is your schedule today?"

"Sergey and I need to work with Victor on some things. My brothers and I also have a meeting later this afternoon."

"Will you be home late?"

"I shouldn't. Why don't I text you when I know the time, and I'll pick up dinner on the way home?"

"All right. And you'll be careful?"

"Of course. Will you feel better if I text you when I get to Maksim's?"

"Yes. Please."

He kisses my forehead then tugs me into his arms. "I'm sorry you have to deal with this."

I circle my arms around him tightly. "Stop apologizing. I just don't want anything to happen to you."

"It won't."

"Dmitri," Sergey calls.

"What?"

"Viktor needs us."

Dmitri sighs then squeezes my ass and kisses my head again. "Duty calls."

"I need to get ready and start work on Nora's pub anyway."

We part ways, and I spend the rest of my morning engrossed in Nora's project.

"Work, work, work," Harper teases and claps.

I jump, startled. "Oh my gosh. You scared the crap out of me!"

She laughs. "Sorry. Couldn't resist. Viktor let me up. By the way, I think I'm wearing him down. I got a happy grunt today."

I snort. "Progress."

"Yeah." She sets the things she's carrying on the table. Then she pins her green eyes on me. "Is Mitch still threatening you?"

"No. Why?"

She wrinkles her forehead. "Then why did I have to go through Viktor after I got past another guy... Peter, I think the building security called him? The other night was the same for the party."

Oh, crap. Why did I say Mitch wasn't threatening me again?

Silence ensues, and Harper tilts her head.

"What's going on, Anna?"

"Nothing." I hate lying to her.

"Anna, something is going on. I'm not a moron."

"I never said you were."

"Okay, then tell me."

My pulse beats so hard in my neck, I cover it with my hand in fear she will see it. "Dmitri is cautious, that's all."

"About what?"

I turn away, not sure how to answer her.

She sits in the chair next to mine and puts her hand over my tapping fingers. "I've known you for a long time, Anna. I know when you lie. Right now, your body language leads me to believe something is going on. Whatever it is, tell me."

I close my eyes, trying to gather my thoughts.

Why wasn't I prepared for this?

"Is someone threatening you?"

"No."

"Someone is coming after Dmitri?"

I sigh. "Things are going on, yes."

"Is this why you didn't come to Vivian's?"

I turn to her. "Yes. Dmitri doesn't want me to leave the penthouse right now. But please don't tell her or my brother. Or anyone else. I don't want it advertised or anyone to worry."

She nods. "I won't. You have my word."

"Thank you."

"So...what is going on?"

"I can't get into it."

Hurt crosses her face.

"Harper, I don't even know everything. If I could tell you, I would. But I can't. I'm sorry."

Something changes in her expression, but I'm not sure what.

"Is there something you want to say?" I ask.

"Don't take this the wrong way."

"Okay..."

"Steven said no one in Chicago messes with the Ivanov brothers."

"What does that mean?" I snap defensively.

She holds her hands in the air. "Calm down."

I take a deep breath. "What else did Steven say?"

"Nothing. He knew Dmitri through the foundation work he was involved in with Vivian. When I told him you were dating Dmitri, he said Mitch better not try to mess with you because the Ivanovs won't stand for it."

"That's true."

"Right. So who is ballsy enough to threaten them to go to these measures?"

I groan. "Harper, you need to drop this."

She sighs. "All right. But I'm here if you want to talk."

I smile. "I know. Thank you. Now can you show me what you brought me?"

Her eyes brighten. She picks up a package she brought with her and sets it in front of me. "Open it."

My stomach flutters. "I'm suddenly super nervous."

"You shouldn't be. They turned out amazing."

I open the flap of the yellow envelope and slide out a stack of pictures. "I still can't believe I did this." I take the cardboard off and stare.

Dmitri's birthday is in a few weeks. I told Harper I want to give him something special but didn't know what, since he has everything and can buy whatever he wants. Harper showed me some boudoir photos her boss Cindy had shot. The only thing I could think of to give Dmitri that he couldn't buy himself was more of me. So I let her talk me into it.

"I still can't believe I did this," I repeat.

"Girl, look how sexy you are!" Harper gushes.

Every picture is sensual but classy. Some photos highlight my breasts, others my ass. "Even my thighs look amazing," I mumble.

Harper laughs. "You have great thighs."

"I can't believe these are me." If I didn't know better, the pictures could be in a sexy magazine.

"Dmitri is going to flip, isn't he?"

My butterflies take off. "I think he'll like them."

Harper huffs. "He's going to love them, or something is wrong with his eyes. Let's go to your bedroom and figure out what to enlarge and hang where."

"What? No way!"

"Ummm...yeah. He's going to want to display them."

"I don't think so."

"Liar."

"Isn't that kind of pretentious? Hey, babe, let me put myself on your wall."

Harper taps the pictures. "Are we looking at the same photos? You're a sex goddess. He's going to want these on the wall."

I cover my face. "Now I'm regretting doing this."

"Why?"

"This is embarrassing."

"I thought you wanted to do something for Dmitri."

"I do."

"Well?" She widens her eyes and raises her eyebrows.

I stay quiet.

"You need to get over yourself. You're super hot, and I already know what pictures should go where. You'll never get Dmitri anything else he'll love as much as this."

"Well, thanks for setting me up for future gift failure."

"Sorry, but it's true." She rises and grabs my arm. "Come on. Bring the pics."

I obey, and we go into the bedroom.

Harper stands in front of the wall across from the bed.

"So, I'm going to lie in bed and stare at myself on the wall every day?"

"Yep. You'll get extra O's for it, trust me."

I laugh. "What?"

"True story. I hung a few on our wall. Steven's obsessed with them, and I get the perks."

"You did a shoot, too?"

"Yep. After we got back from New York, I wanted to give him something to show my appreciation for my engagement ring."

"Seriously?"

She waves it in front of my face. "Yeah. He went all out on this one."

"It is amazing," I agree.

"Plus, it's not really fair. Men give women rings, but what do we give them?"

"Blowjobs?" I tease.

She laughs. "Besides the obvious."

"I'm already happy with my current O status," I assure her.

"So was I. But trust me, we can never get enough O's." She winks.

I put my hands over my face. "Harper."

She organizes the photos on the bed. She points. "This one should go in the middle."

It's black and white. I'm sitting on a fur rug, with one leg bent. The other crosses it, so you get a full view of the back of my thigh and a hint of my ass cheek. I'm wearing stilettos, and it looks like I have nothing else on besides a long string of pearls. One strand is around my neck, like a choker, and the rest hang and touch the top of my thigh. My arms are tucked into my chest, and my breasts are on full display, except for my nipples.

Harper picks up several other photos and arranges them. "Don't deny it. You're beautiful, and these should be displayed."

I can't argue. Everything about them makes me feel sexy. I look confident in them, like a woman who owns her sexuality.

"There's a pewter frame sample I brought. It would be perfect against this wall. Let me go grab it."

She leaves, and I continue focusing on the photos.

Can I really hang these on the wall?

Dmitri will love all of them.

I did this for him.

They do look amazing.

"Look at how perfect this frame is," Harper claims, coming back into the room. She picks up a photo and goes to the wall. She holds an L shaped piece of metal on the corner of one picture against the slate-gray wall. "It's soooo sexy hot!"

"You're right. It is."

She grins. "Yay! Should I order the enlargements and get every-thing framed?"

I've already come this far—no point in stopping now.

"Yes. Can we put a rush on it?"

Dmitri

OBRECHT CROSSES HIS ARMS TO HIS CHEST. "ELEVEN THIRTY AT THE Hornet's Nest in Gary, Indiana."

"What's that?" I ask.

"A strip club."

"Tonight?" Maksim says.

"Yes. If you don't move on this now, the window may not come back around for a while," Obrecht informs us.

My brothers and I glance at each other. But there's no choice. We have to eliminate Lorenzo. He's crossed the line getting our women involved.

"Have you found any connection to Zamir?" I ask.

Obrecht shakes his head. "None. But I will dig now that you believe it is a possibility. If he is involved with Zamir, I doubt his father knows. Whether he is acting on behalf of his father or on his own accord, taking him and his top men out will reduce our risk of a full-blown war.

"We must not assume anything," Maksim warns. "If he is in bed with Zamir and his father does know, we are at great risk."

"Which is why we're going to pin this on Zamir," Boris states.

The room turns silent.

"That could backfire on us. The Rossi family going to war with Zamir could make Zamir more powerful," I warn.

"We make sure it doesn't happen," Boris says.

"How? We've tried for years to figure out how to take Zamir down."

Boris's face hardens. "Let them shed blood. If we need to, we will take out Zamir's top men to level the playing field and keep Rossi in the game. When it is over, we finish the Rossi family off if we find out his father knew about any involvement with Zamir or what he's been up to."

Chills run down my spine. "You're suggesting an ongoing silent battle. The point is to avoid war. We aren't big enough to take down Zamir."

"Killian will execute with me. We can tap into the power of the O'Malleys now."

Sergey and I arrived just as Obrecht did, and we hadn't gotten to discuss what happened when Boris and Maksim met with Killian. I point to Boris's shiner. "He's already gotten over your situation?"

"We agreed it was best for Nora and the baby if we focused on this situation with Lorenzo," Boris replies. "But Killian knows me and who I am. I may not be Irish, but I'm the next best thing for Nora. And he had to admit it."

Maksim shifts on his feet. "Killian is out for his blood. If Zamir is involved and Giovanni Rossi knows about it, Killian will understand the danger."

"Regardless, your window to take out Lorenzo and his men is tonight," Obrecht reiterates.

"How many of his guys?" Sergey asks.

"Three."

"Flavio, Luca, and Angelo?"

They are all the men present at every meeting we've had with Lorenzo. And they were at the restaurant when Lorenzo threatened us.

Obrecht nods. "Yes."

"Killian will come with us. Nora is with him now, but I'll have him drop her off at your place, Dmitri. She can stay with Anna tonight," Boris says.

"I'll let Anna know." I step out of the room and call her.

"Hi! Are you on your way home?" she asks when she answers.

My heart sinks. I hate disappointing her.

"I'm sorry, but we have to deal with our situation. I won't be home tonight."

"The entire night?"

"Yes."

The line goes silent.

I clear my throat. "Boris is sending Nora to stay with you."

"Dmitri..." Anna releases a big breath.

"This has to be done, kotik."

"How will I know you are okay?"

"I will call you when I am on my way home."

More silence follows and further guilt consumes me. "I'm sorry, kotik. You deserve better."

"Please don't say that. I only want you. Do what you need to do and come home to me in one piece," she whispers.

"I will. I need to go. I love you."

"I love you, too."

Hanging up is torture, but there is no point dragging the call out. It's only more painful for us both. I know she's going to be up all night worrying. I can tell her not to, but it's pointless.

This needs to end. All loose ends, including Zamir, need to be taken care of.

I only want my life with Anna. I want to marry her. But until I can assure her safety, I won't ask her to commit her life to me.

She already has.

But she can still get out if she wants to.

If she left, she'd kill me.

I hate the thought of her ever leaving me. But what I'm putting her through right now isn't fair. She shouldn't have to be in a lockdown situation.

Which is why Lorenzo and Zamir both need to be eliminated.

I go back into the room with my brothers.

"Right. See you there." Boris ends a phone call. "Killian is dropping Nora off. He will meet us off I-90."

"Are you sure this is a good idea, getting Killian involved?" I ask.

"Why?" Boris replies.

Something in me is warning me to take precaution. I'm not sure if it's from what we're about to do, or the extra ally we will have tonight. "We've not ever done anything like this with anyone before."

"Lorenzo killed Sean. He went after Killian's blood again. Nora may be carrying my baby, but Lorenzo deserves the wrath of Killian and me. And he's going to experience it," Boris growls.

Sean was Killian and Nora's older brother. It's rumored the Rossi family murdered him. Killian has always believed it was Lorenzo who pulled the trigger.

"I am happy you've come clean about Nora and the baby to Killian. But be careful, Boris."

Boris's eyes turn to slits. "You know we can trust Killian."

"Do not get dragged into the wars of the O'Malleys. Zamir pushed us into this life. We have worked hard to do everything in our power to stay away from it whenever possible. I fear you may lose focus on who we really are."

Boris snorts. "I know who I am. No matter what I do, I will always be the devil. Do not think legitimate businesses and three hundred some days a year of 'appearing normal' erase our sins, brother."

"No one said our actions get deleted. But the O'Malley wars—"

His eyes harden. "Will be part of my child's blood. And whatever I have to do to protect him or her from enemies, I will."

My heart sinks. Boris is right. I wish I could tell him he's wrong, but I can't. And I also know if I were in his situation, I would do the same.

"This is not what we should be focusing on right now," Maksim cuts in. "There is a lot to plan for tonight."

Obrecht fills us in on more details. Maksim pulls out clothes, gloves, and weapons.

All of us have a set at our homes. We're always prepared. After tonight, we will destroy it all. Maksim will replace this set, and we will be ready for our next situation.

Why can't all this just end?

Since the day Zamir held our mother captive and turned us into killers, I've been tired of this. But now that I have Anna, it weighs on me at a different level.

When it's time to go, we get into a black Cadillac Escalade Obrecht arranged. We stop off I-90 and pick up Killian.

He's dressed how we are. His eye is black, which doesn't surprise me. It's quite amazing he and Boris only got one punch in before Maksim stopped it.

Killian has a black hat over his red hair. He nods when he gets in and slides next to Boris. They fist-bump.

Even in the dark, I catch a glimpse of the hunger in his green eyes. It's the same shift Boris has when it's time to do anything immoral. It's a need to destroy the enemy.

What will an Ivanov-O'Malley's eyes be like? Will he or she have an even more intense gaze?

I need to make sure Boris doesn't get pulled into the O'Malley's crime life. Killian was never a part of it until Sean died. Boris doesn't need to fall into their everyday problems.

It would be so easy for Boris.

Maksim fills Killian in on what we've discussed.

"I get Lorenzo," Killian states. "He's going to stare in my eyes when he takes his last breath."

"It's important we find out if they are working with Zamir. I don't know how you do things, but we must execute patience tonight," Maksim states.

"Zamir?" The color in Killian's face drains. "What does he have to do with this?"

"We believe he may be working with Lorenzo to take us down." Maksim informs him about our properties and what we suspect.

"If Zamir is involved..."

"That's why we're pinning this on him. Let Rossi go after Zamir," Boris claims again.

"We haven't agreed on that," Sergey states before I can.

"It's happening."

"Boris—"

"No, Maksim. I'm the one who deals with the debt every year. Not any of you. When it comes to Zamir, this is my decision to make. And Lorenzo's death will be pinned on him tonight."

"What debt?" Killian asks.

Boris sighs. "Nothing."

"No. I want to know. What do you have to do with Zamir? I have a right to know if you're with Nora."

"This isn't the time to discuss this," Maksim barks. "We're here."

The car goes silent. Neon lights flash on a sign with Hornet's Nest around an outline of a woman's body. A dozen cars are in the lot. The run-down building has no windows.

Obrecht drives to the back. As soon as he parks the car, a man steps out from the shadows.

"That's our cue," Obrecht says.

Maksim turns and looks at all of us. "There is no room for error tonight. We torture them until they tell us what we want to know. Then we end it, cover our tracks, and get out of here. Everyone understand?"

We all agree. I wrap my fingers around my pocket knife, sliding them along the cold metal. My stomach twists as it always does in these situations.

This needs to be the last time I kill until the day comes to end Zamir.

"They are in the private rooms with the dancers. Ilia will make sure the strippers aren't in the room," Obrecht informs us.

We get out of the car and walk through the alley and to the back door. When we get into the room, my brothers and I all pull out our guns.

Lorenzo and his three top guys are sitting on the couches, waiting for the strippers. They are half drunk and begin to shout.

But the last lesson they learn is that you should never fuck with an Ivanov or any of our women.

Anna

"Where are they?" Nora paces and frets. It's almost five in the afternoon. Dmitri hasn't called. Boris or Killian haven't contacted Nora, either. I'm trying to keep her calm, since she's pregnant, but I'm having difficulty not worrying.

Where is he?

Why hasn't he called me?

Oh God, what if he's dead?

Neither Nora nor I have slept. I last spoke to Dmitri over twenty-four hours ago. We came into the studio to go through designs because I thought it might get our minds off their whereabouts. It isn't helping.

"You should try to rest, Nora. I'll stay awake and let you know when they call."

"Something is wrong. It has to be. This is too long." Her eyes glisten, and she holds her stomach with one hand and twists her red hair in the other.

"Nora, you need to lie down. This isn't good for the baby." I take her hand. "Come on." I lead her to the bedroom and tuck her under the covers.

"I told Killian not to let Boris go. No matter what was going on, I begged him to stop him. He can't take much more. I know he can't."

I stroke her hair. "They're going to come back."

"What if they don't? This is so long," she repeats. "My baby... I want it to know it's father...to know Boris and be loved by him." She begins to sob hard.

I embrace her. "Shh. They will be back. Your baby will have a father."

She cries herself to sleep, and when I finally leave the room, it's dark outside. Another night passes, and at some point, I fall asleep on the couch.

"Anna," Dmitri whispers and strokes my cheek.

I open my eyes and reach for his face. "Are you really here?"

"Yes."

"Dmitri! Oh God!" Tears fall as he pulls me into his arms.

"Shh. I'm okay, kotik." He scoops me into his arms, and they have never felt so good.

"Where have you been?"

"I'm sorry. Our cells died. There wasn't a charger in the car. We didn't think about it."

We...

My heart pounds hard. "Where's Boris?"

Dmitri smiles. "In the bedroom. He's going to stay the rest of the night with Nora and leave in the morning."

I release a big breath.

"I'm sorry. I know this went longer than I anticipated."

I peer closer at him. His face is worn and tired.

"Is it over?" I ask.

He nods. "Yes."

I cry again, and he pulls me into his chest, then picks me up and carries me to the bedroom.

"I'm sorry. I'm just... I tried not to worry, but..."

"Shh. You did good, kotik. So good. And I'm the one who's sorry. You shouldn't have had to go through any of this."

I put my fingers to his lips. "Don't." I slide them down and press my mouth to his, but he pulls away.

"I have to shower. I have blood on me," he murmurs.

I assess him for the first time and see it on his neck and behind his ear. I get off the bed and take his hand. "Come on."

When we get in the bathroom, his exhausted expression becomes clear. His eyes have something in them I've not witnessed before. I'm not sure what it is, but it scares me. I cup his cheeks. "Dmitri, are you all right?"

He palms my ass, closes his eyes, and holds me tight with his other arm. "I don't want that to be part of my life. I never did. But it is. And I think it's over, but I'm always waiting for the other shoe to drop. I... I don't want to put you through this if something comes up again."

My stomach flips. "Look at me."

He shakes his head and keeps his eyes shut.

"Look at me," I say louder.

He obeys.

I realize what's in his bloodshot eyes and it scares me. It's defeat. "Don't toss me aside."

"I'm not... I'm... You don't deserve to be in this situation. You have an out right now. If you want to take it, I'll always protect you, but I will let you go so you can be free."

I press my hands harder against his cheeks. "I don't want an out," I sternly say. "You are tired and speaking crazy right now. Do not do this and ruin the beauty of us."

"I want you forever, but we aren't married. If you stay, I'm going to ask you. If you say yes, you will be an Ivanov. There will be no going back. It's not—"

"Yes! Yes, I will marry you!"

"That wasn't a proper proposal. I—"

"I don't care. And there is nothing I want more than to be Mrs. Dmitri Ivanov."

"Anna, I don't think you understand—"

"I do. I will be yours forever. You will be mine. The world will know I am an Ivanov. There might be dangers associated with it, but I don't care. I would rather live the rest of my years with you than a moment without you. Do you not understand this? Do you not feel the same?"

He brushes his lips to mine. "Of course I do. There is nothing about this conversation that diminishes my love for you."

"Then stop this absurd talk. I will not allow you to eject me from your heart. We do not do that to each other." I grab his shirt and pull it over his head, then release his pants. I strip, too, then pick up his hand and step into the shower.

The blood washes down his body the moment he steps in.

"Anna, even if you were not physically with me, you would never leave my heart."

I put soap on his head and the front of his body, rubbing my hands over his no past, no future tattoo. "I have made myself clear. Do not talk to me about this ever again. And don't wave marriage in my face and take it away."

"Is that how you see this?"

"Yes."

He stays quiet.

"Turn," I instruct him, and he does. Tears well in my eyes as I wash his back. His talk about ruining everything we've built is a knife shredding my heart. All I want is to be his, no matter the consequences.

He doesn't speak as I wash him.

I make sure every drop of blood is off his skin. "You're clean." I go to step out of the shower, and he tugs me into him. His hand palms the back of my head, and he makes me look at him.

"I don't want you to resent me down the road."

"I'm not a child. I can make my own decisions."

His lips twitch. "No, you aren't."

"Glad you're finding this funny."

His eyes light with fire. He moves me back against the wall. The warmth of his body presses against mine.

Tingles race into my core. It's no different than any other time he touches me. My chest rises and falls faster.

He holds my cheeks and brings his lips an inch from mine. "You are my life. There's no one I love more or care more for. Every moment I've had with you, I cherish. You deserve a man a thousand times better than me. But—"

"No, I—"

He covers my lips with his thumb. "As I was saying, but I'm selfish. And as much as you should run from me, my life, I greedily want you never to leave my side. So I want you to marry me. If it is in the cards, I want you to bear my children. I want all of the world to know that you are mine, and no one can have you but me. So I'm asking you if you'll be a crazy woman and not run from me but instead be my wife?"

My insides quiver. Tears run down my cheeks. "Yes."

"Yes, you'll be crazy?" He smirks.

I laugh. "Yes."

He kisses me then drops his hand to my ass, pulling me as close to him as possible.

When I met him, I was Anna Monroe. Lost. Hurt. A woman suffering in silence who didn't know who she was and hated so many things about herself she shouldn't have.

He changed everything for me. He made me see the brilliance within myself. He taught me what it meant for a man to truly love a woman.

It may not yet be on paper, but I am already Mrs. Dmitri Ivanov. We made our vows in this shower, the first night we were ever together.

Separate, we are tainted, our pasts weaved with sorrow.

Together, we are whole and unbreakable.

And all I wish to do is spend the rest of our lives wrapped in our perfection.

EPILOGUE

Dmitri

Five Years Later

"I'm Anna Ivanov. It's nice to meet you," my kotik says in Russian and beams. It's how she always looks whenever she introduces herself to anyone.

I squeeze her waist then let go. I hug and kiss Zlata Turgenev's cheek then shake her husband, Gabor's, hand after he pulls back from kissing Anna's cheek.

Zlata and Gabor just moved to Chicago from Russia and bought an apartment building they are renovating into high-end, luxury condos. One of their friends is a client of Anna's and recommended her. When she scheduled the meeting, Zlata said they were struggling with some zoning issues. They don't speak English very well, which is also adding to their struggles. Anna suggested I come to see if I could give them any direction.

We're at the Russian restaurant I first took Anna to. The hostess seats us in a booth. We get through the small talk, order our food, and we discuss the zoning issues. I write down my contact in the zoning department who speaks Russian and will help Gabor. His problems aren't that big of a deal, but it's not surprising he's come across barriers without speaking English.

Things turn to the building's interior design, and I sit back, enjoying every minute of watching Anna deal with any hard question the Turgenev's ask, or when they try to lower her rates. Gabor has a bit of male chauvinism in him and addresses me several times. He wants me to step in and agree with him on things, but I say nothing, except to turn the conversation back to my kotik. Anna's in charge, and if he's going to work with her, he's going to give her the same respect he would give me.

Anna's increased her prices several times. She's now the most expensive designer in Chicago. She's still humble but knows her worth and doesn't let anyone push her around.

I couldn't be prouder of her. Maksim is, too, and constantly reminds me he trained her.

We finish our lunch meeting and leave with a new contract. When we get into the car, I pull Anna onto my lap. "I love watching you in action."

She smiles. Her blue eyes light up. "They were nice. It should be a fun project. The views from their building are great. But I think that's the last project I'm going to sign for a while, except for your buildings."

"Why?"

Her lips twitch, and she unfastens the top two buttons on my shirt and traces my no past, no future tattoo. "We've got a slight change in our future."

"Oh?"

She picks up my hand and moves it to her belly, saying nothing.

"Are you pregnant again?"

She nods. "What do you think about that?"

I slide my hands in her hair, which is blonde again. I kiss her deeply until she repositions her body so she's straddling mine.

"Tell Rolan to keep driving until we tell him to go back. I wore a dress for a reason."

"My naughty wife," I tease.

I don't hesitate. I roll down the divider window and give him directions. Before the window is back up, she's unzipped my pants. I quickly tug her panties to the side, and she sinks onto me.

I groan. "God, I love it when you're pregnant, Mrs. Ivanov." Anna can't seem to get enough of me whenever she is. Our son is almost four, and our daughter just turned two.

Vivian and Chase are having a birthday party for their oldest daughter, and we dropped the kids off before our meeting. We're on our way to the event, but there's no rush. And any alone time with Anna, I'll take.

"Dmitri..." she whispers and presses her lips to mine in a slow burn concoction of everything that is us. As always, our bodies sync perfectly, wrapping around the other.

My love for her only grows with time. It surprises me how it can. I don't understand how it's possible. I always think it's at full capacity, but then it deepens again.

We don't go fast, enjoying our alone time. When we finish, we go to the party.

The car stops in front of Chase and Vivian's building. I stroke Anna's hair. "How far along are you?"

"Maybe two months. I made an appointment for Tuesday at nine and added it to your schedule this morning."

I chuckle. "My sneaky wife."

She smiles, lighting up my world and making it brighter. I some-times still wonder how she can know everything she does about me—even the parts I hate—yet love me anyway. There isn't a day where she doesn't give me every piece of her heart. And I make it a priority to do whatever I can to make her happy.

I get out of the car and reach in for her. When I pull her out, I tug her into my arms. Snow is falling in sticky flakes, but instead of running into the building, I kiss her again, putting every part of me into it.

She returns my affection until we're covered in a white blanket of snow.

I can't help the grin on my face. "So we're having another baby, huh?"

Her eyelashes have snowflakes on them. "That's what the five pregnancy tests I took said."

"I'm so happy. Are you?"

"Yes."

I peck her on the lips and quickly guide her inside.

When we get into the penthouse, it's loud. All of the people we care about are there with their families.

Chase and Vivian, my brothers and their wives, Noah and Piper, Xander and Charlotte, Quinn and Jamison, and Steven and Harper.

We find our son and daughter in the chaos and pick them up. I tickle my son, and he screams in laughter. I release him, and he runs back to play with the kids.

Anna's holding our daughter.

I look around the room. I never imagined my life would be full of this amount of love or happiness. I put my arm around Anna, palming her ass, and kiss her on the forehead.

Life is complicated. It's messy and dark at times. You have to choose to let the past hold you back or push you forward. My life is no exception. And Anna and I, we've got secrets between us that we'll take to our graves. But it's part of our perfection: the light, the dark, the gray between it all. It's all in our story. As much as we'd love to erase anything bad, we can't. But as long as we have each other, there isn't anything we can't get through.

I am Dmitri Ivanov. I'm a master of torture. At times, I'm a killer. But the light in me is a lover. And every day, my wife reminds me of the good parts of me and which man I choose to show the world. My children pull even more good out. And maybe that's the beauty of complication. Even through sin and suffering, we get to determine every day what kind of person we are going forward and who we want to love. Without a doubt, I'm the luckiest man in the world, because the woman I choose returns my love with no strings attached.

I'm not sure if fate or luck brought Anna and I together. Whatever it was, I'm grateful for it. When I look into the eyes of my wife and mother of my children, all I see is a reflection of everything I feel for her. Then I glance down and see her sexy little body that I still can't keep my hands off, and the desire I always feel for her swirls in my veins.

What we have is beautiful. It's layers of complication and trust. Others wouldn't understand it, but for us, it's unbreakable perfection.

READY FOR MAKSIM'S STORY? CLICK HERE FOR RUTHLESS Stranger, book one of the jaw dropping spinoff series, Mafia Wars!

RUTHLESS STRANGER - BLURB

He's a Ruthless Stranger. One I can't see, only feel, thanks to my friends who make a deal with him on my behalf.

No names. No personal details. No face to etch into my mind.

Just him, me, and an expensive silk tie.

What happens in Vegas is supposed to stay in Vegas.

He warns me he's full of danger.

I never see that side of him. All I experience is his Russian accent, delicious scent, and touch that lights me on fire.

One incredible night turns into two. Then we go our separate ways.

But fate doesn't keep us apart. When I run into my stranger back in Chicago, I know it's him, even if I've never seen his icy blue eyes before.

Our craving is hotter than Vegas. But he never lied.

He's a ruthless man...

"Ruthless Stranger" is the jaw-dropping first installment of the "Mafia Wars" series. It's an interconnecting, stand-alone Dark Mafia Romance, guaranteed to have an HEA.

Ready for Maksim's story? Click here for Ruthless Stranger, book one of the jaw dropping spinoff series, Mafia Wars!

ALL IN BOXSET

Three page-turning, interconnected stand-alone romance novels with HEA's!! Get ready to fall in love with the characters. Billionaires. Professional athletes. New York City. Twist, turns, and danger lurking everywhere. The only option for these couples is to go ALL IN...with a little help from their friends. EXTRA STEAM INCLUDED!

Grab it now! READ FREE IN KINDLE UNLIMITED!

CAN I ASK YOU A HUGE FAVOR?

Would you be willing to leave me a review?

I would be forever grateful as one positive review on Amazon is like buying the book a hundred times! Reader support is the lifeblood for Indie authors and provides us the feedback we need to give readers what they want in future stories!

Your positive review means the world to me! So thank you from the bottom of my heart!

CLICK TO REVIEW

MORE BY MAGGIE COLE

Mafia Wars - A Dark Mafia Series (Series Five)

Ruthless Stranger (Maksim's Story) - Book One

Broken Fighter (Boris's Story) - Book Two

Cruel Enforcer (Sergey's Story) - Book Three

Vicious Protector (Adrian's Story) - Book Four

Savage Tracker (Obrecht's Story) - Book Five

Unchosen Ruler (Liam's Story) - Book Six

Perfect Sinner (Nolan's Story) - Book Seven

Brutal Defender (Killian's Story) - Book Eight

Deviant Hacker (Declan's Story) - Book Nine

Relentless Hunter (Finn's Story) - Book Ten

Mafia Wars New York - A Dark Mafia Series (Series Six)

Toxic (Dante's Story) - Book One

Immoral (Gianni's Story) - Book Two

Crazed (Massimo's Story) - Book Three

Carnal (Tristano's Story) - Book Four

Flawed (Luca's Story) - Book Five

Behind Closed Doors (Series Four - Former Military Now International Rescue Alpha Studs)

Depths of Destruction - Book One

Marks of Rebellion - Book Two

Haze of Obedience - Book Three

Cavern of Silence - Book Four

Stains of Desire - Book Five

Risks of Temptation - Book Six

Together We Stand Series (Series Three - Family Saga)

Kiss of Redemption- Book One

Sins of Justice - Book Two

Acts of Manipulation - Book Three

Web of Betrayal - Book Four

Masks of Devotion - Book Five

Roots of Vengeance - Book Six

It's Complicated Series (Series Two - Chicago Billionaires)

My Boss the Billionaire - Book One

Forgotten by the Billionaire - Book Two

My Friend the Billionaire - Book Three

Forbidden Billionaire - Book Four

The Groomsman Billionaire - Book Five

Secret Mafia Billionaire - Book Six

All In Series (Series One - New York Billionaires)

The Rule - Book One

The Secret - Book Two

The Crime - Book Three

The Lie - Book Four

The Trap - Book Five

The Gamble - Book Six

Stand Alone Christmas Novella

Judge Me Not

ABOUT THE AUTHOR

Amazon Bestselling Author

Maggie Cole is committed to bringing her readers alphalicious book boyfriends. She's an international bestselling author and has been called the "literary master of steamy romance." Her books are full of raw emotion, suspense, and will always keep you wanting more. She is a masterful storyteller of contemporary romance and loves writing about broken people who rise above the ashes.

Maggie lives in Florida with her son. She loves sunshine, anything to do with water, and everything naughty.

Her current series were written in the order below:

- All In

- It's Complicated (Together We Stand (Brooks Family Saga - read in order)
- Behind Closed Doors (Read in order)
- Mafia Wars
- Mafia Wars New York

Maggie Cole's Newsletter
Sign up here!

Hang Out with Maggie in Her Reader Group
Maggie Cole's Romance Addicts

Follow for Giveaways
Facebook Maggie Cole

Instagram
@maggiecoleauthor

Complete Works on Amazon
Follow Maggie's Amazon Author Page

Book Trailers
Follow Maggie on YouTube

Are you a Blogger and want to join my ARC team?
Signup now!

Feedback or suggestions?
Email: authormaggiecole@gmail.com

CPSIA information can be obtained
at www.ICGtesting.com
Printed in the USA
LVHW110909301122
733858LV00007B/348